SHAME, SHAME, I KNOW YOUR NAME

Book 2 of the Marina Konyeshna Thriller Trilogy

HEATHER HARLEN

Northampton House Press

Cover art by Scott Snyder.

SHAME, SHAME, I KNOW YOUR NAME Copyright 2017 by Heather Harlen. All rights reserved

First Northampton House Press trade paper edition, 2017, ISBN 978-1-937997-75-5.

First Northampton House LLC ebook edition, 2017. ISBN: 978-1-937997-76-2.

Library of Congress Control Number: 2016950599.

9 8 7 6 5 4 3 2

In memory of Bonnie Brush: because you made me laugh when I needed it most.

and

In memory of Vladimir: because this is the ending you deserved.

Better to be slapped with the truth than kissed with a lie.

– Russian Proverb

SHAME, SHAME,
I KNOW YOUR NAME

1

And so there I was, staring up at a huge fiberglass udder. Shaking, gasping.

Cars rumbled by on Route 309 as I hyperventilated underneath this gigantic bovine landmark.

"What the?" someone from the wedding party said.

"What is she doing under there?" another guest said.

"Is that the wedding coordinator lying under The Big Cow?" That was the bride. Her high-pitched voice was unmistakable.

All totally valid questions. I didn't even know the answers myself. I'd seen two different colored eyes. And then I'd crawled under here. Sirens. Car doors slamming. My breath shallow and raspy.

Everything had become spinny and the next thing I'd known, my head was on the cold concrete. It felt amazing to lie down. The twenty-foot tall white and brown bovine blocked out the sun. It used to be the mascot of a long gone dairy and I was now a spectacle under this local landmark.

Bright sun.

Eyes closed.

"Ah, yeah!" I kicked off my heels. I could have been there for five seconds or five hours. Boy, that udder sure had a lot of veins.

"Marina!" someone else yelled.

"Call the ambulance!" That was the bride again.

Someone covered me with a jacket. The lining felt silky. Niiice. Silky reminded me of Arman. I wondered where he was.

Then someone slid my bracelets and watch up my arm. Soft pressure. I only saw a gray goatee through my mostly-closed eyes.

"M'am, I'm a paramedic," said a deep voice. "What is bothering you most now?"

"My life." I squeezed my eyes shut and curled into a ball.

"Um, well, OK. Besides life, what else is bothering you? Your breathing seems labored. Does your chest hurt?"

"My *heart* hurts." It sounded like I was whining into a glass tube. "Does that count?"

He sighed. "Ma'am, what's your name?"

"Marina Konyeshna."

"OK, Marina. I'm going to give you some oxygen now. Then we take you to the hospital. I'll give you an IV in the ambulance. They'll probably do an EKG at the ER. Now—you taking any medications?"

"Adderall. Wait— hospital? EKG? No, I'm fine. Fine. I'M FINE!"

Someone else crouched next to me, soles grating on concrete. I couldn't see who, but the person touched my arm.

"Marina. Marina, Marina. Come on, open your eyes for me."

"Gilly? Why did you leave work? I'm fine. I swear." My best friend. My breath caught in my throat and I gasped, but I was fine. Truly.

Gilly and the paramedic had some conversation just over my head, which I couldn't make out because all I could hear was the monstrous thunder of a coal mine crashing around me. All I could see was my niece's face buried in the shoulder of this guy who had been a link in a chain of gigantic mistakes.

Someone lifted my head and put an oxygen mask over my mouth. Then I was slid onto a gurney and rolled into an ambulance. The sheets were cold.

The last thing I saw as the paramedics lifted me into the back of the ambulance was the bride, groom, and their wedding party all staring at me. The late-afternoon sun made halos around their heads. Their husky was straining on her pink leash, tongue out, panting, as if she wanted to ride along with me.

Then it all went black.

***

Gilly set the bag from Home Depot on my deck.

"Thanks for helping me out yesterday, Gil. And for getting the stain."

"No problem. Let's get to work. It's been warm, so you can still repaint the deck. You can tell me all about it while we DIY."

Gilly decided to stain the railing so he could stand. His knee was better since his injury on the evil geocaching competition this past summer, but not 100% yet. I took the backside of the spindles.

Loud music again poured through the walls of the house next door. *Boom BA boom boom! Boom BA boom boom!*

"My new Mexican neighbors sure do love music," I said.

"Um, how do you know they're from Mexico? Have you actually spoken? Asked them?"

"Whatever, Gilly."

"No, seriously. It sounds...racist. You're better than that, Marina. Especially after Amparo."

"Whatever." I couldn't believe he would bring up the dead girl I'd found in the river. Her family's escape from a gang in El Salvador certainly had nothing to do with my loud and obnoxious Spanish music-loving neighbors.

Boom BA boom boom! Boom BA boom boom! Boom BA boom boom!

Our paint brushes swished swished swished. Otherwise — silence.

Holy awkward.

"So, have you heard from the U.S. Attorney?" Gilly finally said.

"Oh, Pumpernickel?"

"McNichol."

"I like to call him Pumpernickel. It keeps it light. Yeah, he called to check in. Me being the star freaking witness and all."

Gilly dipped the brush in the stain can and scraped the excess Redwood Forest on the rim. "It looks like it won't go to trial anyway. You're probably OK."

"I hope it doesn't." Another cloud of anxiety over my head. My favorite aunt dying, the geocaching competition, getting fired, getting rehired, my sister not talking to me, all of it was all getting hard to take.

"Word on the street is Ruby's going to take a deal. But the competition organizer— no way. He'll take the fall for whatever syndicate he works for. Talk and he's as good as dead. Oh, and you missed a spot."

I frowned. "So, say Ruby takes a plea. Do she and her Botoxed forehead get sent to the hoosegow?"

"Probably. But not for as long as you'd like."

"And in exchange for talking she gets less time to find out what's real and what's fiction in *Orange Is The New Black*?"

"Yeah. Information is currency."

Again with the silence. We brushed away on the deck, the stain soaking into the weather-battered wood.

Finally Gilly cleared his throat. "Looks like you had a cow at The Big Cow."

"Ha," I said, voice as buoyant as a popped balloon. "Not funny."

"Neither is a recycling container full of wine and beer bottles."

"I'm a big girl, you know. Allowed to have a drink now and then."

"Now and then?" He balanced the brush on the edge of the stain can and leaned against a part of the railing he hadn't painted yet. He rubbed his leg. "It's more like now and today. I'm worried. Kendra's worried. We're all worried."

I realized I was shivering and I zipped up my fleece. Fall was on its way. "I had a few parties. Anyhow, what are you saying? That I'm an alcoholic? Really?"

"No." But he didn't look me in the eye.

"Then what exactly? 'Cause you're supposed to be my friend."

"I *am* your friend. That's why I'm here."

"So what are you saying?"

"I'm trying to say that—"

"Hellllll-o?" A stranger's voice called from the front of the house.

Gilly froze. "You expecting anyone?"

"Nope." I grabbed the pink flamingo I'd forgotten to stake in the front yard and bounded down the concrete walkway. "But random people have been stopping by lately, asking for my aunt. Part of her cancer support group or something. Guess they don't know she died."

I walked to the front of the house, Gilly along limping behind.

"Hi. Can I help you?"

The guy was Asian, in an untucked button down that looked two sizes too big and baggy khaki pants. "I'm looking for Yelena?" His voice was nasally and he kept rubbing his palms together.

"I'm sorry. My aunt died over the summer. Let me guess. Cancer support group?"

"Yup." He shifted, rocking from heels to toes. "Sorry. Sorry to bother you."

"How did—" but he was down the front walk and back at his car before I could finish my sentence.

"Weird." Gilly said.

"Tell me about it. He's like the fourth or fifth person who's come by asking for her. And, well, maybe I shouldn't mention this so you're not worried. But I've noticed someone in a hoodie who's been hanging out on my street at night. And, like, staring at my house."

Gilly gaped at me. "WHAT? Have you called the police? What about that Sutton guy?"

Sutton. Just hearing the name made my stomach flutter. "You know, I feel better having said it out loud. I'm sure it's nothing. Maybe just some guy paying his respects to my aunt or something."

"Or someone related to the geocaching event. Hello? If I remember correctly, we were part of busting an international sex trafficking ring."

"I think it's just me being paranoid. A lot of people wear hoodies, right? So many people knocking has put me on edge."

"If you see this creeper again, call the police. Immediately. You hear me?" Gilly gave me the Serious Lawyer Eyeball.

I waited a beat to answer. "Yes, Gilbert. I hear you and will obey your orders."

He smiled. "Anyway, your aunt was a people-person. Everyone loved her. She must have had tons of friends you didn't even know about. And she passed so suddenly. I bet a lot of folks want to pay their respects."

"Probably. I sure do miss her." I pushed the stake of the pink flamingo into the ground a few feet away from the one already planted in the front retaining wall. This one had a rainbow heart painted on one side. I hoped it would distract from the brown patches of grass and weeds below it.

"Nice. A pride Flamingo!" Gilly shook his head and chuckled.

"Only my aunt," I said. Under a tarp in her basement, I'd found ten pink flamingos, each unique. One with a green Mohawk. One with a cigar. And my favorite– the one made of pink Christmas lights. That was always a holiday staple in the Konyeshna family. Black Friday meant two things: shopping and the glowing pink bird. Sometimes,

Aunt Yelena would put it up other months during the year, too. She had definitely been her own woman. God, I missed her. A lot. But she'd left me her house in her will, so it felt like I had a little piece of her with me still. Now, coming home was special, especially since it didn't involve trudging down the stairs to a lumpy sofa bed, like when I'd been broke and crashing at my mom's.

Gilly steadied himself on the peeling front porch banister and sat on the middle step. He stretched his left leg in front of him, massaging around the knee, wincing. Yes, there was always next year's Boston Marathon, but I looked away because the guilt was going to make me cry and I was sick to death of crying.

"Have a seat, Een."

He scooted over and I squeezed between him and the railing. Green paint chips plunked to the grass as I picked them off, one by one.

He took my arm. "Like I said, I'm worried. We all are."

"I'm fine." I huffed strands of hair out of my face and tightened the elastic around my ponytail.

"Do you see that recycling container full of beer, wine, and whipped cream vodka bottles?"

"Well, remember I had that party a few weekends ago? I never took the recycling out."

He sighed. "Marina."

"Gilly."

He grabbed my wrist and unsnapped the thick leather bracelet I'd been wearing for the past few weeks. "You are far from OK."

I wriggled my wrist from his grip and pulled my cuff over the tattoo.

"I just don't want to forget." I didn't want to mention the shame that was creeping through my body like a poisonous vine. That I couldn't stop thinking about the mine subsidence, the cave-in that had almost killed my best friends, my niece, and me. That I wondered every minute of every day about the six people who'd been "prizes" for the geocaching contest. What were their lives like now? It was impossible to forget any of that, so a drink every now and then helped me temporarily not remember.

"Marina. Of course none of us can forget. But your binge drinking, your tattoo...those are signs you're not OK. Not to mention your on-the-job freakout at The Big Cow the other day. A meltdown at a roadside attraction while coordinating wedding photos? You need to talk to someone. You need to give yourself a freaking break."

I leaned back against the step and flung my arms over my eyes. An airplane whooshed overhead. A horn wailed down the block.

"Well, if you don't want to talk, I'm not going to force you," he said. "But me, Kendra, your mom, even Janna, we all love you and feel concerned." Gilly hoisted himself up and started down the concrete steps toward his car.

"Oh, yeah? Really? If Janna cares so much, she can call me herself!" I hadn't spoken to my big sister since Aunt Yelena died, outside of family events where we had to be in the same room. She was never going to forgive me for getting her daughter kidnapped.

And I was never going to forgive myself for letting six helpless children disappear. For putting my best friends in danger. For almost getting my niece killed.

I snapped the bracelet over the five black dots tattooed on the inside of my right wrist. I'd gone to Tattoo You a few weeks earlier and described what I'd wanted. The same dice image The General, a psycho Russian mafiya sex trafficker, had used to mark "his girls." Because I had to do something to remember. Something to remind me, every single day, of my gigantic failures.

2

I **slid invitations into thick envelopes** at Prestige Signature Events the next day. At least my job had been productive, outside of The Big Cow incident. It was the only wedding I'd done in a while, filling in for sick colleagues, since I'd acquired an affinity for coordinating the charity events. Leukemia and Lymphoma Society 5K and Walk. A ball for the Wounded Warrior Foundation. A bowling tournament for Blue Chip Animal Farm. I'd always loved planning any big social events, but something about these fundraisers really got me going. Every nametag, every napkin color choice, every name on the invite list made me feel like I was doing something worthwhile. I didn't have much money to donate until my credit cards were paid off, but I had energy to share. My picture had been in the paper seventeen times this fall due to coordinating such events. My photos would be on the Wall of Fame in the lobby soon enough.

Look out, Prestige Signature Events. I was back.

Derek Longingham, the new executive director, called me into his Ikea catalog-perfect office. Everything was straight lines and clutter-free. He slid out from behind his desk and sat next to me on the sofa.

"Marina, how you feeling today?" Derek had a bird-like frame and a pointy little head. Probably weighed 130 tops. To his credit, he played to his strengths. Boyfriend might never play football but he could manage the hell out of any event and the people running it. When he'd been hired to take over for Ruby, the felonious skank who'd previously run the company, things had changed. Fast. Team building, coaching, seminars on customer service and event planning. This guy was on it. Yet he was nice. He sincerely wanted to know how I was.

Oh boy. Here goes. "Um, better. Much better. It's just — I didn't have anything to eat that day because I was feeling under the weather. The perfect storm, I guess. I'm really, really, really sorry. I can't imagine how the bride and groom felt."

"The good news is, you did such a great job putting their wedding together they were more concerned about you than their photos. Your team allayed their fears and got them refocused on their Big Day. Marina, you have a talent. You unite people, instead of taking all of the glory."

"Thank you. That means a lot." Uh oh. When was the other shoe dropping?

"Here comes the tough part." Tough parts had become part of my daily to-do list. "I'm offering you a paid leave of absence. Take at least a week. After the, ahem, incident with the geocaching, you never gave yourself time to recover, to decompress. Instead, you've buried yourself in work. And don't get me wrong—you do amazing work. But I'm worried you're short-circuiting. I need you. We need you."

I welled up and felt immediately pissed at myself for letting him see me cry. "Thank you, Derek. I see what you're saying. But I'm already seeing a counselor. Not sure if I should have told you that, but what the hey. I am taking care of myself. Truthfully, this job is the only thing that keeps me sane. It takes my mind off...things."

He leaned against the orange cushions on the sofa and put his hands in his lap. "Well, if that's how you feel—well, you know what's best. This isn't about the company, though. It's about you. I want to make sure Prestige employees are taken care of. But, in the end, I trust you to know what's best."

I finally inhaled. "Thanks, Derek. That means a lot."

"You're welcome. Now go get that Arcadia Energy event wrangled. I agree promoting Princess to program associate was a good idea, but she still needs guidance. The charity auction is coming up fast."

"Thank you, again, Derek." He nodded and walked back to his desk.

My heartbeat had slowed and I felt better. It was great to have a true ally behind me. I smoothed my dress, making sure the pleats of the skirt fell where they should have. When I'd put the hot pink number on this morning, I hadn't been feeling bright or cheery. My inner fashionista must have known something I didn't. It felt great to finally feel good. Keeping up with my ADHD meds helped, too. Still, it totally sucked being an adult sometimes. Like that movie my sister liked to watch in college: Reality does effing bite.

At her cubicle, Princess was writing a list. In fact, she had five of them going and was cross-checking each. With one red, one blue, one green and one black pen. At first glance, she appeared a bit of a mess. Hair escaping from her bun. Her taupe-pantyhose-encased feet halfway out of her tan flats. I watched her for a minute. Her eyes darted here and there. She murmured to herself, then clicked on something on her computer screen, nodded and got back to her papers. A yellow Post-It, a green Post-It. She had a real system. I was intrigued.

"Hey, Princess," I said from behind her.

She swiveled in her chair. "Oh! Hey, Marina! How's it going?" Princess adjusted her glasses and squinted.

"So whatcha doin'?" I leaned in. "Derek asked me to come over and see if there's anything I can do for you." Her fingernails were painted neon green with pink hearts. Not my taste exactly, but it worked for her.

"Oh, well, I have lists of everything donated for the silent auction. Now I'm trying to figure out the best way to arrange the items on the tables. For example, when I go to these events at my church, the donations are all over the place. No one cares. In fact, people like me who actually take the time to read, have the advantage, because we notice the free passes to Great Wolf Lodge thrown in the middle while everyone else goes in for the prizes on the end, like baseball tickets. But let me tell you, a weekend at Great Wolf is more fun than sweating your booty off at a baseball game."

"Nice," I said. "What kind of prizes are we working with here?"

There was a huge gap between the buttons of her shirt. Not enough to see her bra, but enough to notice she needed a size bigger. Her gazillion gold bracelets jangled as she pointed to columns on the spreadsheets. "Well, here's a donation of $100 worth of tokens at Zephyr's Family Entertainment Center. Here's a free white water rafting trip in Jim Thorpe—"

"Switzerland of the North," I said. That was what some called it. A cute town nestled in the mountains of Eastern Pennsylvania. Lots of outdoor activities. Totally fun.

"Marina? You still with me?"

"Yes, yes. Sorry."

Princess pointed to a gold envelope. "And this is super cool. My uncle donated five ballroom dancing lessons. He does waltz, tango, cha cha, merengue, bachata and more."

"Bachata?"

"It's a dance from DR."

"DR?"

"Dominican Republic."

It was only then I noticed the red, blue and white flags in the middle of her huge gold, hoop earrings. "Gotcha. You from DR?"

"Nope. This is the Puerto Rican flag." She smiled and pointed to one earring. "So, anyway, that's what I was doing."

"I have to say, Princess, I'm impressed. You're new to this position, but it's like you were born to do it."

She smiled and ducked. "Thanks. That means a lot, Marina. And it's mad cool I get to work with you."

Whoa. "Um—well, thanks. I enjoy working with you, too."

Gold star for me.

Finally.

3

Later that week there was another knock, another someone asking for Aunt Yelena. I had to do the same spiel about her having passed away. I hated having to say it over and over and over and over. So, this latest one, a girl with straight blond hair and Steelers fleece, was officially getting on my last damn nerve.

"Seriously? My aunt is dead!" I mumbled through a mouthful of Ben and Jerry's Karamel Sutra.

"Like, whoa. Whoa." she said. She pushed her aviators down to the tip of her nose, leaned against the banister, and sighed.

"How did you know my aunt?" I asked, pointing the spoon at her.

"Well, I didn't, exactly, I just stopped by now and then for my grandfather, because—well, he asked me to and—" She put a hand over her mouth, a gold class ring gleaming. "Never mind, sorry to bother you."

"Wait. What did your grandfather need?"

"Nothing. Gotta go. He's sick. Sorry." Aviator Chick pivoted and headed down the stairs to the sidewalk.

Jesus Christ. All I'd wanted was dessert and reality TV. Nothing was easy around here. I set the container on a too-dusty end table and jammed the spoon in the ice cream. I opened the front door and trotted after her. "Come on, already. Tell me. What did my aunt have that your grandfather needs?"

She opened the door to her Jetta. "They were old friends. Sorry to have bothered you."

The ignition kicked in and Nicki Minaj was rapping through the windows.

"I literally can't even," I said to no one as she drove away.

I turned to go back into the house. From the corner of one eye, I saw the guy in the hoodie again. He was leaning against the Kazmersky's white vinyl fence. His navy hoodie obscured his face, but his hands were at his side. White male, average height. On the skinny side.

Flight or fright. Or was it flight or fight? My heart pounded and my breath was caught in my throat. My eyes watered.

Oh, no. I was done. This was the moment I'd been dreading. The General had definitely sent someone for me. There was no way I was going down that easily, though.

My feet pounded on the stairs to my house. I knew who to call.

***

When Sutton arrived, I was drumming my fingers on the kitchen table and finishing a Blue Moon. The screen door rattled.

"Marina!" he called as he came in.

"In here!"

"Konyeshna. What's up?" The glass in the china cabinet shook as he walked through the living room and into the kitchen.

His hair was now beachy-brown and short. I liked it. The dreads were cool and all, but this showed off his face. His cheekbones, his green eyes. He was six foot six of yum.

"Um. Some dude's been lurking around my house." I brushed the hair out of my face and tightened my ponytail. Composure was key. There was no way I was going to let him know how freaked out I was. If he knew that, he'd have the FBI, CIA, and Interpol here.

"Did you call the police?"

"Well, duh. I called you."

"But I'm Wilkes-Barre police. Did you call the Edwardsville station? You know, *your* police? They're just down the street."

"Not yet."

"Why not?"

"I could just be catastrophizing it. But people are so small town here, Sutton. Some still have it in for me, from last summer. Like they think I got into all of that mess on purpose."

I leaned against the wall, thinking about the dates we'd been on after The Mess. How he'd found anything redeeming about me I wasn't sure, but we'd had fun together. A few months ago, he took me to a Japanese restaurant and although I'd discovered I didn't like sushi, we'd had a great time talking over warm sake. He didn't even try to kiss me.

Smooching had happened on our second date when we'd gone to the movies. He'd slung his arm around me about an hour in — I'd been wondering when he'd do that — but he whacked me in the head by accident. I'd snorted so loudly, the people in the row behind us shhhhed me. I'd grabbed his hand and we sat like that for the rest of the movie.

Later, he'd escorted me up the steps and thanked me for a fun night. Then touched my cheek and kissed me lightly. As we kissed on the porch, I'd fumbled for my keys, pulling him toward the door. But he'd stepped away, still holding my hands. "Not yet." Then he smiled, turned, and bounded down the steps to his pick-up truck. "I'll call you!"

He called the next day and asked me to go out that weekend. I wasn't free due to work obligations. He tried a few more times but I'd been so busy at work.

And now here we were, face to face again.

"So what happened to your dreads?"

"It's hard to be undercover when you are the only black dude around with hair down to the middle of his back. I blend in now."

"Gotcha. So, um, what do I do about this stalker?"

"Well, I'm going to make sure your windows are secure. And when it happens again, call the Edwardsville police first. Then me. Got it?"

He went outside and circled my postage-stamp sized property, testing windows. Then he came back inside to check things out. It was comforting to hear him knock around the house, from the attic to the basement.

"Hey, Marina!" he called from the basement. I opened the fridge and took out two bottles of Blue Moon. I cut two orange slices and shoved them into the neck. He'd earned a cold one, for sure.

"Coming!" I yelled. The door to the basement squeaked open and the aluminum stairs rattled as I descended. I hated the basement, my dumping ground for stuff I didn't have the energy to donate or throw away. Evidently, my aunt had thought the same idea because some of the stacks were piles of her boxes, too.

Sutton was on one of the lower steps. I sat next to him and leaned my head against his upper arm. He still had that Zest soap smell I remembered from the interrogation room when I'd found Amparo Rivas's body in the river.

It was quiet down here. His bottle clinked on the cement floor.

"So, your aunt paid some good money to get the windows replaced. Even the basement ones. A lot of people ignore those. Big mistake. She didn't."

"Well, that's positive, right?"

"Uh, yeah. Definitely. But do you know how to get in there?" He pointed to the wooden door that led to the old coal room. A fist-sized, shiny padlock hung from a latch.

Honestly, I'd noticed it before but kept on forgetting to check it out. "I bet there's a key here somewhere. I've been meaning to look."

"Well, if you can't find it, let me know and I'll get bolt cutters."

Then there was silence. We sipped our beers and scanned the room. Then Sutton leaned and kissed me. I kissed back. His lips were warm, his touch soft on my cheek. I could taste the orange I'd squeezed into his bottle and his tongue was warm and I just let myself fall into him. I needed that warm skin and so I ran my hand up his stomach and chest and he kind of fell back onto stairs and I fell on top of him. Soon we were a tangle of arms and legs and my hair was out of its ponytail again. I pulled off my tank top and he traced my spine with a fingertip. I reached to undo his belt and he shook his head no.

I frowned. "Dude. Not again."

"No. Just not here. The steps are digging into my back. It hurts."

He eased me into standing and threw me over one shoulder. Laughing, he bounded up the stairs, patting my behind. I flicked off my flip-flops and howled with laughter.

I figured he'd want to throw me on the sofa and have his way, but he made for the stairs. We got to my room and he put me on the bed. We were both breathless with laughter. He took out his phone, pressed an app and Sade played out of the speakers: No place to be ending but somewhere to start.

Old school. Nice.

He pulled his shirt over his head and smiled. My hand moved over his chest. His skin was so smooth. He was so yummy.

But then I sat straight up. "You know I'm a mess, right?"

He pulled back to him. "Yup. I don't care."

"Are you sure?"

"What do you think?" And he grabbed my face with both hands. The afternoon sunlight filtered through the white curtains. He kissed me so deeply I truly saw stars and, for the first time in months, felt relaxed. Felt...here. The sheets were so cold. I shivered as he traced his fingers under my waistband

I did unbuckle his belt then, and then the brass button on his jeans, too.

***

An hour later, Sutton was massaging shampoo into my hair. I closed my eyes to keep the water and suds out. That let me concentrate on the deep timbre of his voice.

"—So then I moved up here for college. I wanted to get out of the DC suburbs. Too crowded, too much damn traffic. My mom was not happy."

"Hmmm." He wrapped his arms around me and I was enveloped. The water streamed over us and yup, he was ready to go all over again.

"Hold on, cowboy. I'm a little chafed. Down there."

"Aw. Let me kiss it and make it better."

I flushed and leaned my head back to rinse off the suds. Yup. He was already past my belly button.

"Nice tan line."

Clean and dirty. Niiice combo.

***

My feet were propped up on the railing of the deck and Sutton was stretched on the lounge chair. I brought us a couple of blankets and we ate dinner in the under the stars, scarfing down a Tommy's pizza and a dozen wings. A laugh track and Spanish were blaring from my new neighbors' TV. A mom was yelling at a kid from a house up the block. The ice cubes in my tumbler clacked together as I finished the last of my mango Malibu and 7-Up.

"Refill?" asked Sutton.

"No, thanks. I'm OK. So, tell me: what the hell are we doing, Officer?"

He came over and crouched next to me, holding both my hands in one of his. "Take this however you need to, Konyeshna. I'm not built for lying. Although the job requires me to frequently fib about my identity, I don't do it in my private life. Heart, meet sleeve. Ever since you crawled through that old bootlegging tunnel at Baldanza with your half-baked, dangerous plan to circumvent the bombs rigged to blow up that restaurant, I've had a thing for you. There's something special, fun, you know, honest about you."

It felt like time was in slow motion as he said these words to me.

"Not to mention you're gorgeous and fun and sexy as hell."

I pretended to dust off my shoulders. "I got mad swag, yo."

He rolled his eyes and laughed. "That's one word for it."

"So... what are we doing?"

"I don't know what you're doing, but I'm chasing after someone I can't stop thinking about. Someone who has kept me at arm's length for a few months. Someone I can wait for, if I have to. I just need a sign it will be worth it."

I reached over and grabbed the neck of his t-shirt, pulling him close to me. I bit and pulled his bottom lip, then kissed him. "Is that a good enough sign?"

"I think you're trying to kill me."

"Not a chance, Officer."

I pulled him on top of me and almost gave our neighbors a free show, so we moved the entertainment to the kitchen floor.

4

Somehow in the mess that was my life, things moved along for a few weeks without any incident. Sutton and I were officially dating, but his job required a lot of overtime, and I was working my tuchus off for charity events. So, we did a lot of texting and I loved the connection. Any connection with him was wonderful.

My mom was a little old school, so she only kind of knew about Sutton. I was worried she'd have a problem with him being black. I didn't care. My friends didn't care. I didn't tell her much. Just kept our relationship vague in our conversations. She'd just have to build a bridge and get over it.

One Sunday in late September, I finally found space in my schedule to see my besties, Kendra Karvinian and Gilly. I had just enough time for breakfast at Canteen 900. Kendra waddled over to our booth. Her baby bump had officially popped out, I noticed as she collapsed onto the seat cushion. Her curly black hair was even thicker and springier than usual, thanks to prenatal vitamins and the hormones running a marathon in her veins.

"Are you sure you're not having twins?" I said, warming my hands on my oversized mug.

"Wait until this happens to you, skinny bitch. But I have to say, being in love looks good on you." She rubbed her belly with one hand and threw a packet of Splenda at me with the other.

"Yup, she's all 'throbbing manhood' and 'pulsing shaft,' these days, that's for sure," said Gilly.

"Geez, am I that bad?" My face felt hot. Thank God the restaurant was loud and we were in an isolated nook in a booth at the immense front window.

My besties looked at each other, laughed, and said *yes* in unison.

I slid lower in the booth.

"Een," said Gilly, "This is good for you. You had a horrible few months. You deserve a guy who worships you."

"Yeah, that Arman character was super-shady. Glad you haven't heard from him."

My spoon clinked on the sides of the mug, turning the heart that was swirled into the foam into a white blob. I was glad Arman was out of my hair, too. Kind of. Yeah, that dude was bad news. He'd brought negative stuff with him, like connections to an awful excuse of a human being who brought a human trafficking ring and arms dealing to the Valley. But he'd also been incredibly intense and intelligent, fighting hard for what he believed in. Almost like a superhero in a silk tie.

His cologne. His accent. His lips. Our chemistry. His—

"Marina? Marina!" Gilly poked my shoulder.

"Yeah? Sorry," I downed some latte and looked at my bff's. Though I'd been fairly consistent with taking my Adderall, I still found myself zoning out sometimes.

"Anyway," Kendra said, "So what's the news from Dr. Campbell?"

No boundaries, those two. They wanted all the details from my counseling sessions. The one's they'd pretty much guilt-tripped me into attending. I was doing fine. Didn't need any head shrinking. But everyone else in my life said I did, including my employer. So I went.

"He thinks a little change of scenery will be beneficial." Let that little bit of chum keep my sharky friends occupied. And cue their suggestions.

"Ohh! Don't Sutton's parents have a condo in Ocean City?" said Kendra as she perused the menu.

"No! Go to an all-inclusive in the Dominican. Pete and I have been dying to go," Gilly said.

"Or just a long weekend in the Poconos! Dom and I did that champagne glass hot tub!" Kendra said, almost cooing, if Kendra ever cooed. "It was fun!"

"Road trip! We could go to New Orleans, like we've always talked about." Gilly slapped the table. "That's totally it! Pete knows someone who has an apartment we could use!"

"Hold on! Jeez! Are you kidding? I can't take any vacation. I have this little thing called a job and it feels amazing to know I had a little bit to do with helping someone get cancer treatments or add a wing onto the Hoyt Library or renovate a playground."

The parking lot outside the glass was getting full. Cars jockeyed for parking spots. This was a popular place. I was folding the napkin into an accordion.

"Marina." Kendra said. "It's taken two weeks to get you to meet us for breakfast. Two *weeks*."

"Some of us work for a living," I said.

Kendra and Gilly stared at each other. "Did she really just say that?" Kendra said to him. "'Cause last time I checked, I'm a nurse and you're a lawyer."

Gilly shrugged. "It's Sunday. Give yourself a break, Een."

"For the love of God, you don't need to take care of me. I'm fine. And I'm freaking sick of everyone telling me what I should and shouldn't do!" I threw my tortured napkin and a twenty-dollar bill on the table, and bolted out to the car. My phone buzzed. I figured it was Gilly or Kendra, but no — it was Sutton.

Let me take you out for the afternoon. For a surprise.

My fingers tapped the phone screen. *Sounds good but gotta go to work. Sorry xo.*

***

Work, work, work, work, and more work and I loved it. Wake around seven, get to the office around nine, leave around eight in the evening. I loved the rhythm. The predictability. Yeah, it put a damper on my social life, but Sutton would come over after to watch Netflix, put his head in my lap, and we'd talk until he had to go to roll call. Night shift weeks also limited our time together, but we were making it. How amazing to have someone understanding. John, my ex, never would have gone for this.

This particular weekend Sutton was on duty, so I was keeping my mom company at the salon. The sour chemicals that helped shape her brunette curls stunk up the area near the dryers. I longed for fresh air. Mom, on the other hand, loved this place. She'd been coming to the Hair Affair for as long as I could remember. She wore the same orange and yellow floral cape each visit and read the celebrity gossip magazines in the same order – first *Star*, then *People*. She always tipped Mary Jo ten bucks and rescheduled for exactly four weeks later, between eight and ten a.m. Anna Konyesha thrived on two things: predictability, and predictability.

Hair Affair was the type of place where the mauve wallpaper was two decades out of style but small-town gossip was always in fashion. Mom got the latest scoop here. Given what people were probably saying a few months ago about me, my ears should have been on fire 24-7.

Pink plastic curlers clanked against the inside of the dryer as Mom shook her head in disapproval. She was reading this week's *Star*.

"This rap star guy. What's his name? Anyway." She huffed and put a hand on my arm. "We had a fun run as roommates, right? We were like No Sex in the City."

"Ma!" I looked around to see if anyone had heard her.

"Don't be such a baby. I'm a hot tamale still, or so I've been told."

Oh Lord. "Holy TMI, Mom. Yes, we were great roommates. You were good to me." It was true. When I'd taken a break from John, who is now my ex, she'd taken me in, credit card bills, student debt and all. She'd fed me and loved me, despite me being the biggest hot mess in Northeastern Pennsylvania.

"Anyhow, what's with this new guy you're dating?"

"Sutton. Remember him from the half-marathon? He took the photo at the end? The cop who helped me out with all of that? Yes. We've been seeing each other."

She snorted. "You need a boyfriend like I need another donut." She poked at the little roll of fat above the waistband of her purple velour yoga pants.

"Mom, honestly. Give me a break."

"Can't you just be alone for a while? I mean, look at John. You broke his heart. He's a good boy. And then you got involved with that guy from Greece."

"Turkey, Ma."

"Whatever. *He* was bad, bad news. And now some new boyfriend? Relax, kiddo."

"Is this because he's black?"

"Oh, really? Black? I hadn't noticed."

"Come off it, Mom. Seriously. Do you have a problem with his race?"

She laid the magazine on her lap and turned her head toward me as far as it could go. Curlers scraped in agony against the dryer hood. Above the drone of the dryer's motor she said, "You should be looking for ways to make your life easier now, sweetie. That's all. I don't care if he's purple with stripes. I just want your life to be *easier*. I think you need some space for you."

"Wow. Everybody has such great advice for me. Take a few days off work. Stop having a few drinks to unwind. Blah blah blah blah blah. Well, I'm fine. I'm fine. My job is finally awesome. I love my boss. I'm finally dating a great guy. I'm out of YOUR basement. I have my own house. And yet none of this is good enough for anyone. I'm FINE!"

By this point, one stylist stood frozen with a foot of newly auburn hair pulled out on a round brush, staring at me. Another was applying color with amazing concentration. I sighed, slung my purse over my shoulder and marched out. I had done so much marching out on people lately, I should have been carrying a tuba.

5

Derek called me into his office** first thing Monday morning. He usually had coffee, read the papers and answered emails until 9 — alone. This was strange.

"Marina, we just received a gigantic contract. A fundraiser for the Pure Water Fund. The person who came in to make the arrangements stressed that you must personally coordinate it. Is that OK with you?"

"Um, yeah. But why? How did they know about me?"

"Apparently, you were recommended."

My heart did a little polka at that. Recommended. Awesome!

"Their mission is to assure clean, safe drinking water for every town and city in America," he said. "Seems simple and straightforward enough. But this contract could ruffle feathers with Arcadia Energy. We've been coordinating their corporate events lately. You may have seen in the news in the past few months that Arcadia's been accused of contaminating ground water during the hydraulic fracturing process. PWF frequently challenges Arcadia, and has publicly tried to discredit them."

"Are you sure you want *me* on such a delicate contract? I mean, I'd love the challenge but…"

"At least you know your strengths and weaknesses, Marina. Not everyone does. And I know you love charity work. You excel. It's your passion now. Do you miss the adventure parties and corporate retreats you used to plan?"

"Hmmm. Not really." It was true. "Right now, I'm loving the charity events, to be honest. It's a buy-one-get-one free deal for me. Like, do a job I enjoy *and* make a small difference."

He smiled "Seems like you've found your niche. OK. There'll be a video conference at ten. Princess will get you set up."

***

I waited for the Skype image to appear from the Pure Water Fund. Who would it be? An older man, or a freshly-graduated program associate? Dreadlocked and tie-dye t-shirted? Or was it a buttoned-up office culture?

The laptop beeped and the screen revealed the contact from PWC. My coffee went down the wrong pipe and then as I coughed, it dribbled out of my mouth

She still had the short, curly chestnut hair. Her office attire was a button-down white shirt and small gold hoop earrings. Cassidy Valeo shook her head and smiled. "I'm glad to see some things haven't changed."

"Cassidy? What the? You work for the Pure Water Fund?"

She nodded. "I'm one of their spokespeople. When we decided to do this event in Pennsylvania, I knew you were the one to contact."

"Um, thanks. Thanks! Wow. I don't know what to say. This has to be the most bizarre networking ever."

"That's one way of putting it. How are you doing, after all that?"

"Fine. You know. It is what it is."

"Yeah. I know what you mean."

I never thought I'd see Cassidy again. I'd met the outdoor survival specialist during the geocaching competition over the summer. She'd given me a hook attached to a pole for the underwater cache at Harvey's Lake, and that had given our team a huge advantage. I felt like I still needed to pay her back. She had been, after all, my hero. But the veneer had been tarnished by our awful shared experience. It's not every day your TV idol becomes your competition in a sinister game of life and death.

There was so much to say but I didn't have the energy to get into it at the moment, so I kept it all business. "So, what is this event about?"

"We have a multi-pronged approach. There'll be a photography contest for people to showcase watersheds across the country. We will feature those photos on our website, Facebook page, Instagram, etcetera. The winners will appear in a spring feature about environmental issues. We're also going to have a kindergarten through twelfth grade poetry contest. Recruiting science and English teachers for that now. We need you for the main event: a concert. A big one. I can't tell you the names we signed on just yet, but we want Prestige Signature to handle all the backstage riders and on-site logistics. Next summer."

"You mean all the contract demands from the performers. Like no brown M and M's and only white sofas?"

"Well, yes. But in a charity event, you'll find there's less diva-tude. Not *much* less, but certainly fewer wild demands. So—what do you think?" She stared at me through the screen. It was hard to say no to her. She was one of the reasons we'd been able to make it to the end of the geocaching competition.

"Where in PA?"

"Well, that's the tricky part. We're going right to the natural gas drilling. Up in the northern counties, near the border with New York."

"You do know that's in the middle of nowhere, right?"

"And that's the point. People need to see what's going on out of sight. We'll offer excursions to drilling pad sites, etc. And anyway, remember: Woodstock was just a random farm town."

"True. True. But still. I'm not in a position to say yes or no. These details are handled by the executive director."

"Derek already said yes. The question is, do *you* want in?"

"Sure. What a great opportunity. Thanks for thinking of me, Cassidy."

"This event is going to face massive opposition. But you and I already know something about struggle, right?"

I nodded. And broke into a cold sweat. "Um, yes—absolutely."

"Great." Cassidy put up an index finger and turned her head. Murmured something to someone off screen. "OK. Have to go. I'll be in town next week. We'll go over some options. See you then."

The screen bleeped off. I turned away and sat in the conference room for a few minutes longer, staring at the traffic meandering around Public Square. Images from the summer passed through my mind. Meeting Cassidy at the estate where the competition started. Cassidy handing me the hook to be able to reach the underwater caches. Running through the collapsing mine. I hoped we'd be creating memories of success this time.

6

The week went by quickly. I was consumed with spreadsheets and guest lists and tweets and posts and everything else I needed to prepare for the events I was already managing. And then I had to meet Cassidy to talk about the concert. The walk to my car was all about trying to stay calm using the breathing technique Dr. Campbell taught me. Inhale. Hold for two seconds. Exhale. Hold for two seconds. There was heavy feeling in my gut, like my body was telling me *just say no*. But I shrugged it off, figuring I was just being a scaredy cat.

I unlocked the driver's side door to my crapmobile. A new or even new-to-me car wasn't in my budget, but I'd managed to save enough to get the driver's side door fixed, so I didn't have to shimmy over to the passenger side to get out. That was a victory.

I popped the Adderall I should have taken with breakfast and pulled into traffic. For some reason, Cassidy wanted to meet in a strip mall. Subway, nail salon, Dollar General, Chinese restaurant. A random location, but hey—she was the client.

A brown Jeep Wrangler parked next to me and when I looked over, there she was. We waved and got out. Cassidy had the same short, curly chestnut hair. Freckles sprinkled her tiny nose. Merrill trail sneakers, brown cargos, blue long-sleeved shirt and plum-colored fleece. Sporty sunglasses, the kind triathletes wear. Five foot two of straight-up outdoors.

I didn't see Cassidy as the hugging type, so I just waved and put one hand in a pocket and the other on the strap of my purse.

"Thanks for meeting me here, Marina. You're the only one I'd want for this."

I stood straighter. Working with Cassidy Valeo, famous outdoor survival specialist, could open more professional opportunities. I needed to not blow this. "Thanks for entrusting me with this."

"Before we get started, I need to show you something," She pivoted toward the strip mall. I followed, and was intrigued even more as she opened the door to the nail salon. Sharp acetone and banana-sweet nail polish wafted through the air. Bells on a red string jangled as the door closed.

"Hel-lo! Manicue and pedicue today?" said the bird-like Asian lady from the counter. OK, I could get used to business meetings happening over a foot scrub.

Cassidy busted out some foreign language and the lady's smile tightened into a straight line. She nodded and called over her shoulder to someone in back. Another Asian, tall with poker-straight black hair to the middle of her back strode to the counter. Gold bangle bracelets circled each wrist and a gold necklace held a jade pendant. Cassidy nodded and the other woman nodded back. They spoke the same strange language and I looked around, noticing a three-foot laughing Buddha with a bowl of fruit and candles around him. Then water stains on the ceiling. I felt wickedly out of place. Clueless.

"Marina, hey." Cassidy tapped my shoulder. "Follow us."

"Sure, um. OK. Uh, what language are you speaking?"

"Vietnamese."

"Oh. How'd you learn that?"

"I've traveled. Picked some up here and there. Come on. I want you to meet someone."

We passed manicure tables where tiny sanders whirred and customers chatted on phones while techs in white masks buffed their nails. Then back into a room with four pedicure tubs on each side. There were two unoccupied. I hoped they were for Cassidy and me. But, no, we went on past and stepped through a beaded curtain. On the right was a small room, its door cracked enough to reveal a cushioned table and a pot of hot wax. On the left was an open area furnished with a small dorm-sized fridge, and a dinette set with mismatched chairs. A girl sat at the table playing with her phone. She looked up, saw us and put the phone down. She and Cassidy exchanged a greeting and hugged. She was willowy, her thighs so skinny that when she crossed her legs, the toe from the other foot touched the floor. She wore dark skinny jeans and a white baby doll t-shirt that spelled out *Hollywood* in pink script.

The lady who'd met us up front motioned for us to sit. She smiled, walked to the counter and began to prepare hot tea.

"Marina, this is Dolly." Cassidy pointed to the woman who'd escorted us back here. "And this is Hong." She then said something to Hong. The girl bowed her head, so I followed suit.

Cassidy talked quietly with Hong, a hand on her arm. Hong's eyes dropped to the floor and she didn't speak. Dolly set steaming clunky pink mugs in front of us and patted Hong's back.

Doopeedeedoo. Twiddling thumbs. Looking at the walls. Awkward. Three other people in the room and no one to talk to. Ladedeeedadeee.

Cassidy turned to me. "Marina, Hong needs to show you something." Cassidy nodded and the girl rolled up her sleeve. On her wrist was a tattoo. Five dots like those on the side of a die. I opened my mouth but the only thing that came out was, "Whrahgh." I gasped and took a sip of tea. It singed the roof of my mouth like fire, so then I coughed. Hong smiled and rolled down he sleeve. Jesus, Mary and the manger. I could always be counted on for comic relief.

Cassidy squeezed Hong's shoulder. My heartbeat stomped through my ribs. The girl in front of me had been marked by The General and lived to tell. Part of me wanted to run out of the salon. Most of me need to know more.

Finally, Hong spoke in a soft voice while Dolly translated.

"I wanted to leave Vietnam. My family was very poor. I worked in a clothing factory and most of my money went to their needs. One night, girls from the factory convinced me to go dancing. I had some extra money, so I said yes. I met a very handsome man, a few years older. He was very respectful. Dressed in expensive clothes. He did not touch or try to kiss me. We made plans to meet for a walk in the park the next day. There, he held my hand and told me I was special. That he had never met a girl like me. We saw each other quite often after that."

"I revealed my dream to go to America to live with my aunt, to go to college. He told me he could make that happen, that his uncle had a connection to the States. Duoc could get me a job and a student visa. He was planning on doing the same thing in a few months and if I wanted to join him, he said we could get married there. It seemed perfect. I would go to America with my future husband. We made plans, but I didn't tell my parents yet. They never would have agreed. The night before I left, I told them, assuring them I would work and send them money. Still, they were furious. Said I was betraying them. I left anyway."

Hong sighed and twisted a gold ring on her thumb. "My boyfriend met me at the airport. But he was acting strangely. I thought he was simply nervous. A man who he called his uncle arrived. He was very well-dressed. He hugged me and said, 'You are as beautiful as my nephew claimed.' I giggled and told him I was grateful he was able to help me make our dreams come true. At that, he smiled and left."

Hong closed her eyes for a moment.

Cassidy said, "Marina, it gets rough here."

"Duoc ordered me a Coca Cola when the stewardess rolled the big silver cart down the aisle. It was refreshing but it tasted funny. He said it was because it was American, which tasted different than Coca Cola in Vietnam. I became very tired and the next thing I remember is the plane landing. Duoc had to help me off. I remember him telling the flight attendant that I had the flu. Then I was put into a car. I woke up in a small room with a bright light on the ceiling. The walls were white, but that light made everything look yellow. I was lying in a bed that sagged in the middle. I got up to open the door but it was locked. I pulled on the handle, yelling for help. My boyfriend opened the door and I was so scared by then that I started to cry when I saw him. He pushed me on the bed. Then he... had his way with me. I begged him to stop but he wouldn't. I heard keys in the lock. And it was his uncle. He shouted at him to get off me. I felt relieved. And then his uncle unbuttoned his pants. I will not tell you what he did. I passed out and woke up bleeding. And in pain. My boyfriend came back and gave me a pill. He stroked my head and told me all would be OK. That had just been payment for the flight. I would be in college soon. College."

Hong rested her forehead on top of her hands and trembled. Dolly rubbed her back, looking at the ceiling, like she was keeping tears from streaming down her face. Then, she bent and whispered into Hong's ear. After they hugged, the girl stood, nodded and left.

Cassidy braced her hands on the table and stared at the wall. "Dolly is the owner of the salon and the woman who saved Hong."

Dolly picked up an empty pink mug. "I watched Cassidy's special about trafficking on CNN, so I Googled her."

I spun my head toward Cassidy. "You had a special on CNN?"

She nodded.

Sheesh. Where had I been? I'd been burying myself in dinner menus, social media, and nametags while she'd been out saving lives.

Dolly sighed. "I was at another salon in New Jersey, visiting my cousin. I saw Hong there. She was more than quiet. Scared, like a little mouse. Every sound, a drills starting, the drawers opening and closing, the jingling of the bells on the door. Many girls who come here are scared. This was different. Then she turned a client's hand over for a massage, and I saw the tattoos."

I fumbled with my leather bracelets, pressing them down over my own inked dots.

"I went to my cousin and asked how she'd come to hire Hong. My cousin said a friend of a friend was giving Hong place to stay. Another relative was coming, so Hong had to find somewhere else to live. I took her in. I had to." Dolly's eyes narrowed. "I am an honest businesswoman. Others? Not so much. They bring women to work in salons as indentured servants. Pay them a low wage. Hold them hostage until they pay it off. They make us all look bad."

"Dolly, do you know who she was forced to work for?" Cassidy asked, arms crossed. "Or how she escaped?"

"Hong will not say anything else except she worked for men who made her do bad things. Nothing beyond that. The fear stops her. I found her a trauma counselor who speaks Vietnamese. They talk. The counselor cannot tell me anything. But he has given me helpful advice. Right now, we are working on making her feel safe, in a routine. And working with the INS to get her immigration status legal. It's a big, huge mess. She cannot go home. She won't tell how she got free. She is just very, very afraid."

For once I was speechless. Was Hong one of the girls we could've rescued? I couldn't even look at the chair she'd been sitting in. The silver wall paper had black stripes. It shimmered and shined. Halfway across the wall, one seam was peeling.

"Marina, hey!" Cassidy shook my arm.

"Sorry," I said.

"We've got a clue."

I frowned, confused. "To what?"

"The assholes responsible. I don't know about you, but my life hasn't been the same since the summer. I haven't slept a full night. I'm focusing too much on work. I have alienated so many people. I can't take it anymore. I have to start doing something. I want to take these motherfuckers out."

My foot tapped the linoleum at a rate that would have broken a drill. I needed fresh air. "I'm fine. Seriously. I'm great. I have a great job. A great boyfriend. I'm totally over it."

The beaded curtains clanked as Dolly passed through and headed back to the salon.

"Marina, you're *not* fine. I can tell by just looking at you. You have dark rings under your eyes. You've lost too much weight. You can't stop tapping your fingers or shaking your leg. You're pale. You're far from fine. Join Arman and me. We're started an organization to take down these trafficking rings, tentacle by tentacle."

Hearing Arman's name made my heart pound so hard it hurt. I couldn't figure out if that was a positive or negative. "I'm getting past this on my own. I did what I could. I'm fine now."

Cassidy grabbed my left wrist so quickly, so tightly I couldn't escape her grip. She flipped the arm and over pushed up my bracelets. "Oh, yeah? Then why do you have this?"

"Fuck you," I growled. "And, especially, fuck Arman."

Dolly strode into the back room and said in a loud whisper, "I have clients, you need to be quiet."

I stood and pushed in my chair. "I'm sorry, Dolly. I'm leaving now anyway."

Cassidy put her hand on my purse. "Marina. Wait."

I yanked my bag away from her and stormed out of the kitchenette. The bells on the door jingled even louder when I threw the salon's front door open.

Then I cried the entire way home.

7

Monday **afternoon, I was watching** dust mites float through a sunbeam down to my office's gray carpet. All of the paperwork for Arcadia Energy's dinner was spread out in front of me. The concert with PWF was going to make for some friction, but whatever. I was still furious at Cassidy. Who the hell was she to tell me how I was feeling?

The only way to cope was to immerse myself in work.

Just then I heard the two loud bangs. Gunfire, out on the street. My town was going to hell fast. So many shootings. Whenever I read an article about another murder, I felt sure someone was coming for me next. The hooded lurker only made it seem a matter of time. Too risky to pull the shades down to hide, so I did the next best thing. I slid under my desk and curled into a ball. It would all be over soon. Either the shooting would stop, or I would.

BANG BANG BANG on the door. "Marina?"

I was pretty sure it was just a colleague, but I couldn't take any chances. What if one of The General's associates was back for revenge, luring me out to finish the job? Only a few months ago, I'd unwittingly broken up a sex-trafficking ring in my sleepy corner of Northeastern Pennsylvania. A few months ago I'd said goodbye to the business-mogul, terrorist (depending on how you saw it), crime-fighting hot guy who'd exploded into my life. Anything could happen now. I'd done lots of research on the Russian mafia. They were patient motherfuckers. I was just glad it wouldn't be an Asian mafia crew.

They'd been known to cover people in hot pepper powder and wrap them in Persian rugs to die.

Ruby, my former boss at Prestige, was locked up somewhere in PA. But she could have had informants on the outside watching my every move. Ruby must want payback for my busting up her money-laundering scheme. Her sentencing hearing was like a guillotine dangling over my head. I just needed it to get over with already.

BANG BANG BANG again on the door. "Marina?"

No. I would not answer. Wouldn't take the chance. I'd told the staff a few weeks ago that under no circumstances should anyone open the door to my office without me saying it was OK. But now I heard the knob jiggle and I sprang to my feet.

I heard Sam on the other side yell, "Jesus! Seriously, Marina...Princess... call Sutton. It's happening again."

Sutton? Why do they need to call him? It's happening again? What's happening again? Bait. That's all Sam was, even though he was putting up a good front. Obviously, someone had a pistol pushed into his back. My picture had been in the media for the incident, and I was all over social media for my job. The General's people would know where to find me.

No more noise from the street. So they were already in the building. Damn. Damn. What would Cassidy do? She always worked with what was available, from using a Frito to keep a fire burning, to crawling into a sliced-open Mongolian yak to stay warm. I slid a hand into a drawer handle and pulled it open millimeter by millimeter, then fished out the shiny brass letter opener Mom had bought me as a present for my first day back to work. Ever the practical worrywart, she'd encouraged me to carry it in my purse, but now I was thankful I wasn't the world's most obedient daughter. I also grabbed the stapler — it was heavy and I could maybe get a shot off one of their temples. The hole puncher would definitely take someone out, too. I was an armed office supply soldier.

Who was coming for me? The General's henchman, The Husky? That skinny livewire with one blue and one green eye, and hands like the business ends of bulldozers. Or was someone new coming to kidnap me? I needed more weaponry, so I pulled the Wite-Out, scissors, a box of paperclips from the drawer, too. I was going out fighting.

"Marina?" It sounded like Princess. She rattled the doorknob. Oh God! They had Princess too! I couldn't let the staff go down with me. The invaders probably had bombs rigged around the entire office. Just like that night at our company gala. I was going to handle this. No one else would be dying or disappearing on my watch.

The desk toppled more easily than I'd expected. My picture frames crashed. Business cards fluttered like dying moths. I kicked off my heels so I could run faster and crouched. I shoved the Wite-Out and paperclips down my shirt. My hands clutched a three-hole punch and the letter opener. My breathing steadied. I pushed hair out of my face, since the French twist I'd painstakingly worked on that morning was now cockeyed and unraveling.

Someone was pounding on the door again. The spot on my shoulder where The General had landed that pickaxe throbbed, a phantom pain that drove into my nerves when felt in danger. A constant reminder of the kidnappings, the mine collapse, my assault. No. *Let it go, Konyeshna.* The doorknob jiggled harder. I tensed my muscles then launched over the desk, brandishing the letter opener like a warrior from *Braveheart* and yanked open the door.

"AGGGGGGGGGGGGGGGGGGGGGGGGGGGG!" I launched the stapler at the hulking figure in front of me and then the hole-puncher thwacked off his temple and I waved the letter opener in an x pattern as I fled down the hall. People jumped back. Why weren't they running, too? My pantyhose snagged on the coarse carpeting and I rounded the cubicle corners so quickly I slammed against the walls, sending files crashing to the floor. The red exit sign loomed just ahead. I only had to get down the stairs, to Bernie the security guard in the lobby.

Someone was closing in behind me. Arms wrapped my waist. I still had the paperclips. I whipped the box back at whoever was trying to kidnap me. A flash of dark skin, green eyes.

"Marina, Marina, it's OK. It's OK," Sutton whispered, pulling me closer.

Oh no. Sutton! *He* was working for them too? Twice I'd fallen for another criminal? How did I not see the signs? Oh, sure, he was working "overtime" all those nights. Right. I flicked my wrist and slapped the clear plastic container right into his face. It slammed against his jaw and pink, white, and blue paper clips flew out like shrapnel.

"OW!" Now he had me by one arm. I drew my other arm back and slammed the Wite-Out bottle into his cheek. I squirmed away, broke grip and made for the exit sign again.

"Awww, shit," Sutton groaned.

I began to fear I couldn't cheat the criminal underground more than once, though. What secret location were they going to take me to? No no no. This wasn't happening. I wouldn't let it. People were calling my name but I wasn't going to let them take me. They were all involved. I grabbed a fire extinguisher off the wall, the metal cold in my hands. Pressed the lever.

SHHHHHHHHHHHHHHHHHHHHHHHHHHHHHHHHHHH.

Sutton and his cronies were covered in white foam. The few seconds they'd need to wipe it from their eyes were all I'd need to make it to the back stairwell.

Instead, his arms were around my waist again, pulling me to the floor. I'd let him think I was giving in and then sock him good. Rough carpet fibers scraped my face. Tears streaked my cheeks as Sutton relaxed his grip.

Princess and Sam pushed through the door with the exit sign above it. Why were they coming into the office rather than fleeing?

"GO! RUN! DON'T LET THEM GET YOU! AHHHHHHHHHHHHHHHHHH!" I struggled against Sutton's grip, but it only grew tighter.

Sam lowered his skinny butt to the floor and sat cross-legged next to me. He laid a hand on my head. He was way too calm. Oh no, that meant—

"NOT YOU TOO!"

"Not me too what?" Sam started stroking my hair.

"You know what!" I narrowed my eyes. "What? Him. Them. You're all in this together!"

Sutton sighed as he flicked fire extinguisher foam off his hoodie. "Oh boy. Konyeshna, you need a vacation. Remember I was going to stop by today to say hi?"

Derek crouched with a paper cone of water from the cooler. All around us eyes peeked over rainy-day-blue cubicle walls. Princess's radio was spewing out the usual reggaeton. The fax machine whirred, the elevator beeped, and the mail cart rattled down the hall. No commandos were pointing AK's at anyone's temples.

"But... I heard gunfire in the street."

"A huge truck hit that big pothole," said Sam.

"Again?" I remembered The Big Cow. Aw, shit. Not again.

"Again," Sutton kissed the top of my head and started picking out little circles of hole-punched paper that had stuck in my hair. "So I guess you want me to call Dr. Campbell now?"

"Jesus in the friggin' manger." Then I closed my eyes because I just didn't want to see anyone.

Shame, shame, I knew my name.

And I also knew I was so tired of being this hot, embarrassing mess.

***

I scanned the packing list Cassidy had emailed me the day before: no baseball hats, no sneakers, a black coat, dressy clothes. I purchased a bunch of Pennsylvania tchtochki at the kiosk at the mall: t-shirts, a mug, pencils. Deodorant. Adderall refill? Check. Plenty of pills to get me through fourteen days in a different country. I tucked my new passport, mysteriously expedited through an Arman connection, into my purse. I was excited about getting out of town for a fresh point of view, just like Dr. Campbell had suggested. He'd been telling me for weeks, "Take some time off work. Give yourself an opportunity to process all of this." Well, here was my chance.

My family, friends, and Sutton weren't quite as pleased as my shrink. They'd all arrived to my house in a group at eight a.m.. The car Cassidy was sending for me was coming at nine, so I only had to deal with them for an hour. I'd dealt with worse.

With a tug, I wheeled the suitcase out of my bedroom and stopped at the door to give my room a final glance. I'd actually made the bed and put my dirty clothes in the hamper. It looked like the bedroom of a bona fide adult. High five, Konyeshna! I double-checked all the upstairs windows again to make sure they were locked, twisted the wands on the blinds to make sure they were closed tight. OK, all secure. I took a yoga-worthy breath and went to the top of the stairs.

They'd stopped talking down there. Great.

"Well, if you're all going to hang, can someone at least help me get my suitcase down the stairs?"

No one answered.

"Whatever. Fine." I hit the first step. The suitcase flopped down behind and knocked me forward, forcing me to lean on the metal banister. It wobbled, and my arm shook. Still, no one came to help. I couldn't see their faces, only Sutton's black boots, Gilly's sneakers, Kendra's burgundy Coach purse next to the TV. I could smell my mom's White Diamonds perfume.

My suitcase and I were a duet as we descended to the first floor: *thud sigh thud sigh thud sigh thud sigh thud sigh thud sigh thud sigh*. Finally, step by shag carpeted step, at the bottom of the stairs.

"Geez, a room full of people and you'd think one would help."

Sutton crossed his arms over his chest and looked at the ceiling. My mother was pretending to read an issue of *Runner's World* from the end table. Kendra and Gilly were the only ones who looked at me. Well, to be honest, stared me down.

"Whatever, then! I'm going to make a coffee. Help yourself. Sorry there's no food, but I cleaned out the fridge since I'm going to be gone for a couple weeks."

Silence. I left the suitcase next to the curio cabinet of my aunt's Madame Alexander dolls, even their creepy gaze telling me I wasn't thinking straight. But whatever. I was going.

I walked into the kitchen and jammed coffee pod into the Keurig. The machine buzzed.

"Mom, you'll still pick up my mail, right?"

No answer. The Keurig gurgled as if someone were strangling it. Great.

"Sutton, are you still able to take my trash out Wednesday nights?"

Cricketcricketcricketcricket. If there were a sound effect for my morning, that would have been it. That, and the guzzling, shaking Keurig. I unplugged the machine and sighed.

The glass window of the china cabinet vibrated as I marched back to the living room. That noise was getting on my last nerve, too.

"What's the deal?" I was now shouting. Not good, but I couldn't hold back. "I told you Dr. Campbell said a change of scenery would be beneficial. He's been telling me this for months. There's nothing going on with the court cases. I'm allowed to leave the country. I'm finally doing what he told me to do. You've all told me to make space for myself. And now I'm doing it. And it's still not ever enough for any of you!" I stared at them, out of breath, choking back tears.

"Marina." Sutton stood and walked toward me. I put my hands on my hips and glared at him. He stopped. "Listen, this trip isn't exactly what Dr. Campbell had in mind. We need to talk."

"Oh, really? So you were there at my therapy sessions? Funny, I never saw you there. You must be the best undercover cop in the world!" The corners of his mouth turned up a half a millimeter, which made me snarl. "This isn't funny, Sutton! Dr. Campbell's exact words were 'take some time from work for yourself. Take a little trip. Do something new.' Now I'm doing that and you're all acting like I'm on a shuttle to Venus."

"Marina, for Christ's sake." Kendra hoisted herself from the loveseat, one hand bracing her lower back. She tilted her head toward her belly and said, "Listen, little one. Your Auntie Marina is batshit crazy sometimes. But we still love her."

Gilly leaned his head back on the sofa. "Going to effing *Russia* was *not* what Campbell meant. Yeah, I offered my friend's parents' condo on Sanibel Island in Florida. You could go sit on the beach, collect seashells and go kayaking every day. But no."

I was waiting for my mom to chime in but she kept her head buried in that running magazine as if she were training for a marathon. Her face had flushed, however, and her green eyes looked glossy.

"Well, Cassidy offered me this cool opportunity to go with her. She's paying all the expenses. Some type of write-off for her. It's going to be super-cool. I'll be shadowing her for her projects with the Clean Water Fund. Plus, like I've said before, this will give me an idea of how large-scale events are managed. There's no master's degree in event planning, so fieldwork is the only way. I can't learn how to hobnob with the big guys if all I do is stay in stupid, small-town Northeastern Pennsylvania."

Gilly took off his glasses and pinched the bridge of his nose. He squinched his eyes and shook his head, "No. This is not what Dr. Campbell wants you to do."

"And what if you have another panic attack over there, Marina?" Kendra said. "Who's going to take care of you?" She was holding one of my aunt's old blue and white Gzhel figurines. One perk of my trip to Moscow might be a chance to add to my collection.

Sutton's voice went soft. "Marina, this is not the best idea you've ever had—"

"NOT THE BEST IDEA SHE'S EVER HAD?" My mother erupted from the chair and the magazine went flying. She never yelled. She usually served me The Business with a side of quiet guilt. "What are you *thinking*? Russia is not a short drive away. We can't just come GET you when you have another episode."

Sutton put a hand on my elbow, steered me into the kitchen and out the back to the deck before I could either cry, yell or both. I paced back and forth, undoing and redoing my ponytail, snapping the elastic like gunfire, muttering, "Why can't I ever make anyone happy?"

I caught movement in the corner of my eye as a curtain twitched in my new neighbor's window. Great. I had an audience for my pre-flight breakdown.

"Marina. This is bad timing. But I need to talk to you."

I let my hair down and rolled the elastic over my hand to the wrist. The crisp fall air felt beautifully cool on my burning face. I leaned against the railing. "Ow!" A stupid sliver. I picked at the shard of wood embedded my palm. "What?"

"Listen. This wasn't how I meant this to happen, but you've been totally unavailable this week, and I can't do it over a text."

My eyes shot up to his, still squeezing on the sliver in my hand. Boy, it stung. "Jeez. Sorry. Your schedule isn't exactly easy to deal with, either, you know."

He sighed. "Seriously. Listen. I got that promotion."

I squealed and hugged him. "I knew you'd get it!"

"Well, thanks. I wish I'd had that much faith in the process. Anyway, it requires me to go undercover. For a big operation."

"Ooooh! What's it about?"

"I can't tell you. Sorry. But...here are the hard parts."

There had been a lot of hard parts lately. "Oh boy."

"Yeah...Well, I'm going to have to be incommunicado for at least a month. Maybe two. Or three...possibly."

"*What*? They expect you to just, like, delete your whole life?"

"It doesn't always work that way. But in this case, yes."

"Well, if that's what you have to do. I have no right to tell you what to do. Can you maybe check in with me once in a while?"

"That's the problem. I'm going deep undercover."

"Well, I kinda dig you, you know. I'll hang around." I nuzzled up to his cheek and slid my arms around his waist. God, I loved his soapy man-smell.

Sutton stepped away.

Oh boy. I sensed bad news.

He inhaled deeply. "We need to take a break."

"*What?*" My nostrils flared and I took a few steps back and bumped into the railing. "You wait to tell me this now? Minutes before I leave to go halfway around the world?"

He stuffed his hands into his front pockets and looked down. "Like I said, I wanted to discuss this earlier in the week. But you made yourself pretty unavailable."

"You know, you could've told me it was important."

"I *did*. I tried. But you were so preoccupied—"

I slid down the railing to the floorboards of the deck and started to cry.

Sutton's knees popped as he slid down with me and put his arm around my shoulders. "When I get back, let's talk about making a serious go of this relationship. Until then, I need to figure out what I want professionally. If it's even fair for me to expect you to wait for me. And also—"

"I can handle it. Look at everything else I've handled. We can do this, really. I know we can."

He sighed. "Do you know how many of my buddies are divorced, or serial monogamists? And the drinking...my mentor killed himself, Marina. I never told you that. I'm not sure I can put you through all that and if I can hold up my end of a relationship while doing this kind of work. And—"

I put my head in my hands. "Can't we just—"

"Marina. *Please*. Stop interrupting me. I'm not done saying what I have to tell you."

I crossed my arms out over my chest and scooted away. "Fine."

"Even without my new job, even if I was writing traffic citations, I don't know if I could do this. You just don't seem to have time for a normal life. I love every minute of our takeout, Netflix Saturday nights, our conversations. But I don't consider texting while you're working late to be a quality relationship-building technique. I don't know if we can give each other what we need."

"Of course we can! I had no idea this wasn't working for you. I can make space!"

"You can make *space* for me. Space. Like for a new vase or a pair of shoes in your closet. That about sums it up." He lumbered up and dusted off his jeans.

"Wait. I didn't mean it like that."

He stared down with light green eyes. I'd never realized how much that gaze meant to me. "Yes, you did," he said. "If I'm going to commit to making something work, I don't want someone to have to *make space* for me. And I don't want to disrupt your career. You're talented. You love what you do. Who am I to get in the way?"

I shook my head. "No. I'm really sorry. Come on. Let's talk about this."

I heard a car roll to a stop in front of my house. A door opened and closed. Footfalls up the steps. The ding dong of the doorbell.

"Well, you have to go. I have to go," he said. He offered me a hand and I took it, so warm in mine. "Maybe we can talk about this later, when I'm done with this assignment. Until then, think about what you want. But I would rather have a clean break for right now."

"Marina! Your driver's here!" The storm door screeched as Gilly opened it. He looked at us and bit his lower lip. "Oh. OK. Uhhhh….um, I'll tell him you'll be out in a few minutes."

As soon as the door was shut, Sutton put a hand on my cheek. "Marina, for the record, you know I love you." He kissed me on my forehead and left.

Sadness. No, anger. I picked up an empty flowerpot and winged it at the toolshed. It bounced off and plopped into a puddle. I sulked back into the house, grabbed my suitcase, phone, carry-on, new coat and tossed Gilly my house keys. "Lock up. And there's been some guy lurking around the house. Good luck with that. Thanks. Bye."

I slammed the front door and got into the Town Car idling at the curb. That sliver from the deck stung my palm and I tried to squeeze it out. As the vehicle whooshed up the mountain to the Turnpike, I adjusted the gold bangles covering the five dots tattooed on the inside of my wrist. It was going to be a long ride to the Philadelphia airport.

8

Cassidy yawned and raised her seat to its upright position as the pilot announced it would be forty-five degrees on the ground. "Be sure to play it cool with Ksenya Sultanovna. She's all business. Formal. We're not in Pennsylvania anymore."

"Point taken." My ears popped thanks to our slow descent to Moscow. Our flights had been surprisingly easy. But now it was hitting me: it was so strange to be somewhere where people weren't speaking my language. I was the one in the minority now, the stranger.

The announcement system crackled and the pilot announced in Russian and then English we were approaching some airport that sounded like Sherry Met A Va. I wanted to ask Cassidy what the airport was called, but popping a sleeping pill washed down with bourbon hadn't done much for her chatting skills. Cassidy yawned again and tightened her seatbelt. Strips of lights marking the runway appeared through the fog. As we descended toward them, I prayed prayed prayed to Jesus, Mary, Joseph, Buddha, and Krishna that the plane would land between them.

With a jolt and a skid, we touched down. The passengers erupted in cheers. My mouth hung open. I'd never been on an international flight before, but what the hell was the safety record of this airline if passengers clapped when the pilot did his job? Ms. Sleepypants yawned again. She clearly wasn't concerned.

I zipped my black fleece and stretched my legs out. At least I hadn't been forced to make room for someone next to me on the flight over. Passengers were snapping open the overhead bins and unloading laptop cases and duty free bags laden with tax-free perfumes and bottles of Jack Daniels.

On the ground, airport workers flung suitcases and bags onto carts. It was pouring. Their thin raincoats and hats didn't seem to be doing much to keep the workers dry. I'd actually expected snow. I wanted to buy a big fur hat to wear with my long coat with the fake fur sleeves and collar. I needed a picture of me looking like a Russian princess. Oh, well. Nothing much had been going my way, anyway. For now, brown Uggs and skinny jeans would have to do. I also wanted a pumpkin coffee. Fall in PA meant hoodies, college football, and pumpkin coffee. I was missing that stupid place already.

The runway was packed with planes from LOT and KLM, whatever they were. The rain pounded harder. I had that heavy coat with the faux fur hood, as many different work outfits as I had been able to cram into a suitcase, but no damn umbrella. Of course.

We filed into the terminal. The funk of sweat, wet coats, and too much cheap perfume greeted us. I tried to make out the words on the signs in the airport. My iPad Russian lessons on the way over helped me decipher some of the letters. The circle with a vertical line through it made an F sound. The M was an M. The P was an R, and the backward R sounded like *ya*. So, essentially, if the word sounded like *fmrya*, I was fine. Otherwise, not so much.

That condo at the beach offer from Sutton's family was looking better and better. But I wasn't going to admit that to anyone I knew.

I pulled out my phone. "Hey, Cassidy. How do I get on wi-fi?"

She frowned. "Let's worry about that later."

"I want to let my mom know we landed."

"Seriously. Just wait. We have to get through customs."

I rolled my eyes and continued down a long hallway showcasing posters of forest landscapes and huge historical buildings painted pastel greens, blues, and yellows. Chills ran through my body when we passed one of Red Square, the red and green domes of that famous church spiraling against a bright blue sky. I couldn't wait to see it for myself. Me, Marina Konyeshna, from Nowhere, PA, here, in Moscow. A few months ago, I'd been camping out in my mom's basement and now I was going to work for the richest woman in Russia for a few weeks. My life was an adventure, for sure.

A woman with high cheekbones and brassy blond hair ordered us to "Proceed to za custom control" and pointed to double glass doors that opened into a large room. A sea of backs of people's heads waited in front of us. The lines didn't seem to be moving.

"Um, Cassidy, what the hell is going on?" I wiped sweat from my forehead and hugged my purse closer to my chest.

"Welcome to Moscow. This is customs. You had the required medical tests, you have all the documentation. This is your first culture lesson on the overwhelming friendliness here. Lines are optional. Just stick with me. Don't talk any more than you have to. I know that will be hard for you to not blabber on to anyone who'll listen, but please —just keep quiet."

I rolled my eyes and sighed. Where the heck was the Starbucks? Caffeine would've really taken the edge off.

There were so many languages being spoken back and forth, Russian, some French, Spanish, maybe Italian. Some stumped me. They sounded more like guttural spits and jags. My heartbeat quickened. My palms grew sweaty against the plastic handle of my carryon. If I'd wanted to be comfortable, I could've stayed in Pennsylvania, right? Could have become Mrs. John Pernitsky, clipping coupons and teaching Sunday school and driving a minivan but calling it a crossover and having parties where women would come to buy brightly patterned, monogrammed bags.

A man's sharp voice clicked me back to reality. I had to suck it up, buttercup. And fast. "Meeeess. Come." Thick gray hair swooped over his forehead head and a gold tooth glinted from behind a grimace. He held a hand out from behind a waist-high desk. I gave him my passport. "Konyesha. Marina," he muttered.

Was it a question? "Um—yes."

"Eeenteresting last name. Means 'of course'."

"Yes, I know."

He grunted and clicked away on a keyboard. I glanced back at Cassidy, behind me. She shrugged and went back to looking at her phone. The customs dude inspected my photo again, then picked up the phone, keeping an eye on me as he dialed three numbers. He didn't speak to anyone, just hung up.

"Is there a problem?" I asked, looking around the crowded room. Each booth was manned by one person, one official stamping all those passports, inspecting, barking questions.

He looked at me without expression, but I felt some major heebie-jeebie action behind that Michael Myers mask of a face.

Two tall, blond men in olive drab uniforms appeared at my side. "Please to come weeeth us," said the one with more stars and bars on his shirt.

"Wait. Where are we going?"

"Please to come weeeeth us," the other officer repeated.

"Where?"

"Over there. We have questions for you."

I turned. "Cassi—"

Cassidy sighed. "It happens. Don't worry. I'll wait for you."

The men's sharp jawbones and ice blue eyes scared me. It was like being escorted by two Siberian wolves. I gulped and said, "OK."

The last time I'd looked at gazes so piercing, they'd been the eyes of The Husky, the man who had followed me, intimidated me, and kidnapped my niece. My breathing was shallow. The room was spinning. I practiced my square breathing. Inhale, one, two, three, four. Hold, one, two, three, four. Exhale, one two three, four. Hold, one, two, three, four. Inhale.

They pushed open a new set of double-doors. In this hallway fluorescent bulbs without covers buzzed overhead and the ceiling was what must have passed for Soviet décor: sections of pipe cut and arranged in rows. They guided me to an interrogation room with a single chair and a small table. A woman with black hair in a bun nodded to a wooden chair. A black bra was visible through her white blouse, along with the roll of fat resting on waist of her navy skirt.

"What is reason for coming to Russia?" she said through yellowed teeth. Her accent was British, and very clear.

"Work." I handed her my letter of invitation and the cover letter I'd had to write. Cassidy had been firm: if I didn't have those, I'd be utterly screwed.

"For whom are you working?" Her pencil slid down the cover letter, then the letter from the organization.

"Kcenya Sultanovna Myodskaya. I mean— I think that's how you pronounce it."

"I see. How long do you plan to be here?"

"Two weeks."

"And how did you hear of job?"

What in the hell did any of this have to do with getting through passport control? My intestines were currently rolled up into one big ball. I took a deep breath. "What's going on? Am I in some kind of trouble?" My heart was pounding. I'd only been in the airport for twenty minutes. Even *I* couldn't have done something seriously stupid in this amount of time.

"Miss Konyesha, Russian government reserves the right to ask foreigners any questions it wants to, upon their entry. To my mind, is best you answer all fully so you can get leave quickly."

"A friend, Cassidy Valeo, invited me to work on this project."

"Hmm. I see record for leprosy test." Yeah, that had happened. Leprosy? Come on. That should have been my first signal this country was bizarre. "Unfortunately, we have no record of mandatory HIV test."

"I took it. I swear."

"Is not on paperwork."

"What?" I couldn't believe this was happening. I was going to have to take a blood test, a blood test I'd already paid $100 for before I left home?

A man in a white lab coat entered, snapping on rubber gloves. Without asking he grabbed my arm, pushed up my sleeve and pressed for a vein. He went straight for a syringe, no alcohol wipe. I fought back tears.

Then another person entered, whispered in the woman's ear. She in turn talked to the guy with the needle, who left.

The lady looked over my shoulder. "I regret the inconvenience. You may go."

Fear and fury whirred around in me. I was ushered out another exit, right into the chaos of baggage claim. Cassidy was leaning against a post, surrounded by our bags. I shook my head and ran over.

"What the hell, Cassidy? They wanted to give me another HIV test! Without cleaning my skin. Without my permission! What the hell is wrong with this place?"

She laughed. "We could talk about *that* for hours. I'll fill you in in the car. Come on, here's your stuff." She grunted as she wheeled the biggest bag over. "And you know we're only here for a few weeks, not a year, right?"

I rolled my eyes and steadied the carry-on on top of my extra-large roller suitcase. Cassidy had a roller carry on and a small duffel bag. I wished my baggage was that light — including the baggage that wasn't visible.

I rubbed the five dots tattooed on my wrist and walked on, following Cassidy.

Then my heart literally leaped. The beacon of The West. The green and white sign of civilization. "I want a pumpkin spice latte. I need some caffeine. Let's go to Starbucks. It's right there!"

She stopped so suddenly I plowed into her. She glared. *"Pumpkin?* Good luck with that here, sweetie. Just look for a driver with our names on a sign. That's your job right now."

Sheesh. She was majorly PMSing. Actually, I was beginning to suspect Cassidy had permanent PMS and that "Scowl" was her middle name. But here, she fit right in. Everyone looked pissed off. People rushed past, bumped into me. They were even smoking in the airport. Hello, 1970. Old ladies with floral scarves over their heads, gray hairs poking out as they wobbled through the terminal. Business people in suits strode past, yammering on cell phones. Men in patterned sweaters, track pants and hurachi sandals were yelling, "Tak-SI! Tak-SI!"

After twelve hours travelling, now this airport ruckus, I needed some sensory deprivation. The lights were so glaring, the noises so loud. I slid my oversized sunglasses from forehead to nose, adjusted my ponytail, and put in ear buds. I clicked on a playlist I'd made with Kendra for a road trip to Ocean City, Maryland. Then zipped my fleece and popped the collar so it was touching the bottom of my nose, which kept the stale funk out, like a turtle's shell. Inhaling remnants of Tide and Bounce, I cruised through the crowd. All I had to do was follow Cassidy, Empress of the Crankypants Kingdom. I didn't need to hear anything. All I had to do was follow.

Just then someone tugged on my elbow. I squeezed my purse to my side with one arm and hurried up, afraid of getting pickpocketed. But Cassidy was right in front of me. I would be fine. I shook the hand off, turned up the music, and continued at my breakneck speed-walker stride through the airport, looking for our driver.

Another shake on the elbow. I shrugged it off. Not going to talk to anyone. For once, I was going to keep my mouth shut. I mean, I'd read people here would assume, because I was American, that I had money. Hahahahaha. The joke was on them.

I followed Cassidy to ground level doors as her head swiveled left and right, searching for the driver. Men in dress shirts and pants were holding signs, some in English, some in Russian. I was too tired, too over-stimulated to be helpful. If Cassidy had truly climbed K-2, she could surely get us out of an airport.

But when I heard screaming over my music, I pulled the ear buds out. What was going on? Cassidy turned, too, and set her duffel on the floor. I spun and saw about dozen people crowded in behind me. They were screaming something that sounded like, "Olya! Olya! Olya!" plus other words I couldn't make out.

A girl shoved a phone in my face and pushed in for a selfie. She was crying and shaking. Now someone else was hugging me. "Hey! Who—"

"Olya! Olya!"

Flashes from cameras blinded me. Cell phones shoved in my face. My heart was beating beating beating and I couldn't take it anymore, having all these people in my personal space. "No!" I said. I pushed everyone off. One guy with greasy hair and a black Adidas jacket lunged in, trying to kiss me on my cheek.

"Dude! Back off!" I screamed, and shoved him. He fell backward onto an old lady gripping a gargantuan red, white and blue plaid bag. She started swatting him with a rolled up newspaper.

Cassidy yelled something in Russian. The people around me froze. Some started laughing. Others wiped tear and sniffled. A few men with creepy rat-faces carrying huge cameras shuffled away, shaking their heads and grumbling.

"Where's our driver?" Cassidy tapped her foot.

"Um, what the hell did you tell them? What as that all about?"

"That you were not this Olya woman they were all yelling for. Just an American tourist."

"Who's Olya?" My heart was still thumping, but slowing now.

"Her." Cassidy pointed to a huge ad on a wall. Outside of surgically-enhanced lips and boobies, the woman pouting in the liquor ad she could have been my sister. Same green eyes, same brown hair, even the same tiny nose. It was like looking in a mirror.

Cassidy pointed to words under the image. "It says, if Forbes Vodka is good enough for Olya, it's good enough for you. You're the doppelganger of a Russian celebrity."

"Huh?"

She rolled her eyes. "Twin. You look just like this Russian chick."

I heard someone down the concourse scream, "Olya!"

"Jesus, Mary, and the manger. Where the hell is that driver?" I pushed my sunglasses up onto my head and sighed.

***

The hotel was amazeballs. Marble, gold accents. California king-sized bed with a heavy white down comforter, a ginormous flat screen TV, a Jacuzzi and a view right down into Red Square. The colorful domes of that famous church and the walls of the Kremlin were visible. For little old me to see. I felt like a queen. And most importantly, wi-fi. The little bars on my phone lit up and I was so happy to be connected. I Facebook messaged my mom, Gilly, Kendra and Sutton, letting them know I was fine. I kept it short. I didn't have much to say. I was here to sort things out. Distance was fine. Except from Sutton. I called him. Left a message.

I didn't have to see Crankypants Cassidy until the morning, so I showered and passed out in bed. Finally, peace and silence. I hadn't expected everything here to be so loud, so dirty, so crowded. I got that it was the capital of the biggest country in the world, but still. Thank God for quiet. I needed it.

Ultimately, all I wanted to do was sleep. And sleep it was.

9

After Cassidy met me in the lobby, the driver zigzagged us through busy streets clogged with both Mercedes-Benzes and little sedans that looked like they were from some old timey 1960's movie.

"Nice ride! So what are we doing today?" I asked.

She tapped on her phone and said, without bothering to look up, "You're meeting Kcenya Sultanova Myodskaya, one of the richest people in Russia. The richest woman in the country."

"Whoa," I raised my eyebrows and bit my lip. Better get my awkwardness under control, for sure.

"Whoa is right. She, too, finds all of this trafficking in Eastern Europe, Russia, and the former Soviet Union abhorrent and is willing to go toe to toe with the government, the mafia, and anyone else involved. I'll explain more later. Right now, I just need a minute." Cassidy began to type on her phone.

I got the vibe. Miss – excuse me – Ms. - Crankypants didn't want to elaborate, so I just stared out the window, watching the people on their morning commutes shuttle in and out of buses and metro entrances.

A minute or so later, Cassidy broke the silence. "OK, Marina. Here's the deal. Business meeting start times are fluid here. By the time everyone arrives, pours tea and asks about each other's families, thirty minutes will pass. It'll give you an opportunity to learn about everyone. Use that time wisely."

The driver deposited us in front of a skyscraper of steel and blue glass. It twisted into the sky and made me feel suddenly very small.

The cavernous lobby was an expanse of backlit sea foam green and sea glass blue. The men were dressed anywhere from jeans and a button-down to three-piece suits. The women were dressed up, from skirts and blouses to pant suits. Heck, I could have people-watched in the lobby all morning and felt like I had a productive day.

The elevator beeped and we entered, along with a throng. Where I was from, folks smiled or nodded at each other in elevators, so I just did what I always did and smiled at the ones who looked at me as they entered. They returned glacier-like stares and turned their backs, scooting as far away as they could.

"Jeez," I muttered under my breath.

Cassidy rolled her eyes.

We got out at the eighteenth floor. Cassidy pushed the doors to a conference room. Heavy wood with shiny brass handles that extended diagonally from each panel. People were pouring tea from a gigantic silver urn with ornate scrolls and handles on top of a credenza. A woman with ice blue eyes offered us some. My cup was so delicate sunlight filtered through. Pink roses with gold filigree ringed the top. I was loving this already.

It was easy to spot the boss. Kcenya Myodskaya was tall and thin, not a healthy thin from yoga and pilates classes, but the type of skinny that implied a high metabolism and lots of coffee. Wide cheek bones, deep brown eyes. She wore a winter white suit and was bending over the table, pointing at items on a document. In the past twelve hours, I'd noticed many Russian women liked to bleach their hair, but Kcenya clearly had the means to have it done well.

A skinny man with greasy hair was nodding like a metronome to her every word. Her employees seemed to be trying hard to maintain a casual air, but they kept glancing her way, like, every ten seconds. Well, I supposed you didn't become the wealthiest woman in Russia by being Natasha Homemaker.

"Cassidy! Welcome to Mother Russia!" Kcenya put a heavy silver pen on the table and strode over to us. They kissed on both cheeks. "And you must be Marina." Kiss kiss on my cheeks. "Please, have some tea." And with that, turned away to talk with a dour man in a grey suit.

The skinny guy with the greasy hair skittered over to me and extended his hand. "Khello, Marina Styopanovna!"

"Hi. Um, nice to meet you, but my last name is actually Konyeshna. Sorry for the mix up."

"Meex up? There is no meex up! You see, here in Russia, we don't use Miss or Mrs. We use first name and a variation of father's last name. I am Fydor Abramovich. You are Marina Styopanovna. Or, to my mind, that's what Stanley would be in Russian."

"But...how do you know my dad's name?"

His olive-colored suit was too big for his matchstick frame and pastry crumbs dotted his scraggly mustache. He smelled like a mix of dollar store after-shave and sweaty socks. "I am former KGB." He paused and I froze. "Just keeding! HA! No, we found out you were coming with Cassidy Ivanovna. I was told to research you. Not to investigate like big file in our basement but to learn about you and to make you feel comfortable. Social media is very useful and interesting tool."

Great. A stalker. "Well, OK, Fydor Abram—" I gripped his hand and leaned back, hoping he'd get the hint I wanted space between me and his deodorant-less self. Instead, his moustache grazed both cheeks as he kissed me in a very warm, Russian greeting. I got a close-up of the dandruff that salted his shoulders.

"Uh-bram-oh-veech. Is OK, is hard to say. No worries. You will get it."

"Please, call me Marina."

"Ok, Marina. I hope you have good morning here in beautiful Mosk-VA, my hometown."

Kcenya clapped. "Ok, everyone. Let's get this meeting started." She took the seat at the head of the table, flanked by a set of stern men and women. Two Olympic-sized heavies in dark suits drew the doors closed, remaining outside.

"Please welcome back Cassidy Valeo. Also welcome Marina Konyeshna. As I told you, they will be part of our team for the next few weeks. You all have an agenda. Since our guests only speak English, we will conduct the meeting today in English. We have only an hour today. Thank you for coming in on a Sunday. First item. Marina and Cassidy, please sign the confidentiality agreements."

A woman in a black suit began speaking about the next hotel to be built in Dubai. The last time I'd put my autograph a contract, I'd signed myself and my best friends up for a dangerous competition. My hands shook as I scrawled my name this time, despite Cassidy assuring me it was normal. "Just sign it already," she whispered.

"Next on our agenda." Kcenya adjusted her reading glasses. "The Kitchen. Galina."

A tall, angular woman with bony arms read from a report. "Our client workload has increased by thirty-five percent in last week. We have enough supplies for rest of month but will have to go out again soon. Staffing level is good."

"More clients. What a pity," said Kcenya, shaking her head.

What was The Kitchen, some sort of restaurant? And why would Kcenya be upset if there were more? Weren't more customers a good thing?

"Remember, no one mention The Kitchen or my association with it. It falls under another arm of my business. It cannot be known I run the project. You understand?" She then rattled off something in Russian and her employees nodded. I had no idea what she was talking about, but even I nodded because Kcenya punctuated the sentence with a fist on the table that made the teacups rattle.

When the meeting ended, I wanted to know about more about The Kitchen. Galina was still there, zipping her bag, so I stood next to her.

"Excuse me, Galina. Galina Pet—"

"Petrovna. Galina Petrovna." She turned, and her deep, brown eyes jarred me for a second. So still, so serious. Then I noticed the over-plucked eyebrows and bad dye job. Her hair was supposed to be red, but the roots were light blond and from chunk to chunk flowed into various shades of pink and red as it coiled into a bun at the base of her head. That hot mess made her a little less daunting. She shoved papers into a folder. "Yes, Marina."

"Um, I was wondering if you could tell me about The Kitchen. I mean, what is it, exactly?"

She cleared her throat. "Perhaps later." She slid the strap of her bag over her shoulder and walked away.

What? Did I say something rude? I couldn't figure out what I'd done. I had a history of opening my mouth and inserting my foot, but this wasn't one of those times.

"Excuse me, Marina Styopanovna." It was Fyodor. I could smell Sir Sweats A Lot even as he approached. Now Marina, be nice, be nice, I scolded myself.

"Please call me by my first name. It's fine."

"OK, Marina. Can I offer you a, how you call it, a cook-ee?"

"Thanks for asking, but I'm OK."

"Ah ha. Thanks for asking. Now I know another way to say no thank you. I learn so much colloquial English from you, Marina Styopanovna. I mean Marina." More crumbs caught in the moustache, but I didn't have the heart to tell him. Still, he was growing on me.

"Glad to help with your English."

"I overheard you and Galina talking about Kitchen. Please forgive her. She takes her job very seriously. Follows all directives from Kcenya."

"Phew. I thought I offended her or something."

"Oh, Galina is very serious. To my mind, she needs night of dancing and drinking. You like salsa dancing?"

Was he asking me on a date? "Um, I've never been."

"Well, you must to go. My friends and I go tomorrow night. You are free?"

Meet some people, dance, have a few drinks. I could do that. "Sure, that would be fun."

"Yes. Great fun. I phone your room tomorrow afternoon." He walked away.

My phone vibrated in my purse. Messenger alerts. From Mom: *I miss you honey. Sorry I was mean when you left. I love you.*

From Gilly: *Glad you are safe. Still don't think this is your best idea but you'll figure it out, I guess. PS – no lurker.*

From Kendra: *happy u arrived in one piece. stay that way. xoxo*

From Sutton: nothing.

I shoved the phone back into my purse and then one more cook-ee in my big, fat mouth.

10

When we got back to the hotel Cassidy said, "I have work to do, so you're on your own for a few hours."

That was my cue to explore the city, so I settled on taking a walk. I hadn't expected people to dress so formally here, although Cassidy had mentioned it. Dress pants and skirts. Nice jeans were OK. Forget the sneakers, she told me. But today would be a long walk, so I opted for jeans, fleece, and sneakers anyway. Plus, my favorite pair of skinnies made my butt look a lot firmer than it actually was.

Just as I was about to stuff a key card into a purse pocket, my phone buzzed. "Marina, it's Galina. If you want to find out more about The Kitchen, meet us in lobby in ten minutes." She hung up.

Galina was as soft as a Brillo pad, but — whatever. At least I wouldn't have to spend the day alone. It would be with the Ice Queen, but I wouldn't be wandering around a strange city by myself.

When I got to the lobby, it turned out Galina was dressed casually too. Well, casual for a Russian woman, I was learning. Black pants and a button-down shirt. Black short trench coat, black rain boots. She looked me up and down, sighed and without saying a word turned toward the revolving door and exited. Whatever. Lord. I liked my bright green sneakers. I followed, wondering about this secret kitchen. Probably one of those exclusive restaurants, like maybe a trendy pop-up you see on TV. Perhaps Kcenya didn't want the competition to be on to her. I picked up my pace and followed through the revolving door. The afternoon was surprisingly warm and muggy for fall but storm clouds were gathering in the distance.

I sidled up next to Galina, who was waiting at the curb. "So where are we going?"

"You'll see when we get there. You must to remember to keep Kcenya's name out of it." Galina opened her bag and perused a sheaf of papers that appeared to be in French.

Wow, I thought. She might not look incredibly impressive with that mess of striped hair and chipped nail polish, but Galina knew at least three languages. But since she wasn't going to win the award for friendliest tour guide, I turned my gaze from her pile of paperwork to the city bustling around us.

A black Mercedes pulled up. Sure beat my Crapmobile. We got in and the driver took off without saying a word. The colors of the older buildings were a surprise. Pastel greens and peaches mixed in with the unpainted, cold concrete of Soviet buildings. We drove past one of the Seven Sisters, hulking buildings around the city dating to Stalin. I'd read that on some tourist website. The style was called a wedding cake — nice. A good omen for this event planner, I'd thought. These ornate monuments to Soviet glory loomed over Moscow with an almost reverential and powerful vibe. They had wide bases and towers at the top. They reminded me of dogs hunkering down. And they also looked out of place next to glass skyscrapers and luxury sedans zipping through the streets.

When our driver didn't actually gun it through a yellow light for once, I had a chance to study a woman sweeping the walk of an apartment building. The old lady's kerchief pinched the droopy skin under her chin. She hunched over a broom made of one big stick that came to only her knees with dozens of smaller sticks lashed to the business end with twine. She pushed the twig broom back and forth, clearing the dust out of the way of the steps but making piles on either side. I couldn't help but wonder if this was what the Konyeshna side of my family looked like. But heck, that probably wasn't even their real last name. I had no way of knowing. When my grandfather came over from Russia, family folklore had it he'd lied about his name, a fresh start, hiding. He'd chosen Konyeshna. Probably because he had a good sense of humor. I'd definitely inherited that.

The car lurched forward and our driver pounded the horn. I couldn't see the old lady anymore, but I still thought of my grandmother, how neatly she'd kept her home. Nothing ever out of place. When someone was coming over, it was full hostess mode. Best dishes, best silverware, best tablecloths. What would life have been like for me if my great grandparents had never fled? I might have been one of the young moms pushing baby carriages with their girlfriends, going to the market. Or maybe steely and brazen, like Kcenya. Maybe as sharp and mean as Galina. I had a lot of wonderings. Maybe I'd come to Russia to deal with my fears. Maybe I'd come here to ignore them. Only time would tell.

One thing I did know is that Kcenya fascinated me. After Ruby, the boss who'd kept me ignorant of the double-crossing and all of the money she was skimming of the top of contracts for Prestige, I was eager for a better role model.

"Marina. We've arrived."

"Arrived where?" We were parked across from a gigantic train station that loomed over the boulevard. Its entrances were tall arches and people streamed in and out like ants. Where was the kitchen? All I saw were kiosks of electronics or prepackaged snacks for people getting ready to board trains to places I'd never even known existed. I kind of wanted to jump on one see where it took me.

"Come. Let's go." Galina got out of the car and plowed through the throngs milling around the station. A woman tottered with a toddler in one hand and a red, white, and blue square in the other. Two out of every three people had those bags, some shiny and new, others grimy and stuck together with duct tape.

I followed Galina around the side of the station. We stopped at two old ladies selling steaming food from cardboard boxes lined with garbage bags. Galina told me it was homecooked and the ladies brought it to the train station in hopes of supplementing their meager pensions. They wore brightly-colored cotton kerchiefs and felt boots. I suspected they were younger than they appeared, but years of living on low incomes and poor nutrition had etched deep lines into their faces. But they had glints in their eyes, and laughed with their customers. Gold teeth flashed. Ah ha . . . Russian *Golden Girls*.

Galina brightened as she talked to them. She bought two breaded things that looked a little like an eggroll.

"Here. Have real Russian food. *Pieroshki.* Yours is potato."

"Thanks. I'm starving." It was warm and sounded like pierogi, so I was in. And yet....it felt like a condom stuffed with white-hot mush. I was dubious.

"Isn't it wonderful?" Galina asked as she dabbed the corners of her mouth with a white paper napkin. "Just like my babushka's."

"M-hm," I bit into the soggy mess. And — yes! It was fabulous. The texture left a lot to be desired, but man, comfort food was comfort food in any culture. Warm mashed potatoes and a savory fried dough wrap. Heavenly.

The kiosks seemed to mostly be manned by non-Russians, their dark skin and thick moustaches different than the faces I'd seen near the hotel. The men selling CD's snapped their fingers and flicked their wrists to the whirling Middle-Eastern music that played through the speakers rigged on their stalls.

Galina sped on ahead of me and the noises from the bazaar area were fading. Now we were curving behind the train station, into a creepy, muddy, trash-ridden wasteland. What the heck were we doing back here? What was going on? A restaurant, here?

Then I saw a coach bus with red letters on the side: *Guérison de l'Humanité.* That was familiar....yeah...I'd seen them on TV specials. The volunteer medical group called Healing for Humanity that went around the world to provide health care in dangerous areas. Wait. Dangerous areas? But we were in Moscow. Then a tall guy in a white lab coat stepped off the bus, poking at an iPad.

"Bonjour, Dr. Jean!" Galina's eyes lit up as she waved to him. "This is Marina. She will be working with us."

"Nice to meet you." Dr. Jean shook my hand. He reeked of cigarette smoke. *Zhan.* I was guessing he was French or something.

We walked around the bus. On the other side stood a minivan with a line of people stretching at least three hundred deep. Many were teenagers or younger, but most were senior citizens. The rest fell into a gray, ashy middle ground. Could have been twenty-five or fifty. They all had one thing in common, though: a look of despair at a depth I never could have imagined. Eyes hollow, sad, angry, afraid. I couldn't seem to move. I felt stuck to the ground.

"Well, come on. You wanted to know what The Kitchen was," Galina said as she pulled on my sleeve. "Now you know. And now you work." She handed me a pile of paper plates. "Give to clients."

A skinny black man with gold wire-framed glasses perched on the tip of his nose was doling out steaming mounds of a hot porridge. "Greetings, mademoiselle. My name is Frederick. Welcome to our first-class dining experience. Today we have kasha with ham."

I considered the bubbling pot of beige glop. People lined up for this? *This* was the fancy restaurant? "Um—I'm Marina."

"Well, it is very nice to meet you. Today we are also serving hot tea, a bottle of water, and an orange – special donation. Very exciting! Oh, and a vitamin. Then if they wish, Dr. Jean and his team will see them."

The faces in line reminded me of the movie version of *A Tale of Two Cities* we watched in ninth grade. Their skin was sooty, hard. This was no restaurant. It was a *Grapes of Wrath* soup kitchen.

Galina cleared her throat and clapped. She shouted to the crowd, hands raised in what looked like prayer. I bowed my head and thanked God for all I had, because even when I'd been camped out in my mom's basement, I had a million times more than these people. Shame tightened my throat. But no time for that nonsense. No time for a pity party. The dinner rush began.

Little cherubic faces smeared with dirt said, "Khello, *Amerikanka!*" then giggled and hid behind their mother's legs. The moms smiled and nodded. How did they know I was American? I passed out plate after plate, smiling back. I smiled and said, *"Priviet,"* which meant "hello." Many of the women and children had darker skin, like from the pictures of gypsies in my grandfather's National Geographic magazines. They wore shabby but brightly colored dresses peeking out from their coats. Their little girls had pixie haircuts and gold earrings. I smiled at them until their mothers shooed them along the line.

Then, the old ladies. They shuffled along in boots and kerchiefs. They should have been in their favorite chair watching their favorite soap opera, not here. I choked back tears thinking of my Aunt Yelena having to line up for food behind a train station.

After them, the single women. More open to returning grins. But with black eyes. And bruises. Bandages poking out of sleeves. A few had gauze taped over an eye. Oh my God, I didn't want to know.

Next came the old men. Fingernails rimmed with grime. Three shirts layered under a suit coat three sizes too big. Stubbled cheeks, knotted knuckles. Quiet, understated. Teeth like vandalized graveyards. Gold caps. Or no teeth at all.

Then the single men, last in line. Rambunctious, antsy. Lean, hungry, mean. Or chests like barrels. Arms in slings, sleeve pinned where an arm used to be. A few with gauze taped over their eyes, too. A tussle in line here, a shout there.

One man grabbed for two plates. "DVA!" he growled. I couldn't look away from his yellow, bloodshot left eye. His right was covered in grimy bandages, the edges of clear surgical tape crusted with dirt.

"Alexey!" Galina shouted, her eyebrows furrowed.

He backed off. I breathed again. She spoke to him in Russian. He grunted.

"Hmm," Galina said, watching him shuffle away with the bread clenched between his teeth. "I have noticed many people lately with these gauze patches over their eyes. I am trying to get information but no one will tell me anything. Hmmm. Well—let us continue."

As I smiled and passed out plates, I had plenty of wonderings myself. Where did all these people come from? Where did they go afterward? As clients scraped every last morsel off their plates, some were laughing, some talking, others silting alone on small retaining walls.

"What's with the boots?" I asked Galina after I'd noticed a lot of people wearing dark-green boots that could have been left over from a Doc Martens convention. Rounded toes, thick black soles with white stitching.

"Oh, a company had overstock and donated them to the Kasha Kitchen clients."

A little boy, no older than my seven-year-old niece Piper, with blond hair and bug bites all over his face said, "*Davai, davai*!" I had no chance to think because three other children were yanking my hands, pulling me toward a cleared patch of mud where other kids were kicking around a soccer ball. I hadn't played since high school, but when I kicked the ball with the toe of my sneaker, the children cheered and raced after it with such energy I felt like David Beckham. One little girl stayed, though, clinging my hand.

I crouched to look her in the face and said, "Hi, sweetie."

Her almond eyes widened. She whispered, "My name is Katya."

"My name is Marina." How did she know English?

"Marina. Hello. My name is Katya."

"What a beautiful name, Katya." I tried how to explain how my grandmother was Russian but my linguistic limitations just made the girl giggle and squeeze my hand harder. She didn't know beyond some basic phrases, but that that was OK by me. I didn't know beyond the basics of her language – or much else – either.

The group of mini soccer stars came tumbling back, shouting. Probably about playing some more, so I kicked the ball and they went screaming gleefully off to it. PlayStations, iPhones, video games on most every American Christmas list, yet all these kids needed was a half-inflated ball.

A shout from Galina made me snap my head back toward the van. I couldn't understand what she was saying, but whatever it was made everyone clean up and clear out fast.

"Bye-bye Marina," said Katya. Her mother waved to me, then they trotted down the path by the tracks.

"Come on, Marina!" called Frederick. "The police are on their way. We have to clean up, quick!"

We jammed everything into the van. With a slam of the door, it tore out of the lot and merged into Moscow traffic.

"Damn police. Thanks God for Vlodya." said Galina. She wiped sweat from her brow and leaned against the side panel.

"Who's Vlodya?" I asked.

"My cousin who works for the local *militsia*. Whenever he finds out they plan to raid us or shake us down for money – or worse – he calls and lets me know. He's a brave boy."

"Aren't the police supposed to protect you?"

Galina sighed. "You are so naïve, Marina."

Ugh. But I had to be nice to my host. Time to use one of my super powers: lightning-fast topic changes. "Where do they go, Galina?"

She frowned "The police?"

"No. The clients."

"Oh. Yes," Galina said. "Well, they live in metro tunnels, in parks, abandoned buildings, shacks in the woods. Some have apartments but little food."

"Doesn't the government help them?"

"Our government only cares about itself. Money and power. If you have both, you are in luck. If not, well, you are nothing but fly that needs to be swatted or ignored until you die. Well, to be fair, there are ten municipal shelters in Moscow. But people are turned away if they have a fever or a rash. And if you have no proper documents to prove you are a city resident, you cannot get services. It is terrible system. The police have started to come by the kitchen and ask for documents. That's where Vlodya helps. I am very happy they all received their meal today."

There was nothing to say to that, so I was silent as we sat trapped in a traffic jam.

"Will you come back to help us? Many do not. I understand if you do not return to The Kitchen," Galina said as she typed on her phone.

"Yes, I will. I would like to. And I want to see what I can to do help after I go home."

Galina put her phone on her lap. She tapped the back of the driver's headrest and said something Russian. He nodded. "Well, in that case, you can come along to our second location, then. I never let the authorities get to me. "

I smiled to myself as she resumed typing. I was cracking Galina's veneer, icicle by icicle.

11

The second stop was on the outskirts of the city. A landscape of tall white apartment buildings, some shops, a lot of squat metal warehouses and smokestacks burping clouds into the sky. Women holding shopping bags hunched over to battle the wind as children ran alongside them. A few men stood around a metal food kiosk, smoking and drinking beers. Our driver turned onto a muddy path and stopped at a graffiti-covered train platform. Old advertisement posters peeled off the walls. Chip bags skittered like mice, propelled by the wind.

"Ah, Galina!" said a soft, male voice behind us. His chin was sharp, hollow cheeks stubbly, his thick glasses smudged. Gray hair stuck out of his black stocking hat as he limped over, hand out.

"Pavel Andreovich!" Galina's eyes turned bright. She was suddenly a whole other girl: happy, joyful. They embraced.

"Marina Konyeshna, meet Pavel Andreovich, one of our volunteers and clients."

"*Ochen priyatna*," I said, hoping the pronunciation was clear because my Russian was baaaaad.

"It is a pleasure to meet you, Miss Konyeshna," Pavel Andreovich said softly, perfectly, with a trace of a British accent.

How do so many people know English? "Um, wow. Your English is wonderful. Where did you learn it?"

He smiled and said, "I am just a good student. So tell me, Galina, in English, please, so Miss Konyeshna can understand. What is on the menu?"

I listened in awe as this volunteer and client helped Galina unload and set up. I was assigned the plate job again. Pavel erected the folding tables and set the coolers on top. He wore a long navy wool coat with black stitches where holes had been mended. Underneath, I could see a cardigan, a turtleneck sweater, gray dress pants. His heavy black boots were too big for his feet.

Within minutes, a crowd of kids gathered. Pavel and Galina laughed and cooed over the children in line. Child after child took a plate from me and returned my smile. Five women stood at the end of the line. Galina said they ran the orphanage.

"Orphanage? Wait? They don't have enough food there either?"

Galina's voice dropped to a growl. "The government has slashed expenditures on orphanages. Charities rely on non-governmental organizations to pick up extra costs, but these NGO's are often kicked out of the country. Then government limits international adoptions. We make sure we come to *cirostvo* number 432 at least once a week. Irina, director of orphanage, is old friend from school days. We do what we can."

The children wolfed their steaming kasha as the adults fussed over them, pulling down hats and cinching ties on hoods. These boys and girls were clean and dressed warm. Their clothes were shabby but their smiles were beautiful. The kids sat in a semi-circle around Pavel, who perched on an overturned crate. They sat on logs that seemed to have been arranged for this purpose. He pulled his arms back to his sides, over and over, like he was pulling something out of the ground. The children giggled, eyes wide. When he was done, he bowed to applause muffled through mittens and gloves.

After the kids were back inside the building, I asked Pavel what story he'd told.

"A story about a farmer and his wife. They have to pick a *repka* or turnip because it is very big and will feed their family for days. But the husband can't pull it, so the wife joins. By the end even the little field mouse helps. With everyone's effort, the turnip comes out and everyone gets to eat a little more."

Galina smiled. "All right, Pavel Andreovich, enough charming our *Amerikanka dyevushka*. We will see you tomorrow at Wednesday place?"

"Yes, Madame. You will."

She raised an index finger. "Before you go, Pavel Andreovich — one question. Why do so many clients have gauze over their eyes? No one will tell us."

"I have my suspicions but cannot exactly say." Pavel bowed and turned up his collar. Dry leaves crackled underfoot as he limped into the trees behind the apartment buildings.

"Where does he go, Galina?" I asked once his dark coat had blended into the shadows.

"I have no idea. He will not tell. I don't understand why. To my mind, he is very intelligent and interesting man. He could get a job. He could translate. His English is perfect. *Davai*, let's get packed up before authorities are called."

I grabbed the trash bag and flung it into the back of the van. "Why would anyone call the police?"

She snorted. "I wish I knew. When the *militsia* come, the children are so frightened."

"One more question," I said.

"OK," Galina hoisted herself into the back seat of the van.

"Why is Pavel like this? I mean, he seems to have the skills to pay the bills."

"Yes, you are right," A flicker of a grin, at me! Finally! "I like that expression. He does have the skills to pay the bills, as you say. Some people think he is former KGB. Back in the Soviet era, one had to be government official or KGB officer to live in English-speaking countries. Alas, he will not talk about it. He might also have, how you say....mental health issue. But all we care about is we get to feed him and give him purpose by helping us with operation. Like story he told, it takes a chain of people to get job done."

Right. The proverbial village. "One more question."

She narrowed her eyes. "You said that was your final question."

"I was wrong."

"OK. What about, then?"

"What will happen to these children? When they grow up?"

She looked out the window and said in a whisper, "I do not know."

12

I was dressed to kill by nine o'clock. Fydor was coming to pick me up. After an emotional day, I needed some regular, old-fashioned fun. From what I'd seen from the car, if all those Russian girls prancing around in skirts and heels during lunch hour — well, I couldn't even imagine what club attire entailed. I put on my strapless black minidress and the red peep-toe sparkly stilettos finally unearthed from a box in my mom's basement. I'd known intuitively I'd need them. Cassidy hadn't understood when I told her I was going out. She'd been glued to her laptop. I'd invited her, but she was in for the night.

"Be safe, Marina," she'd said, all big-sister-like. My hero – Miss Boring. No, wait. Ms. Boring. I'd received that lecture on the flight over. Oh, well. My hair was down, my eyeliner thick, my lips glossy. Miss Good Time. Ack! Ms. Good Time. Whatever. I'd promised her I'd meet her in the lobby at nine the next morning, so I double-checked my alarm.

Meeting Fyodor in the lobby was not at all like when I'd met Arman at the Olmstead. That night, I'd wanted him to put his hand up my dress. Tonight, I had to be mindful. No mixed signals, no matter the number of empty glasses in front of me.

Fyodor entered the hotel in jeans and boots. Not just any boots, but snakeskin cowboy numbers with pointy toes. He wore a crisp white long sleeved shirt and a bolo tie with a gigantic hunk of turquoise embedded in the sliver slide.

"Well, howdy, cowboy," I said, batting my eyes.

"Well, khowdy to you, pretty lady!" Fydor tipped an invisible hat. I had to smile. He *was* kind of charming. His black goatee was freshly trimmed and he smelled like Dollar Tree cologne. Oh, he was sweet. Very, very sweet. I was such a jerk sometimes.

"*Davai!*" I said, yanking his arm.

"*Ochen khorosho*, Marina Styopanovna! Very good!"

I blushed. "Aw, thanks. I know a few words: yes, no, beer, and let's go."

"All important words to know. *Maladyetz*. Good job."

I was ready for some fun.

The club was a few blocks away. Two doormen the size of gorillas were on crowd control. They said nothing as we passed through metal detectors. Again, I'd read that was commonplace. Lots of organized crime. Lots of guns. Safety first, I told myself. But I was going to dance. I'd already had enough organized crime for the rest of my g-d life.

When I took out my wallet, Fydor clucked at me. "*Nyet*. You are my guest, my new American friend."

My calculations said cover was about twenty bucks each. Wow. That was a lot, here. I'd take him to lunch one day to pay him back.

The thump-thump-ta-thump of Latin music turned into full mariachi blare as we entered the club. It was a converted theatre. The band had commandeered the stage, along with two couples spinning each other like they were on *Dancing with the Stars*. The women wore red one-shouldered dresses with more sparkles than the New Year's ball in Times Square. The fringe at their hems, which stopped at the tops of their thighs, twirled and shook. Their male partners' shirts were unbuttoned to their belly buttons.

The crowd was full of three kinds of people: those who could dance, those who tried, and those who sat at tables and drank. A lot of bottled blondes and fake boobies. I wished I'd brought those chicken-cutlet falsies I'd bought in college for a sorority semiformal. I felt a little unimpressive up top compared to these babes.

The cigarette and cigar smoke was choking me, though. I wasn't used to that. Fydor scanned the room and found his friends. We sat down at a table with two other women and two men, all of whom seemed nice enough. I couldn't hear a word over the trumpets and singers. But since I wouldn't have been able to understand what they were saying anyway, I just smiled, shook hands, kissed cheeks. I settled in and looked around to amuse myself while they chatted.

Men in expensive-looking jeans and dress shirts sat in groups in booths that lined the dance floor, pouring from bottles of Courvoisier and making eyes at the girls dancing. They shook their shimmies, all hair extension, false eyelashes, and tight dresses.

I poked Fydor and yelled over the music, "What's the deal with all these older men? They're creepy."

Fydor scooted closer and yelled back, "The women are looking for Forbeses."

"Huh?"

"Forbeses. Like *Forbes* magazine for successful businessmen. They want rich boyfriend."

I took a sip of my vodka and pineapple juice. "Huh. So this is basically a meat market."

"Meat market? What is that?"

The trumpets were blaring and the singers' voice crescendoed. "I'll explain it later. Too loud now."

In a corner booth, a smooth looking guy waved his hand with a snap. A server in a French maid outfit sauntered over and took his order. I couldn't stop staring. I mean, outside of the movies, I'd never seen anyone sit in a half-circle booth with four porn-worthy women worshipping him. They smiled, fawned, and poured shots from a liquor bottle at intervals so regular it was alarming. He seemed relaxed, like he owned the place. He leaned back and sipped an amber liquid that might have been whiskey. He had a sharp, wide jaw and high cheekbones and olive skin. His eyes looked Asian beneath the long bangs that swept his forehead. He laughed and smiled, scanning the room once in a while. His long fingers tapped to the music. Dark gray suit, deep purple shirt and dark purple tie. The dude oozed money, and he was hot as hell. And way, way out of my league.

I'd stared a second too long, because our eyes met. A jolt of electricity went up my belly and made me choke on my drink. My drink dribbled down my chin and I wiped it with my napkin. He was still looking at me.

"Marina! Marina!" Fydor poked my arm this time. "*Davai!*"

All six of us scooted out of the booth and out to the dance floor. I would have been happy to bob back and forth at the bar, but Fydor and his friends would have none of that. He grabbed my hand and we pushed our way to the middle. Red and blue lights flashed and then the music just enveloped me. Trumpets, bongo, words in Spanish I couldn't understand, but as soon as Fydor took my hands, I understood. His face changed – his eyes lit up, and he seemed taller.

"Do you trust me?" he yelled above the music.

I nodded. And we were off. However he positioned his hands on my arm and back made it like I had been motorized and my two left feet were actually working. He crinkled his nose once when I stepped on his foot, but that was it. He mouthed the words of the song and guided me to a few spins. I wasn't fast and not anywhere near as good as his friends, but it felt great. Truth be told, I would've been wholly satisfied just watching everyone else dance, but it was freeing to be in the middle of this swirling, smiling crowd. Fydor raised my hands above my head and then put one of his hands on my waist, pushing me. I twirled and laughed.

"God wouldn't have given you maracas if he didn't want you to shake 'em!" I said as he pulled me in.

"What?" Fydor said.

"Classic American movie line."

He smiled and nodded, spinning me again. I felt like Baby at the Sheldrake. Fydor was my dandruffy Johnny Castle. I was lost in the music, the drums pounding with my heart. Life in PA was miles away. Literally and figuratively. Now it was just me, the trumpets, and the trickle of sweat dripping down the small of my back.

The song ended. We clapped and cheered. "They are one of the best bands in Moscow," Fydor said, wiping his forehead. "You are very lucky to see them."

"Fydor, this is wonderful. You have no idea. Let's take a selfie!"

He smiled. We put our heads together and I snapped a few photos, a souvenir of the night.

Maracas whirred and the band struck up a slow number. Just as I was about to grab Fydor's hand again, his eyes grew wide and he froze.

"What? Don't you want to—" Puzzled, I turned around.

And there was the Don Juan from the booth, flying solo without his Big Boobie Posse. I came only to his shoulders. I had to tilt my head to see him. He nodded. Fydor nodded back and left.

"Wait!" If anyone would've told me about this earlier in the day, I wouldn't have believed that I didn't want Fydor to leave my side. But he'd disappeared, enveloped in the crowd.

The dude leaned into my ear and said in Russian-accented English, "Please. Dance with me." He didn't wait for an answer. Simply grabbed my right hand in his, and held it next to his heart. He wrapped his right arm around me and swayed. My left hand hung limp at my side as I shuffled back and forth with him. I didn't have much of a choice, unless I wanted to stomp on his foot or nail him in the jimmies, but I decided to hope the song would be short. I couldn't hear him hum, but I felt the rumble in his chest.

"She used to love salsa," he muttered into the top of my head.

"Who?" My cheek rubbed against his silk tie. He didn't have the best rhythm. I tilted my face up again and examined angles of his cheekbones and the intensity of his gaze. He was one model-worthy man. The last time I'd associated with a gorgeous hunk who smelled this delicious— well, I'd ended up escaping from a collapsing mine tunnel. "Hey, you. Fred Astaire. Who used to love salsa?"

"My ex-girlfriend." He stepped me back and then to the side. I stood on tiptoes and noticed the Silicone Sisters staring at us. "I miss her," he added. "We used to go dancing every weekend."

"Oh," I said. "Well, sorry it didn't work out. Thanks for the dance. I have to get back to my friends."

He released me. Tears lined his brown eyes, making the eyelashes clump together. "You just look so much like her. I saw on Twitter you were here and I had to see for myself."

"Twitter? What? Who exactly was your girlfriend?" But I had a feeling I knew. The airport mob scene flashed through my mind.

"Olya. There is a hashtag. Olyaornot. You look just like her." The accordion fanned in and out. "The resemblance is certain. You could be sisters."

"Oh boy. Um, gotta go. Thanks, Big Guy." I was a hashtag. Jesus, Mary and the Carpenter.

"Wait. Please. Your name?"

A bongo solo punctuated my pivot as I broke free, wondering what that weirdo's deal was.

I trotted to the bar to rejoin Fydor and Friends. "Sorry. What the junk? I need a drink."

"Do you know kwhoo that eez?" said that one I thought was named Vika, eyes narrowed as she sipped a martini.

"Some heartbroken playboy who enjoys vodka with silicone and says I remind him of his ex-girlfriend, some pop star named Olya." I was getting tired of shouting above the music.

Fydor's friend Alexy tapped a cigarette into the ashtray and took a long drag. "That, my new American friend, is Dmitry Daurenov. Oil tycoon of Kazakhstan. We have been trying to get interview with him for a year. And he comes right up to you and asks you to dance in club."

Vika chimed in. "He and Olya were the Beyonce and Jay-Z of Russia."

I grabbed my phone and opened Twitter. #Olyaornot had 1000 tweets. I swiped through tweets, some with pictures of me dancing with Mr. Sad Rich Dude. I suddenly felt very, very watched. I shoved the phone back in my purse. As if the lurker at my house wasn't bad enough.

"He seems pathetic for a millionaire," I said.

"Billionaire." Vika killed the last gulp of her martini and raised her hand for another.

"No. WAY. Me and rich men don't mix."

She rolled her eyes. "Only American girl would say that."

"Listen, you have no idea—"

She curled her lip at me. "Listen, Yankee. You have no idea what is like here. Ever since fall of Communism, western countries flood us weeth promises and lies. Here I am, with master degree. I am journalist. I am interested in truth. Instead, all newspapers, magazines and news stations are puppets of government. I spend my days and nights writing regime-approved garbage. And the twenty dollars Fydor here spent on you would make a *babushka* selling herbs at the subway very happy for a week. Instead, you complain about rich man hitting on you."

I felt my face flush. This time the embarrassment wasn't from passing out under The Big Cow. It came from understanding I didn't understand much at all.

Fydor put an arm around Vika. "Why so serious, my friend? None of our problems are Marina's fault. Let us dance. Night is young. And so are we. Come on. *Davai*!" He glanced at and mouthed "sorry."

Then he looked at Vika, flicked the side of his throat and frowned. She rolled her eyes and took a drag off Alexey's cigarette. I had no idea what the throat flick meant, but I hoped it meant *shut your fat trap before I punch you in the throat.*

"Hey, Fydor!" I pointed to a bathroom sign. I'd earned a break from Venomous Vika. Plus, the vodkas were creeping up on me.

The music faded as I wobbled down a neon-lit hallway to the bathroom. I stood in line and leaned against the wall, doing the pee-pee dance. The door slammed open and two women holding cell phones teetered out. One looked at me, her black eyeliner smeared under her eyes. She screeched and grabbed her friend's arm. Their phones were in my face. All I could make out was "Olya!" So I leaned against the wall and posed. Give the people what they want, right? I raised my right hand and made a peace sign. They finished their photo shoot and exited the bathroom. Then it was my turn to break the seal.

13

Instead of going to the Kasha Kitchen the next day, I met Cassidy in the hotel lobby. We went to a park and sat on a bench. In the rain. It was miserable.

"What are we doing here?" I was already antsy. I switched my umbrella to my other hand.

"Waiting. Watching."

"For what?"

"Talk quietly. Pretend you're showing me something in your magazine. We're just two gal pals enjoying the fall weather."

"Fine," I scooted toward her and pointed to an ad of a woman dangling a cherry into her mouth.

"Here's the deal. If we are going to take down a trafficker, we need to do surveillance first. We have to know his routines, his patterns, right?"

"Um, OK, makes sense." It was a lie. I still didn't get what sitting here had to do with anything. There were no shady guys lurking around the park. As far as I could tell, *we* were the weirdoes, sitting on a bench on a dreary day where anyone with sense was inside.

There were only so many minutes I could re-read the magazine she gave me, count the number of ducks, marvel at the height of the women's stiletto boots, and keep my own boots out of the mud lake surrounding our bench. And there was only so much to talk to Cassidy about because she wasn't exactly winning the Miss, I mean Ms., Congeniality Award. I mean, I loved her on her TV show, *Wild Woman.*

She was so engaging, so awesome. In real life, she was an intense dud. I couldn't take it anymore.

"Cassidy, what the hell? This is ridiculous." I was beyond bored. And getting cold.

"So you know Pavel, the guy you told me about from the orphanage?"

I smiled. "Yes! He was so sweet telling the children that cute story about the carrot or something!"

"Right. Well, he's been following some suspects for us. He says this park is where a lot of exchanges go down."

I glanced over my shoulder, palms suddenly sweaty. "Really? Isn't that dangerous?"

"Maybe, but he is poor. Just wallpaper. He sits on the bench and no one pays him any attention. He speaks Russian, he speaks English, he has a beautiful mind. And no one notices him. He's a perfect spy."

"Why does he do this?"

"I don't know. A sense of justice? Something to do? A way to feel like he matters?"

"Hmmm," I said.

"Look over there, three benches down. See the guy lying on the bench?"

"Yeah."

"Well, that's him. Pavel. Permanent fixture. No one notices. Not even you."

My heart sank. I stood to go over to him, but Cassidy flung an arm across my lap to bar the way. "No! Citizens here don't just go up to homeless people. He's fine. Just wait."

"For what?"

"The guy who's going to be our broker for the sting often meets his clients here. Brings his daughter for a walk in the park most days at this time. He will predictably meet up with at least two or three friends, talk and move on, all with his adorable little girl holding his hand. There."

Cassidy nodded toward a dude in a black leather coat who was indeed holding the hand of a child, her blond hair in pigtails. She licked an ice cream cone and skipped along the pavement. A white-haired old man with a hunched back and a cane hobbled toward them. The girl came to a halt as her dad stopped to greet the adorable old man.

They gave each other two kisses on each cheek, then talked and laughed.

"We're going to take a photo of you. For your scrapbook," said Cassidy.

I flinched. "Huh? I don't have a scrapbook."

"Trust me, Marina."

"Fine." I got up, hand on my hip, smiling.

"To your left. A little more. Perfect."

I sat down and watched the two men talk. Then the old guy strolled away, smiling.

"Awwwww," I said, "He made the little old man so happy."

Cassidy whispered, "That 'little old man' is one of the heads of the Organizatsiya, the Russian mafia. Strip off his overcoat, cardigan, and button-down shirt, and you'll see a world map of prison tattoos. He's *not* a cute codger. He's a monster. He's a big player in the red market."

"What's the red market?"

"The underground system of selling human bodies, in full and in parts. Trafficking, blood, organs. Anything can be sold here, with or without your permission."

I turned my mouth down and pulled my coat tighter. "Eeew."

"You have a way with words, Marina."

As she finished the sentence the old man ambled past, his cane a metronome on the pavement. I ducked my head and pretended to read my magazine until he was just a speck of gray in my peripheral vision.

Cassidy took out her phone and typed. "Here's your picture." There I was, with half of my face cheezing into the camera. Most of the frame was filled with the two men talking.

"Kcenya will find this very interesting. Get up. We have to go somewhere else and watch."

***

I spent the next day with Cassidy as well, pretending to be happy tourists but really on stakeouts for criminals. I'd cheese in pictures, she'd get maybe my ear in the corner, and capture a thug in a black leather jacket talking or standing with another goon. Sometimes getting into a car, sometimes walking out of a store. It might not have been the most exciting gig around, but if it could be the link in a chain to get even one of these monsters in prison, I'd chill on every bench in Russia.

My phone buzzed. Fydor. "Marina, can I please to take you out for dinner tonight?"

"Sure! Where? I should be back at the hotel by seven."

"I want to take you to Georgian restaurant. You know Georgian food?"

My mouth watered. "Like fried chicken and peach pie?"

Fydor laughed. "No, my American friend. Food from Georgia, a country south of Russia."

Duh. Of course. I pulled up a world map on my phone to look for not-fried-chicken-Georgia.

We agreed to meet at 7:30. Fun with Fydor again. He was such a nice guy. Sutton was nice, too, in so many ways. Nice to talk to. Nice to hang out with. To look at. To sleep with. But I screwed up nice. I was always screwing it up. I'd had a nice relationship with my sister. Gilly used to have a nice chance of a strong finish at the Boston Marathon. Even my old living situation with my mom had been nice, but I hadn't realized it.

Compared to what I'd seen so far here, I'd been lucky as hell to live in my mom's basement. At least it was warm and clean, my own space. Fydor told me he still lived with mother, father, sister, aunt *and* grandfather in a two bedroom, one bath apartment. My own coalcracker house in Edwardsville wasn't going to win any awards in *Better Homes and Gardens*, but it was a country club compared to that.

At seven, Fydor texted me the address of the restaurant and said he'd have to meet me there. I found it myself. All by myself. I navigated the metro by myself, took the correct exit and even found the restaurant. It was housed in the ground floor of a gigantic cement block of an apartment building. Fydor knew I wouldn't be able to read the sign, so he said to look for building number fourteen and go through the red doors.

I settled in on a stool at the bar and ordered a glass of wine using my limited Russian repertoire. Hey, I had linguistic priorities. A girl needed her wine. And the red was amazing. Thick and sweet. So there I was, after an uneventful solo excursion through Moscow. I was feeling a little proud as I scanned the room. There was a bar on one side, a dining room connected to it and then two small private dining rooms with curtains on either side. It was intimate and lovely. Gold-flecked mirrors caught the candlelight. Red linens draped the tables.

It was actually comforting how I couldn't understand everything spoken around me because the body language, the laughter, the leaning in toward each other, told me so much. Dark-haired men, women dressed up with carefully-done makeup and sparkly jewelry. Families laughing, clinking glasses.

A ping in my heart for my own family. For sitting around my mom's kitchen table, admonishing Piper when she made sculptures with her mashed potatoes. Holding the baby. Oh, the baby. He was already three months old. Janna hadn't forgiven me and the distance was making me so, so sad. How do you convince your sister you didn't mean for a crazy, murdering maniac to kidnap her daughter, although you'd known it was a possibility? I'd wanted to feel in control, that I could've solved the problems on my own. I'd been in denial that anything horrible would have happened.

Well, I'd certainly learned a lot about control when The General and Ruby had tried to kidnap Piper and then we'd all almost died in a cave-in. So I was done solving problems — I simply wanted no more of them. I'd come here to Moscow to help Cassidy with her vendetta because I'd thought I had one, too. Maybe it was true, but I think the ache in my chest largely came from the pain I'd caused others back home.

It was then, as I was thinking this, I recognized him. The broad back, that silver in his hair. And just like that, my body felt warm. I registered his touch even though he was sitting in a booth with curtains pulled up on the sides. His back was to me, so I could indulge myself in a spying session. The sleeves of his bronze dress shirt were rolled up, to expose the flex of his forearms. The strong hands connected to the forearms. And how the fingers connected to those hands had felt on the inside of my thigh. He was focused on whatever he was typing on his phone. I shifted on the vinyl seat, and watched him laugh at something on the screen.

I looked down and checked my own cell. Fydor was now officially late. The universe had meant for Arman and me to meet up.

The bartender cleared his throat and said something that probably meant, "What would you like?" I smiled and held up my glass. Once it was refilled, I took a deep breath and walked over to Arman. Thank

God for beer guts. Or wine guts. I twirled the tassel that held the curtain back and smiled. Arman lifted his head and blinked. His mouth dropped open and then he smiled. Those eyes were still deep and bright, just as I'd remembered.

"Konyeshna," he said, standing to hug me.

No one had ever made my last name sound so sexy. *Of course*. It had always seemed so silly before – who would want their last name to mean *of course*? In this context, it made sense. He grabbed my hand, and sat back down. Without breaking his voodoo eye contact, he patted the cushion. I obliged with my breath caught in my throat.

Then he leaned in so close his breath glided off my cheek and flickered on my collarbone. "I'm glad fate brought us together tonight. I wasn't planning on seeing you until later this week, my Marina."

My Marina. Wow. I swore I'd never ever succumb again, but he was so smooth in a place where I felt so out of place. "Um, yeah."

He chuckled. "This is a long leap from Pennsylvania. What made you want to become so involved in Cassidy's work?"

Had he forgotten my crooked boss and her Russian mafia sex trafficking ringleader friend? The dead Salvadoran child? The geocaching competition where the prize was a harem of young girls for the sex trade? My niece being abducted? Hello?

I took a deep breath. "Well, after our adventure, I'd thought I could just settle back into my old life. Unfortunately my subconscious kicked in, what seemed like PTSD reared its ugly head, and I, uh, had some freak outs." By then, my hands began to shake. My wine was jumping in the glass. Arman took it and covered my hands with his. "Then I met a woman who'd been forced to work for The General."

"I am certainly glad you are with us. I think it will be good for you. For all of us, to give these criminals what they deserve. So let us not darken this reunion with talk of sadness. Why are you at this restaurant?"

The anise and vanilla of his cologne. I'd forgotten about that and it suddenly relaxed me. "Supposed to meet a co-worker. Nice guy. Looks like he's not showing up though. Why are you here?"

Arman straightened his cuffs. "I'm meeting someone, as well." He cleared his throat. "But when it is over, we must see each other outside of our professional obligations. How long are you here with Cassidy?"

"Ten more days." Ten long, wet, freezing, and probably snowless days. What was the point of coming to Russia if I wasn't going to see any snow, for God's sake?

"If ever you need me, I am available."

Holy Merry Christmas. That freaking glint in his eye. This man was like crack for my libido. Earlier I'd been pining for Sutton, but now I couldn't think of anything but Arman unbuttoning that bronze shirt. And in the mirror I caught Fydor walking in. Shit shit shit.

"My friend's here. I have to go. But you can find me later tonight." I wrote down my hotel and room number on the back of my business card, not giving Arman the chance to get another word in. I slid out of my seat before the awkward duty of introductions: Fydor, meet Arman. We make out and get into trouble. Arman, meet Fydor. He has a crush on me and I let him because he takes me out to cool places.

I felt like the most horrible person in the world.

After leaping from the booth, I pivoted and pretended I was just walking from the ladies' room. My heart was still fluttering from seeing Arman when I kissed Fydor on both cheeks.

"*Prostemenya*, Marina. I'm sorry to keep you waiting." Fydor pulled my chair out for me.

"No worries. It gave me some time to think and enjoy a glass of wine."

In a few minutes our table was filled with dishes I'd never heard of: *khinkali, lobio, khachipuri*. Dumplings, a kidney bean casserole, and cheese bread. But I almost choked on a dumpling when I noticed Arman stand to hug a gorgeous woman in a long fur coat. Beneath her little black dress was a body to rival a *Sports Illustrated* swimsuit model. Hmmm...his hug lasted a little too long for any "business meeting."

"Marina, why is your face red? Is this too spicy?" he said, looking concerned.

"Uh, no, Fydor. Sorry. I think the wine might be getting to me. So tell me more about your summer cabin in the woods."

We chatted for a while, and then his phone buzzed. Fydor frowned. "Sorry. Allyo?" He stood and put up an index finger, asking me to wait. I shoved another dumpling down my gullet and watched Arman talk. To the beauty queen? I felt more jealous than I'd ever expected to be.

Fydor ended the call, suddenly serious. "I am sorry, Marina. Kcenya needs me at the office. I will take care of the bill. Enjoy yourself. Thank you for accompanying me."

"But—"

He went to the front desk faster than I could get up. I sighed and dove in for another piece of cheese bread, preparing myself for a night of pay-per-view movies in my room.

A few minutes later, Arman's date stood. He kissed her surprisingly chastely on one cheek. Then a hug, too. Hmmmm.

As soon as she left, I sauntered over to his booth. "So where are you headed now?" I said, trying to be as casual as possible, knowing I was failing in an epic manner. *Hint hint, come back with me to my hotel.* I played with the gold fringe at the hem of the curtain surrounding the booth.

"Well, my Marina," Arman said, sliding a money clip into his suit coat pocket, "Unfortunately, I have a meeting."

"Bor-ing. Come to my hotel for a drink. We can catch up."

Oh, he gave me that eagle stare again. No talking for a few beats. Just staring. Then it was over. "A raincheck. I must leave." He peered at his phone, shook his head and gave *me* a very chaste peck on the cheek, too.

I put my hand on his lower back and he paused. "I cannot. I must go now." His mouth was in a straight line. Not even a hint of a smile. "I will be in touch," he added.

Well, there went my night. It was back to the hotel. Alone.

He left and I got an idea. What was this international man of mystery up to? What *was* his part of our operation? I was in the dark about so much here. I was already an expert on bench sitting, potato chip eating, and fake photo-taking. I wanted a new challenge, so it was time to see if I could apply the surveillance techniques Cassidy had taught me.

So I left, too, staying far enough behind him to see where he was going but not be too obvious. The cobblestone street in this touristy part of town was packed with people out for a walk in the brisk fall evening. I turned my coat collar up and watched Arman get into a black Mercedes. Faithful Hasan, his assistant and bodyguard, was at the wheel.

A taxi was about to cruise by, so I extended an arm. The shiny yellow Ford screeched to a stop and I slid in. The inside reeked of cigarettes and sweat.

"Where to, Mees?" Ca-ching! He spoke English! How had he known I wasn't Russian?

"Follow that Mercedes." I pointed.

He nodded and turned up the radio to some crazy Indian-Russian-Middle Eastern noise parade. I sat back and smirked.

The streets became less brightly lit and wider. We drove through canyons formed by tall pale gray apartment buildings, block after block of stacked balconies. Soon we were reached an industrial district — a strip of warehouses, short and squat. The driver tapped his cigarette out the window and stared at me in the rear-view as he exhaled smoke. I waved ahead. His eyes went back to the road.

Hasan turned left onto a small access road. My taxi driver hung back without being told. My heart thumped and I couldn't stop tapping my fingers. What type of meeting did Arman have here? Some of the dark warehouses had broken windows. Grimy and beat-up for sure, yet the street was lined with high-end cars. Gleaming BMW's, Mercedes Benzes, Maseratis, other models I couldn't identify because they were atmospheres above my social circle.

Hasan stopped in front of a building with the number sixty-one on the door. A guy big enough to be a pro wrestler stood outside the entrance under a yellow light. Arman got out. Someone stepped out of the shadows. Small, short, in a long dark coat. A woman. It looked like Cassidy. Huh? She'd told me she'd be working in her room all night.

Cassidy nodded at the bouncer-looking guy. Arman shook his hand.

"Mees, I don't have good feeling about thees," my driver said.

"Me, either. But let's stay a little longer."

"You have cash, so you are boss."

I gulped. Right. There was no meter. Hopefully he took Visa.

I powered down my window and listened. No chatting among the bouncer, Arman and Cassidy. But when the bouncer cranked open the huge metal door, I heard cheering.

14

s soon as the door slammed, I told my cabbie through the
rolled down window, "Please wait here." He shrugged and
scanned the street.

I was assuming this was some type of sporting event — maybe
boxing —something bookies loved. Maybe Arman bet on fights. I
would work my feminine wiles on the bouncer, get in there and see for
myself. My charm seemed to work everywhere else.

The dude's gleaming, bald head turned toward me. The pink
bubbly scar that zagged from the top of his skull and ended at his chin
didn't make me feel more confident. But whatever. I had to know what
was going on in that warehouse.

"Hi, handsome. I'm with Mr. Ocalan."

"*Nyet*." He pointed to my taxi.

"I was supposed to meet him here earlier, but I was running late.
He's expecting me. And we all know what happens when Mr. Ocalan
doesn't get what he wants."

The gorilla in a suit grunted and grabbed my upper arm.

"Hey, let go!" I wriggled to free myself, but he only squeezed
harder, pushing me back toward my cab. Just then came a loud bang
further down the building and then the cheering again.

Light flooded the narrow street and a figure stumbled onto the
road. The bouncer gave me a final shove and stomped over to the guy.
A drunk, I supposed. I was probably the least of his problems. The
door was still open and light spilling out illuminated the figure now
heaped in the middle of the road. Boy, this dude was wasted. He'd
have a hell of a hangover in the morning. I winced in sympathy.

I trotted after Gorilla, who moved more quickly than his size would have indicated. The cheering from the building turned into a roar. The figure on the ground wasn't really moving any more, just sort of …twitching. He was wearing only black pants and boots. Wait – green boots. The kind they'd given away at the Kasha Kitchen.

That was the first thing I noticed. The second was the blood smeared all over his chest and arms and face, and the broken nose pushed to the side of his face. One leg was twisted in a way it shouldn't have been. Both eyes were swollen shut. His mouth hung open, gasps escaping like air from a punctured balloon. Blood bubbled over his lips.

"What? Oh my God! Help him!" I screamed at Gorilla.

The bouncer just pressed a finger to his earpiece, then kicked the beaten man. The guy didn't respond except for twitching fingers. Then he started shaking and making a noise that was between moaning and crying. I wanted to run to him to help, but three other monster-sized men flew out from the warehouse, shirts smeared with blood. One huffed in annoyance. The trio picked up the guy as if he were roadkill and hauled him away around the back of the building.

Footsteps behind me. I squeezed my eyes shut. There was nowhere for me to run. This is what I got. I just should have gone back to the hotel. Now I was going to disappear behind the building, too.

"Marina!" Cassidy hissed in my ear. I didn't have turn to look to know she was pissed. *Super* pissed. "What the hell are you doing here?"

I gathered the guts to turn. Her fists were on her hips, feet wide.

"I – I – I was curious. Just, um, wanted to see where Arman was going. I dunno. I wondered what he was up to."

Arman put a hand on my elbow and ushered me back down the dark sidewalk to the taxi that was miraculously still waiting. I stared at the puddles in the street, which reflected the few streetlights with a rainbow-greasy shine. I felt like I was gliding along on autopilot. *The green boots. Those green boots.* His eyes swollen shut. The hissing from his lungs.

Cassidy tapped on the window and the driver looked up from his phone. They spoke in Russian. I didn't understand a word. All I know is the driver put both hands on the steering wheel and wouldn't look up at us. Cassidy took out a hundred dollar bill and put it on the passenger seat.

"He's going to get you back to the hotel. And this is it for your little spy adventures. Understand? I hope you're happy," she said. "You follow *my* lead, just like I told you before. Jesus!"

I sank into the seat and pinched the bridge of my nose. "OK. I get it now. I just wanted … What *is* this place? Is that what you do for fun?" I was now connecting dots, realizing that there might be more to Arman and Cassidy than I'd thought. Something sinister and dark I'd managed to overlook in some stupid, stupid way.

Cassidy threw her hands in the air. "Oh my God. I give up!" She slapped the roof of the taxi, spun, and walked away. A car alarm chirped somewhere in front of us as she disappeared into the darkness.

Arman sighed and crouched to look in at me. He scanned the street and then said, "Let us make this quick. No time to banter back and forth like we normally do. I knew you were following me."

"What? You did?"

"Marina, you have many gifts. Subtlety is not one of them. Do not plan on a career in spying."

"I can see how you might say that." My face turned hot.

"I knew you were behind me as soon as I left the restaurant. I was going to meet Cassidy. I texted and told her. We both decided that if you wanted to know what was going on, you'd have to see for yourself. We weren't going to stop you."

"My mom always told me to watch what I wished for because I just might get it. Lesson learned."

"Well," Arman patted my leg and kissed me on the temple. His lips felt warm. "I have to go back inside that horrible place and finish my business. Get out of here before people get too suspicious."

"Wait. What's going on in there?" My voice was shrill. "That man, that man! What happened to him?"

"Marina, do you really want the answer?"

I turned my head and wiped my eyes. "Yes."

"All right." Arman sighed. "Anything can be bought in Moscow. Drugs, sex, even death. There is an underground blood sport here. Rich men pay poor men to fight each other close to death. Not *to* death, usually, but tonight was a horrific exception. The winner gets some money. Enough to buy more vodka or a night in a cheap hotel.

Sometimes they come back. Other times, well, they don't. But as you saw at the Kasha Kitchen, there is no lack of desperate men looking for ways to make a little money."

"But — but — but — if they have money to pay them, don't they have doctors on standby in there?" I pointed to the warehouse, my index finger shaking.

"Marina, no. This is not legal. This is extra-legal. Politicians, business leaders and other, as you say, big shots, are inside, right now."

I pictured the beaten loser lying in the street, the blood all over his body. My stomach gurgled and wretched. I opened the door and puked, mostly on the sidewalk, somewhat on his nice shoes.

The cab driver shouted something. Arman spoke back in calm Russian. As he stroked my head with one hand and fished something out of his pocked with the other, I puked again. Chunks of cheese bread tinted pink with red wine. I couldn't get the beaten, swollen face out of my mind. Arman leaned me back against the seat and smoothed my hair from my face. He wiped my eyes and mouth with a cloth square. Handkerchief! Really! The man carried a handkerchief. He handed me a mint, too. He was a walking drug store.

"Listen, Marina. Cassidy and I were there to find out how this so-called sport works. Who is there. Who participates. Who makes it all happen. Then try to shut it down. We unfortunately had to see for ourselves first." He was quiet for a few beats. "I cannot do anything for the fighters. Not tonight, at least. Oh yes, I could call for an ambulance, but they know to ignore calls on Tuesday nights from this location. They are paid handsomely to do so."

"What? But — paramedics are supposed to help people!"

"Marina, you are no longer in the United States. The rules are different here. Now go back and get some rest. We will talk more later. I have to get back inside."

As he smoothed my hair one last time, I leaned my cheek into his warm palm. After a few seconds, he closed my door. The driver gunned the car so fast my temple slammed against the window. It hurt like hell. And I didn't care.

15

S leep wasn't happening. I couldn't get Sutton out of my mind. I just couldn't. Back home he'd become my safe place. But he hadn't returned any of my messages. Either he was truly deep, deep under cover or absence wasn't making the heart grow fonder. With me out of the picture, I'm sure his life was less complicated. I felt like an idiot. I'd let a good one slip away. I also couldn't block the images of the bleeding body dumped behind that fight club. Thinking about Sutton so deliberately helped push that out of my mind. What horrible things had *he* seen I'd never bothered to ask about?

Layer upon layer of shame and guilt.

I fumbled around for the AC remote and turned the air down. Maybe sleeping in a morgue would make me fall unconscious. The sheets were so soft, the bed so comfy. Kcenya's company spared no expense. Besides investing, she had a chain of luxury hotels around the world. Maybe I could work for her for real.

At any rate, I hoped cold plus cozy equaled sleep. Cassidy had said our next surveillance adventure would be at two p.m. and to get some rest, so I decided to start being a good listener. Pillows puffed around me as I settled into the white sheets. This hotel was so quiet. And the sheets felt so lovely on my arms and legs, why not see how they felt everywhere else. I slipped off my tank top and underwear. Too bad I didn't have anyone to share this with. I checked my phone one more time. What if he wasn't answering because he was injured? Oh my God. I sent another text. *Please just let me know you are safe.* I tucked the phone under a pillow and closed my eyes.

I woke to a knock at the door. "What," I mumbled. What's my mom doing here so early? I told her I'd pick her up at four. No, wait — I was thousands of miles away. In Russia. Alone.

Probably the wrong room. Happened the night before, drunk Irish-sounding dude with a much younger woman trying to fit his keycard into the hole, jamming it in and out, swearing because it wouldn't work. Probably an omen of how his night had ended.

Wondering how you say "wrong room" in Russian, I wrapped a duvet around my shoulders. In the mirror, I was the Staypuft Marshmallow Woman With Bedhead. I dragged myself and ten pounds of goose feathers across the room to look through the peephole.

A drunken Irishman it was not.

Arman. Staring right into the peephole, knowing I was there. OK, then. I wasn't expecting him to show, especially after the hottie at the restaurant. And who would feel like boning after all that bloody business at that illegal fight club?

"Hold on." I didn't care about the morning breath. Giving him my room number had simply been a mistake and I wasn't going to let him in. If lack of an invitation to cross the threshold worked for vampires, it should stop Arman. I grabbed the terrycloth robe from the hook near the bathroom. I'd open the door, body block the entry, and tell him to leave.

I popped the lock and leaned into the jamb, arms crossed over my chest. His smirk said it all. Arman one, Marina zero. I stepped aside. So much for my plan. His eyes were sad as he stepped into the room. I snapped both locks shut. He ran a finger over the top of the settee by the door. A few more silver hairs intertwined with the black in his hair.

Lord. He was gorgeous. I pulled the robe tighter. "Arman."

He turned. He didn't speak. Neither did I — for about a half a second. And then I launched into it. "So that GIRL you were with tonight. She get you off and now you come to me for sloppy seconds? I mean come on. Really? What the hell?"

He shrugged out of his gray cashmere coat, draped it over a chair, and shook his head. "Sloppy seconds? Another wonderful American expression. I have never heard that before but I understand through the context. Hmm. Sloppy seconds." He leaned against the closet. "*She is my daughter.*"

I could hear his watch ticking, it was that quiet. The silence lasted for about five seconds. "Your daughter? WHAT? I thought Lerzan was dead?" His Kurdish girlfriend had been killed by a Turkish military attack. They'd had a daughter? He'd forgotten that teeny-tiny detail.

"Yes, Lerzan is dead," Arman said. "But I still had a life after her. Sabine is my daughter from a relationship with a German woman I met in the years after."

"Why didn't you introduce me tonight?"

"Imagine that awkwardness. I do not get to see Sabine a lot. I did not want to confuse her. She looks older than she is. She is only 18."

"She dresses like—"

He rolled his eyes. "I know. It is a rebellious phase. Her mother asked me to check on her while I was in town. She is a model, working here. Sabine is also going to university to be a lawyer, like her mother. I do not approve of how she dresses, but no— she is her own woman now. All I can do is sit back and watch. And hope for the best."

"Huh," was all I could manage. He couldn't have told me he had a daughter younger than me? I mean, that was a little creepy. Guess I wouldn't wanted to have met me, either, if I'd been in her place.

Tick tick tick went his watch. And then he went for it. Arman pressed his mouth into mine. His warmth and his cologne enveloped me. Whenever I touched him, time stopped. No need to talk. No need to discuss the months between our lives, the secrets, the disappointments, the loneliness. What had happened that terrible day last summer.

He grabbed my hands and led me to the bed. I wanted to say I was happy to see him again, but he put two fingers over my mouth. There was something about his loud silence, our breath, the blood pounding in my skull—it made me dizzy. I bit his lip and remembered. I got up and went to the closet, found my suitcase and opened up one of the compartments.

He said, "I want to see all of you."

And so I handed him the condom and waited for him to put it on. I dropped the robe and we stared at each other for as second. I walked over to him, my mind calm for the first time in days. I straddled him and we both sighed. I leaned into him, letting myself collapse over and onto him. I wound my fingers through his hair and pulled his head back just enough to kiss his neck. He ran a finger down my spine, our breathing in rhythm. Over his shoulder, through the hotel room window, Red Square was lit up like magic through a misty rain.

***

When my eyes cracked open on the mucky sunlight that passed for a fall morning in Moscow, the domes of St. Basil's were like a landscape painting in a museum. I took a moment to stare at the beautiful architecture in my window. If I hadn't broken up with John, I would have been looking out at the back of the Hoyson's house, watching their crazy German shepherd run around their yard. Or a path of Joe's socks leading to the hallway. Monday, Tuesday, Wednesday, Thursday, Friday, all heralded by a trail of Gold Toes. But now I was propped up on foreign pillows that must have cost more than my entire comforter set at home.

"Did you know the architect who made those beautiful domes was blinded?" I smelled the coffee before Arman entered the room. His scent lingered on my skin, all Turkish spice market and mystery. He'd wrapped a white towel just below his belly button, revealing a scar from shrapnel when he'd fought with the Kurdish resistance. His hair glistened from the shower and now he smelled like soap. He handed me a mug of coffee.

"How did you know I only like cream?"

"Because you taste too sweet to need any sugar."

"Oh, Lord." I rolled my eyes and stuck out my tongue. "You are literally the cheesiest of the cheesy. So tell me more about this poor architect."

Arman set the tray on the nightstand and crawled behind me, nestling close so his chest was against my back. He fumbled with his phone and Led Zeppelin provided background music. We both gazed out the window. "The tsar hired a famous architect to build this grand church. And the architect, of course, wanted to make sure the tsar was pleased. He intended to do a beautiful job. And as you can see, he did. But to make sure nothing quite like it was ever made in the world again, the tsar had the architect's eyes gouged out so he could never create such a marvel for anyone else."

"That's disgusting." The red spires that had seemed so royal last night now only reminded me of clotting blood.

"As you say in America, the road to hell is paved with good intentions. And as you learned last night, this country can have scant regard for human life."

The beaten-up man with the green boots. I thought of Gilly's knee injury from the zip line. Piper being kidnapped. Janna keeping me at a distance. All because I'd thought I was doing the right thing by not going to the police, by handling it myself. I took a deep breath to hold back the tears. I hadn't had a solid cry since that day under my desk and certainly didn't want it to happen now, especially with Arman there. I was in Russia to move forward from those traumatic events.

He squeezed my hand. "Marina, that horrible situation you saw last night is a small extension of The General's widespread enterprises. Well, those of the people he works for."

"Wait. Isn't he dead? Wasn't he killed in the mine subsidence?" I shuddered. Flashback to an underground ballroom in an anthracite coal mine, the cracking of timber, the cascade of coal, the dust choking me.

"His body was never found. Cassidy seems to think he is alive. And still running his businesses – drugs, weapons, and people. But not with so much influence now."

Memories of his gold incisor, his beard against my face. His grip on my niece's arm. My diaphragm tightened and my chest heaved. This was the feeling that had defined the past few months, my breath bottled up like shaken soda. It all came spewing out. "The death of my Aunt Yelena has hit me so hard. Sometimes I feel so ugly inside, so dark. I left everything I knew. The nights of insomnia are the worst, the nights I flip through channels for hours and on nights I played enough Sudoku to make all the numbers blur. I didn't know how to be alone. And that cop that helped with the case, Sutton? We've been dating. But he broke up with me before I left. Was he a quick fix, a finger in the dam? What pulled me here? I'm just an event planner from Kingston, Pennsylvania."

I couldn't believe I was telling all of this to Arman. He just listened, tracing circles with his finger tips on my arms. "Shhh, shhh. My Marina. It will be fine. Everything will be fine. Time heals all wounds. This I know."

"I'm sorry. I'm super-sure this isn't exactly what you'd expected while taking your shower, and making me coffee."

He squeezed me tighter. I turned to him, pushing a leg between his thighs, wondering about his other lives, his other homes. "What are we doing? This would never work. You're old. I'm ridiculous."

His belly vibrated as he laughed. "I do not know, Marina. Sometimes you can't fight an attraction, even if it is complicated. Sometimes the best answer is the most simple. I like you, you like me."

"That's one way of looking at it."

"There is no need to over-analyze this. Let's just enjoy the moment."

I nodded and nestled my head below his collarbone. "I have a question."

"Yes, of course you do."

"So how are you not tied up with court cases from what happened last summer? Or not checking in with a U. S. Attorney? One calls me every week."

"Well, it turns out I had some useful information for law enforcement. I told them what I knew. We made a deal and, well, here I am."

"What kind of deal?"

"That is a story for another day." His hold loosened.

The energy in the air changed and I suddenly felt a tension I didn't like. I sighed and he pulled me closer.

"One of my favorite poems is called *The Cinnamon Peeler*. It is by a writer from Sri Lanka," Arman said as he kissed the top of my head. "It is about a man who wishes he sold cinnamon so when he touched the woman he loved, she'd carry his sweet scent. One line says 'left with no trace as if not spoken to in the act of love as if wounded without the pleasure of a scar'." He moved my fingertips across the long scar on his torso and then rested them over his heart. "'As if wounded without the pleasure of a scar.' You and I, yes, we are both wounded. Our challenge is to find the beauty in our scars."

There was nothing to say after that. I let his words sink into my brain as he fell asleep, arms warm and tight around me.

I reached for my phone, hoping for a message from Sutton. Nothing. I sighed and watched St. Basil's blur as the rain started to pummel the window.

16

Arman snored into the late morning. Well, hot damn. He *snored.* Too funny. And pretty loudly, too, like a bad muffler. Once I got him to roll over, I drifted off again. And then the loudest alarm clock in the universe blared me awake. I shook Arman, but he just kept sawing away.

"Arman! Turn your stupid phone alarm off. It's like a goddamn air raid in here!"

"Huh? What?" He lifted his head, one eye open.

"Come on. *Your alarm.* I don't have to be anywhere until two."

He jolted up. "That is no alarm clock. Get your clothes on. We must vacate the room! It is a *fire* alarm. Moscow isn't exactly known for its amazing fire department. It's probably nothing but let us not take a chance."

I bounded out of bed as naked as the night was long here. I yanked on my Uggs and threw on a robe and shoved my phone in a pocket. Arman pulled on pants and a button down, and slid into his shoes. He pulled me toward the door.

"Wait! I need my purse!"

"No! Let's go!"

We rushed out, the door slamming behind us. We were alone in the hallway, so I guessed most guests were already out for the day, probably. The respectable ones, at work. We trotted down the stairs, the echo of shouting above us. Down, down, down. Through the gilded and mirrored lobby, with hotel employees waving the way out.

We tumbled out onto Teverskaya Street. Cars zoomed by in the cold drizzle. A siren in the distance. Hotel workers directed us to the small park. Arman put his arm around me and guided me to a bench. I pulled my robe tighter and watched as flames pushed through a top floor penthouse suite, sending glass crashing to the sidewalk. Tongues of fire whooshed out and licked the side of the building, leaving a black smear.

Arman made a call and said, "Hasan will be here soon."

"That man deserves an effing raise. We should help people. Come on." I jumped off the bench and grabbed his forearm, tugging him back toward the hotel. People were now streaming out, wearing lanyards and 'Hello, I'm' nametags. I'd forgotten about all the conference attendees, servers.

"No. Trust me. Hasan is a few minutes away. Please."

His phone buzzed. "Yes, she is fine. I have her with me," he told the caller. "Yes. OK. Yes. Yes. Please text me the address."

"Who was that?" Throngs of people gathered, heads tilted back, to watch the black smoke billow out.

"Cassidy. She said Kcenya wants you to go to her mother's flat."

A black Mercedes screeched to a stop. Arman opened the door and we slid inside the warm sedan.

"Hey, Hasan. Just like old times," I said, remembering how he'd chauffeured Arman around the Wyoming Valley.

He looked in the rear-view and nodded, then merged onto a highway. Evidently the white lines to mark each lane were optional, as were turn signals and any speed limit.

Arman squeezed my arm. "Mother Russia is never dull."

"What the hell is going on now?"

"Kcenya is not only one of the richest people in Russia, but the richest woman in Russia. As you can imagine, she has enemies. The latest one has been setting fires in her hotels. Four so far, from Vladivostock to here. This is number five. Never big enough to cause a lot of damage, but enough frighten her guests, hurt business, and make her investors question their investments."

"Holy shit. Would've been nice if someone could have given me heads-up about the fire bug problem. What the junk?"

He smiled. "You have such a way with words."

***

The lobby of the apartment building had puke green tile on the floor and halfway up the walls. The rest of the way up was painted grungy beige. Graffiti in black Sharpie decorated parts of the walls, some in Russian, some in English. A teenager with stringy brown hair and acne locked a mailbox, stared at me in my robe, nodded and skulked out. The worst was the smell – someone had taken a whiz or three and never cleaned it up. That mingled with the stink of rancid garbage. I pulled the collar of my robe to my nose and gagged.

"Russians can be ambivalent about public spaces," Arman said.

"Clearly."

He pressed the up button at the elevator. The doors thunked open part way, shut, and then finally opened all the way. We stepped in and he pressed fourteen. Gears cranked and strained as we ascended. What the hell were we doing here? Finally, a thump. The doors flopped open on the fourteenth floor. Well, a few inches above it. I stepped down and the elevator shook. More graffiti, more urine stench. A man wearing a fur hat looked at us, shrugged, and stepped up into the elevator.

"What was that about?"

"No idea. Come on. Apartment 1456."

A fire hose was covered in dust, unattached to its brass valve. "Um….what if there's another fire?" I pulled my robe tighter.

"Don't think about it."

"But—"

He pressed on a black doorbell. A few seconds later, a lock clicked on the other side. A dozen scuffed footsteps later, once-white, now gray, curtains were pulled back by a woman with a brow as straight as a shotgun barrel.

"*Priviet, krasavitza!*" Hello, beautiful. Oh, come on, Arman, I thought.

Her face relaxed. A beaming smile revealed a few silver teeth. The pane shook as she unlocked the door and ushered us into a long hallway.

We stopped at the door numbered 1456. Arman and the woman kissed on both cheeks. "This is Marina Konyeshna, our visitor from America."

"Ah! Marina! Welcome to Russia! We take good care of you! Come een! Come een! You will catch a cheell out khere!" She opened a heavy black door with vinyl padding. Buttons studded the front, offering a faux-leather quilting effect. A television blared from inside.

"This is Liudmila Sultanovna, Kcenya's mother. She will take good care of you. I have to leave now."

"You're leaving me?" I asked through gritted teeth, still smiling.

"My Marina, yes. I have business to attend to."

"You always do. Convenient."

"Don't behave like a petulant child. You will be safe here."

"Wait...safe? What do you mean?" My molars ground and I shoved fists into the robe's pockets.

"Cassidy and I will be occupied today. You are staying here now. You will be safe here."

I was thousands of miles from home in a country nothing like I'd imagined. Cassidy was training me for undercover operations. I was back in the arms of Arman Ocalan, International Man of Mystery and Mayhem. My hotel was a target of arson. I was wearing a flipping hotel robe and staying with silver-toothed strangers.

The pink udder of The Big Cow flashed through my mind. Then the dusty, disconnected fire hose. Everything slid into pinholes and the last thing I remember feeling was my head hitting the floor.

17

I rolled over and pulled the blanket up to my nose. Warm, in my own cocoon. It felt marvelous to be back in my mother's basement, asleep on the old sofa bed. Why had I been so eager to get out of here, anyway? But it didn't smell like my mom's house. No cinnamon candles, no fabric softener-scented blankets. I knew what would ground me. I yelled for our dog. "Stosh! Come here boy! Come here boy!"

KUH-THUD! A hot tongue the size of a hot dog roll licked my cheek, and leaving a trail of slobber. That wasn't Stosh's kiss. When I opened my eyes I was nose to nose with a panting German Shepherd. His black and tan snout sniffed my hair. He was the size of a large 5th grader. This was no Stosh. Stosh fit in a grocery store basket.

"OK, boy. OK. Nice doggie," I said as I patted his head. Shit. Did he even understand English?

Then he stuck his cold, wet nose into my ear. I tried to push him off, but he just wagged harder.

The door popped open. A woman in a tan blouse and a black skirt said something in Russian. "Foo" meant "Shoo" I guessed, because the dog fooed his way out of the bedroom.

The woman brushed a brown lock of hair out of her face and took a drag off a cigarette. "Sorry. Dickie is friendly and also quite nosey."

Dickie. What a name. "That's OK. So, um, what exactly happened? Where am I?" My head throbbed. I glanced at a clock on the table next to the sofa bed. 5 P.M. Apparently I'd been asleep for a few hours.

She exhaled and crossed an arm over her waist. "I am Katya, Kcenya's older sister. I don't live here, just visiting my mother and grandmother. I don't understand why they still live here in our old neighborhood."

I sat up. "I'm Marina. I'm working with your sister. Looks like she's making me stay here due to the latest fire at her hotel."

Katya's mouth slid into a straight line. "I have nothing to do with it. Or any of Kcenya's nonsense. It's all my mother's doing." She gestured at me with her cigarette and arched her eyebrows. "Anything bad happens to my mother, I come after you, *Amerikanka*."

She exited and I leaned back on the pillows. A brown and gold carpet was tacked on the wall behind the couch. From one sofa bed in PA to another in Russia. The more things changed, the more they stayed the same. A wooden entertainment stand ran the entire wall opposite, filled with ceramic figurines and photos of people refusing to smile. A large flatscreen TV. A pair of brown pleather slippers on the floor. I slid my feet into the grooves in the insoles made by countless other feet. Eww. I tried not to think about it because Cassidy had explained how Russians wear house shoes. A large mirror by the door revealed I was wearing a bright skin-tight orange velour tracksuit with "Joocey" written in rhinestone script across the butt. I had no recollection of trading my robe for this monstrosity. Fabulous.

I sighed and padded into the hallway. To my left, through a doorway, was a living room with sofa, television and a coffee table. Another doorway revealed bunk beds. To my right, the front door and two smaller doors. Clanging pots and pans came from the kitchen. The air grew humid as I approached it, as if something was boiling. Good. I was starving.

"Ah, Marina! Sit, sit, sit! Please! Enjoy! Let me get you drink!" It was Kcenya's mom. Liudmila Somethingovna. She was wearing a pair of bright green slippers and a pink and white striped housedress, complete with oversized pockets and a ruffle around the collar. "You must be very hungry, my dear."

"Yes, thank you."

Liudmila stirred a pot and hummed to herself. "I am making something very special. It will remind you of home in Amereeka." She turned around with a steaming bowl full of spaghetti with red sauce and chunks of what looked like sausage discs. Outside it was raining and gray, so a hot meal was perfect. *"Priatnova apetita!"* I was hungry enough to eat my slippers, so I dug in.

My taste buds told me the meat was cut up hot dog and the sauce was ketchup. I put on my best pageant smile and said, "MMM. Delicious." Oh boy. Between my Joocey butt and the ketchupy pasta, I hoped Arman was coming back for me soon.

Liudmila leaned back in her chair. "Please to enjoy, my new American friend."

"Liuda! LIUDA!" It sounded like a woman calling, but with the scratchy voice of a lifelong pack-a-day smoker.

Liudmila shouted back something I couldn't understand. She looked at me and shook her head. "Mothers."

That was something I could understand, so I nodded and choked down another forkful of Russian spaghetti.

Liudmila left the room. I leaned against the chair and watched rain fall onto the lot below. The cars were ants pulling in and out of tiny parking spots. Aphid people walked in and out of stores, carrying bags. *Shopping.* My favorite therapy.

I rinsed my dishes and followed Liudmila's voice to the other room. She was sitting on a brown loveseat with someone much older. This lady had dark eyes, deep wrinkles that would have been laugh lines on anyone else but were frown lines on her. Gray hair, mostly hidden under a floral scarf. She looked me over and scowled.

"Mamichka," Liudmila stroked her arm. Mamichka scowled. I felt way unwanted.

"Thanks for dinner, Liudmila. I'd like to go for a walk if that's OK. I need a little fresh air."

Her eyes widened. "My dear, is raining and you might catch cold! Plus, we are having company soon."

"I just need to get some air. It's not raining too hard."

Mamichka said something to Liudmila and she shrugged. "My mother says he needs to go to *apteka.* Can you walk her across the street? I have work before guests arrive."

The last thing I felt like was a party. "Guests?"

"Yes, my niece and nephew are visiting. Kcenya promised to come for party tonight. To my mind, she can take two hours from her *precious business* to visit family. I don't understand why my daughter will not give me grandchildren. Only work, work, work. Now, to *apteka.*"

I had no idea what *apteka* was, but we were on our way within minutes. I at least got to cover my Joocey butt with a long black quilted coat that just barely zipped. Mamichka pulled on a black trench coat and tightened the floral scarf over her head. She looked at me, sighed, and wobbled to the front door. When we got to the elevator, I pressed the down button and she grabbed my arm as we stepped up. A plunk and we sank a few inches. I gasped. Mamichka just stared straight ahead, pursing wrinkled lips.

Inch by inch, she and I made our way to the shopping area across the street. She gripped my arm as if it were all that kept her from floating away. After what seemed like a half hour, we arrived at a shop with a green cross on the front. Mamichka stopped at the door and glared at me.

"Oh, sorry," I said, opening it to let her in.

The apteka turned out to be a pharmacy. Bottles and packets lined the shelves of a store as big as a gas station mini mart. I couldn't understand a word on any of the signs, so I just stood by the door and waited. Mamichka hobbled back from the counter with a plastic bag. I reopened the front door. Mamichka threaded her arm through mine and turned toward another store that apparently sold food. Remembering my cue, I opened the front door with an arm flourish like a butler. Mamichka did not get my sense of humor, as she didn't even crack a smile. We entered a small grocery. Shelves of boxes and cans and what looked like a dairy and meat counter.

My phone buzzed. A text from Gilly! *Een – Took our ur trash and I saw someone in backyard. Neighborhood kid? Lurker? Not sure.*

I responded with *Ty for garbage. Ugh about Lurker. Call Eddie Jankovich. He's my go to guy with Edwardsville popo. Xoxoxoxoxoxo x 1000*

Great. What the hell did the Lurker want? At least I wasn't home. He could take whatever he wanted. I didn't have much, anyway. Maybe if he broke in, he'd be disgusted at my poor housekeeping skills and at least run the vacuum.

Then a hot guy with ice blue eyes and short blond hair walked down the sidewalk and stopped in front of the shop. We locked eyes through the storefront window. He waved. I waved. He put a cigarette in his mouth and lit it. To be honest, I was distracted, admiring his butt, when two men in black leather jackets pounced on him and knocked him to the ground. Everyone in the store turned at the ruckus, but I was the only one who dashed out to help. The boys in leather pummeled Blue Eyes with their fists, then kicked him in the lower back.

"Hey! Stop!"

They glanced up and continued the beat down. I took out my phone and snapped photos. That way the police could get these thugs. Out of all of the work I was doing with surveillance, I couldn't help myself. At last the attackers strolled off to their black Porsche Cayenne. Blue Eyes picked himself up off the ground. I crouched next to him. "Are you OK? Do you need help?"

He wiped blood from the corner of his mouth. His English was rough as sandpaper but totally understandable. "Phone, please."

"OK, OK, sure," I handed it over, the screen showing the images I'd caught of the brawl.

He lumbered up and flicked through, poker faced. He then threw my iPhone on the sidewalk and crushed it under the heel of his boot.

"What the hell?" I yelled. "That's mine! I don't qualify for an upgrade until next year!"

He pulled out a pack of cigarettes out of his coat pocket, lit one, and limped away in a haze of smoke. I stared at the shattered glass and plastic on the sidewalk.

"*Davai, Amerikanka,*" Mamichka said as she handed me a plastic bag filled with produce and a long roll of some meat product poking out of the top.

I freaked out as the old lady latched on to my arm for the walk home. "How is anyone going to reach me now? Sutton will think I'm blowing him off if he ever responds to my messages. Jesus, Mary, and the Carpenter. What the hell?"

Mamichka shrugged. Not like she knew what I was saying, anyway.

We trudged back to the apartment, into the stanky lobby, up the rickety elevator, and then stepped down to the 14th floor once it clunked to a stop. I had no way to contact Cassidy or Arman because, to me, their phone numbers were "Arman Cell" and "Cassidy Cell." Sweat was pooling in my bra, so I unzipped the heavy quilted coat.

When Mamichka opened the door to the apartment, classical guitar slapped me in the face along with the smells of fried onions and butter. My heartbeat slowed thanks to that familiar scent of home cooked comfort food. People were talking and laughing in the living room. Great, I thought as I slid my sneakers off and pushed my feet into the slippers. Now I had to be nice to strangers.

But it wasn't all strangers. Arman, Cassidy and Kcenya were at the table with Kcenya's mom, her sister and some others I didn't recognize. When they saw me, they clapped and cheered.

I took a step back. "And I deserve this because?"

Kcenya stood with a champagne flute in her hand. "It's OK, Marina. Come on. It's time for a real Russian celebration."

"But—"

"Later, later. You must enjoy some hospitality." She untied her purple floral apron and hung it over the back of her chair. An apron. The richest woman in Russia wearing one, like she was Betty Crocker or something. This country was full of surprises.

A long rectangular table had been moved into the living room, the other furniture pushed to the side. Three vases of white and pink stargazer lilies were set on the lace tablecloth. The table was loaded with platters and bowls of food.

Kcenya tapped a glass with a fork and everyone got quiet. She stood and smoothed her black pants. She raised a shot glass and said in Russian and then in English, "Please fill your glasses to a toast for Marina, our American guest. We are happy to have her join our business ventures. We hope she enjoys her stay here. We wish her great health, true happiness, and many children!"

Awwwwww. Warm fuzzies. I wasn't sure about the 'many children' part but I was down with the health and happiness. The people around the table raised their glasses higher and downed their shots of vodka. Mine burned my throat like a mofo, so I choked and coughed. Mamichka sighed and held a piece of brown bread in front of my nose. I inhaled the rich molasses scent and it took the edge off. What a surprising chaser. Mamichka winked and poured herself another.

Arman stood. Oh boy. Mr. Talks A Lot had a captive audience. Kcenya translated as he spoke. "To Kcenya Sultanovna. A brave business leader who will do her country proud. Her wisdom is only eclipsed by her beauty." Again, raised glasses, and down the hatch. This time, Mamichka shoved a pickle in my face. I bit the salty gherkin and, again, a perfect chaser.

Thank God that was the last round of toasts. We began eating. I needed to sop up the alcohol because I never made a good impression when wasted.

Kcenya leaned over and pointed with a spoon. "This is my cousin, Boris, and his wife, Anastacia. They are visiting from Samara, in the South. I'm happy we can all welcome you together."

Mamichka pushed a bowl of soup over to me with a thin broth as red as blood. Slices of potato and onion floated on top. She added a dollop of what looked like sour cream and then sprinkled dill. She looked at me and then at the soup. I took a spoonful and gave a thumbs-up. Delicious! Mamichka gave a hint of a smile and started on her bowl.

"So you like my mother's *borscht*?" Kcenya said.

"It's amazing." I then tilted the bowl to my lips to get the very last drop. Mamichka then piled my plate with food from the platters. I couldn't say no. With every deposit accepted onto my plate, she smiled a little more. The way to her heart, revealed! And boy, could I oblige.

Kcenya continued. "OK, Marina, here is the guide to your plate. First, those pancakes are called *blini*. *Smetana*, Russian sour cream, and caviar on top. Don't frown. Try it. Then you have pickled vegetables, some dried fish, some *pyelmeni*, hot meat dumplings. And here." She poured a brown liquid into a fresh glass. "*Kvass*. It's made with fermented brown bread. An acquired taste, but one cannot go to Russia without at least trying it."

I gave myself time to acquire all of it. Every delicious last bite. I even liked the *kvass*. We talked, we laughed, we toasted. I got hugs. It felt awesome to be accepted, a real part of something. Fydor had been nice to me, but this felt like a home. Even Kcenya's sister's Ice Queen façade broke. She was clearly flirting with Arman. She smiled and brushed her hand on his arm as they talked. Remembering what he'd done with me last night made me blush. It was kind of hot to see him flirt with someone else. What was wrong with me? Fifty shades of Arman. Oy vey.

I finished off my second bowl of *borscht* and couldn't fit anything else in my stomach. I leaned back to rub my food baby, and realized I'd even forgotten about the hideous orange tracksuit I was wearing. Now I appreciated its elastic waist.

"Ahem." Boris stood and straightened the bottom of his blue sweater. He said something in Russian. Everyone clapped and passed around a tray of what appeared to be animal parts in orange Jell-O. Oh boy.

Kcenya leaned in. "Mmmm. This is *kholodetz*, a gelatin with meat. Very Russian. Very good for eating when you drink vodka. Boris brought it from the best butcher in Samara. He is very happy to share with his new American friend."

"*Spacibo*, Boris!" I said with a forced smile as the slices of slippery meatoid stared at me from the plate being passed to me.

"*Na zdrovya!*" Boris raised his shot class and we all dug in: meat, then vodka. It was abhorrent, but just when I was about to spit gunk into my napkin, Arman gave me The Eye. I held it in my mouth and swallowed. Another shot of vodka. Arman nodded and smiled. I narrowed my eyes and gulped water.

So this is how they survived in this crazy country – fun parties, food, strong vodka, and good people. I was smiling. I'd almost forgotten about my phone.

I got up and teetered over to Arman and Cassidy, using the backs of peoples' chairs as a lifeline.

Cassidy grinned. "Nice Joocey butt."

"Shut up. Whatever. So, yeah, some thug stomped my phone to pieces today."

Arman took a slice of sausage dotted with fat. "I love this stuff. Anyway, yes. We know. We will get you a new one later today."

"How do you know, Mr. and Ms. Super Spies?"

Cassidy wiped her hands on her napkin. "Pavel texted us."

"Pavel? Who's Pavel?"

"The guy from the Kasha Kitchen, who helps at the orphanage."

"Wait. The homeless guy who speaks English? How did *he* know?"

Cassidy popped an olive in her mouth. "Remember we were at the park and you didn't even realize he was there, too, on the other bench?"

"OK....but why was he there? That's super creepy."

"We paid him to follow you," Arman said. "When there was a fire in the hotel, we wanted you to be safe. Sending you here to the outskirts of Moscow, to Kcenya's mother's apartment, was a holding place. We have been employing Pavel since we started surveillance."

"Consider him your guardian angel today, Marina. I'm not sure what you were thinking when you decided to videotape that mafiya shakedown. If it had gotten ugly, Pavel would have stepped in," Cassidy said.

"To do what?"

Arman leaned in. "Pavel will most certainly fight when he needs to."

Cassidy nodded. "And you have cloud storage, right? Then when we sign in on your new phone, we should be able to retrieve the photos. Could be helpful one day."

Just then, a pop. Kcenya and her sister poured champagne into flutes and it was time for another toast. Kcenya put her arm around her grandmother and spoke. Mamichka smiled so wide her eyes narrowed to tiny creases. We raised our glasses to Mamichka's health, and started on pastries and cakes.

Afterward, Kcenya came over to me. "I could use your help in the kitchen, please."

Cassidy, Arman, and I exchanged glances and followed her.

The kitchen wall of windows was steamed up, green counters covered in pots and bowls. To me, all signs of a good party.

"Arman and Cassidy, I have scheduled that important meeting for tomorrow."

"Excellent," Arman said. Cassidy nodded.

"Marina, here is where you come in," said Kcenya. "Just be yourself and trust us. This meeting could seal the deal for a very important partnership to further our work against trafficking rings. Your part is not dangerous. You should be able to go back to the hotel tomorrow evening. One more sleepover with Mamichka. And I promise to get you non-Joocey pants."

I rubbed my hands on the orange velour. "I'll do anything if you get me out of this outfit. Let's get the bastards."

18

Cassidy told me to meet Arman and her the next morning at some long metro name I couldn't pronounce. Luckily Liudmila was home and could point out the station on the metro map. All I had to do was turn right, walk ten minutes to the platform, and get on the train on my right. Easy enough.

Inside the metro station were vaulted ceilings and marble statues: a man with a dog and a rifle, a woman crouching with a discus, and another woman reading a book. This place was so weird yet oddly cool at times too. I got on the train and found a seat on the vinyl bench.

Kecnyna had sent over some real clothes and I'd been all too happy to shed my tangerine Joocey pants. Now I was wearing skinny jeans, a black sweater, kitten heels and a black coat. I felt less conspicuous and safer. Like I blended in more. Men in leather jackets, women in heavy black coats, older men with glasses, all reading a newspaper, bobbing their heads to music, or tapping their phone screens. It was eerily quiet. Then a woman's voice came over the speakers, the doors slammed shut and with a jolt, we sped to the next stop.

Forty minutes later, I met Cassidy on the platform of our rendezvous station. "Nice scarf," I said, trying to be breezy with her. I did like the black and white checked cloth edged with fringe, draped over her black leather jacket just right. She didn't know her way around a cosmetics bag, but Cassidy had adventure-chic just right.

The escalator took us to street-level. This part of the city was all skyscrapers and glass. It was so modern, so beautiful. So easy to forget we were in a crazy country. Cassidy texted someone and we entered a building with huge mirrored windows. The foyer was marble and gold...amazing. People whirred in and out, talking on phones, dressed for work or for some very expensive, casual play. A few women had little yippy dogs stowed in their bags. We boarded an elevator and Cassidy pressed a button. I still didn't really know my Cyrillic, so the symbol on the button looked like an end table. Or a staple. Or a...

"Jesus, Marina. Come on," Cassidy said, shaking my arm. The doors had opened to white marble floors, gold accents everywhere. The wall-sized windows revealed a breathtaking panorama. The gold domes of Orthodox churches, the glossy windows of skyscrapers, the gray sky like a watercolor painting. Kcenya and Arman were on a cream sofa, drinking out of delicate pink teacups.

"Olya!" Kcenya said, voice echoing through the cavernous room.

A rat-tat-tat of heels from behind us and there she was: *the* Olya, the Olya I'd been mistaken for in the airport. She could have been my long-lost twin, chomping on gum and finishing a text. She held up a bejeweled finger and finished her message. OK, so maybe she was firmer in all the right spots, as evidenced by the fluorescent pink cropped tank top that showed off a diamond belly ring, and the low-rider black boy-shorts that hinted Brazilian waxes were part of her grooming routine. So thongs were over, commando was in. Bedazzled gold-heeled flip flops showcased her bejeweled pink pedicure.

"OK, guys, so—" She finally pulled her eyes up from her phone. "Oh. My. God, Becky!"

If her next words were, "Look at her butt," her skinny ass was going to be smeared all over the hardwood floors.

"Sorry. I love that American song. I am covering it now in my concerts." She giggled and put her hands in the air in some type of made-up gang sign with her fingers crossed over each other. Oh boy. She shoved the phone into the back of her shorts and skittered over to kiss me once on each cheek. "Marina! Yes! You are twin! This is fantasteek! How much you have SAVED me since your arrival. Nobody can figure out where I am. I went to *movies*. My bodyguard sat in back, not next to me. I hate when he sits next to me. He chews popcorn so loud. I saw people taking pictures of you on a train. Thank you! Thank you! *Spacibo, krasavitsa*! You are so beautiful! Come here!"

She grabbed my wrist and pulled me to the mirror that wrapped around the elevator. Same height, same green eyes, same build. She had a firmer body, obviously courtesy of a personal trainer, bigger boobs and bigger lips, but other than that, it was freaky. Side by side you could see the difference, but to the average Ivan walking down the street, who'd only seen her on TV or the internet, it would be easy to confuse us. She smiled a huge whitened smile, wrapped her left arm around me, pulled me close and gave a thumbs up. My weak grin seemed to float right over her head. In the mirror, I could see Kcenya, Arman and Cassidy stifling giggles. I glared at them.

"I must have photo of this madness!" She took a selfie. "*Otlichna!* I love it! You are sister I never had!"

I already had one sister and that was more than enough for me. I let her hug me and kiss my cheeks again, but I stood rigid as a mannequin. Next on my to-do list: to slap the smirks off Kcenya, Arman, and Cassidy.

"Now, Marina. No — can I call you Masha? We have just met, but our psychic energy is so intertwined. Is not just happening by chance. Is fate!"

"Sure, you can call me Masha." Masha-ed potatoes. That was what I felt like next to this pop goddess.

"OK, so Masha. I am having first movie role. Can you believe? Working with Swedish director. Is Cinderella story about homeless girl who becomes princess."

I thought about the homeless I'd met so far in Moscow. Nothing fairy tale-ish about their lives.

"The director made arrangements for me to research. Kcenya is letting me volunteer at her kasha kitchen to learn mannerisms of *bomzhi*."

"Olya. We've talked about that word." Kcenya's frown even put me on notice, and I, for once, hadn't been the one to say something stupid.

"*Protismeya*, Kcenya. Sorry. Yes. Old habits hard to break. Not bums, but *byezdomni*. Homeless. Has been very interesting and useful to spend time there. My heart is so broken. To my mind, I can to help the *bomzh-* I mean homeless people. Is one problem. And I really, really, really need your help, Masha. Please. Your arrival to my country has given me some freedom and I cannot give it up until I go to movie location."

"So what does that have to do with me?" I shifted my gaze from her toned tummy to her green eyes.

"Come here, Masha." She grabbed my hand again and led me to the living room where we walked across what appeared to be a very flat polar bear and then sat on a white sofa. "Masha, I need your help. I wish to have one more day of peace. Can you be me so I can spend time my *babushka,* before I leave? I miss those days of walking in park with my grandmother. Fame has brought many wonderful things but I am also prisoner."

"Um...."

Cassidy came to the couch and. "Olya, we appreciate all the help you've offered us. So yes, Marina, I mean MASHA, will assist with whatever you need."

Help from Olya? Why wasn't I let in on this before? Cassidy mouthed *trust me.* I bared my teeth and grrred back. Snapped back to Olya and smiled. "Sure. Let's do it."

"*Spacibo bolshoi,* Mashinka!" So now I was Mashinka. Wow. That was a fast nicknaming session. "I will call stylist now. She will be here with team soon." Team? I needed that much help? "Please to make yourself comfortable. My chef will make us lunch."

Olya grabbed the cream throw blanket and her toned butt clip-clopped out to the terrace. Blanket draped around her shoulders, she picked up a pack of cigarettes and lit up. She leaned on the railing, a plume of smoke trailing her like a floating scarf as she talked to someone.

"What the hell was that?" My eyes darted among Kcenya, Arman, and Cassidy.

"Olya," Cassidy said, "is our ticket to stopping a trafficking ring."

I looked out at Olya, who was still chattering on her phone and inspecting a fingernail. She was going to be the key to bring down a criminal organization?

"Listen, Marina." Cassidy sighed. "I know Olya seems like a class A ditz. But she's not. You don't get to be that famous for so long without also being smart. She's not the celebrity who lets people take crotch shots of her getting out of a limo at a club. Not the celebrity who will stage a strategic nip slip or beat up a paparazzo. She came from nothing and remembers that. She won't let anyone break this glass castle she built from the ground up."

Arman chimed in. "Also, her management team is very trustworthy. And she has a personal grudge against traffickers." Vendetta; I could understand that.

"Two of her friends have been taken in by men who offered bogus modeling contracts. She hasn't seen or heard from them since."

I glanced onto the balcony. Now Olya was scowling at her phone. Her cigarette tipped up as she pursed her lips.

Arman continued, "These criminals have connections. Enough money to keep the police chief and regional administrators quiet. No one cares about poor girls in an oil-refinery town. She does not talk about it much, but said we could share her story with you."

No one had cared about Amparo Rivas, the girl who escaped El Salvador with her family to avoid a gang, until she washed up dead on the shore of the Susquehanna River. No one had cared about Hong. And their stories were not unique. Thousands of girls all over the world were in the same position. My fingers dug into a throw pillow.

"I haven't been able to ask this. I guess I didn't want to know, but...is The General involved? I'd assumed he didn't survive." The movie in my mind showed a flash — him limping behind me in the cave-in.

Kcenya said, "My contacts report he is running his racket now out of a Moscow suburb. It seems his business skills haven't had much — what is the word? — smoothness. He not a favored son in the Organizatsiya anymore."

Arman jumped in. "His mistakes in trying to establish a foothold in a quiet corner of the USA backfired. He has lost a lot of respect. His trying to redeem himself through drug trafficking. However, he has angered other leaders. They used to have some porous borders in the city with dealing drugs such as heroin and ecstasy, but he is being boxed out, little by little."

"We hope to trap him in a corner," Cassidy said. "And I personally doubt he's totally out of human trafficking. He's too much a psychopath to let that arm of his business fall away."

A cocktail of sadness, anger, and shame filled me. "At the beginning of the summer, I was complaining about my break from John, about living in my mom's basement. I would give anything to those being my biggest problems now."

"Would you, though?" said Cassidy. "Yeah, those problems seem so much simpler. But now you see the world differently, you know what goes on."

"I'm not sure. It was kind of nice not knowing."

Arman stood and walked to the bar. Ice cubes clinked in the class. "Whiskey, ladies?" We all nodded. More clinking, the pop of a decanter. He came back to the sitting area with three glasses. We sipped in silence.

"Yes, my Marina, it's nice not having to know. Yet when we find out what is going on around us, we are able to do more with our lives. I grew up thinking the Kurds were less than me. Then I met Lerzan and learned about her struggles, struggles put upon my own government. The blindfold was off and the light of the truth hurt my eyes. It still does. My life hasn't been the same since."

"Marina, you know me as your favorite outdoor survival specialist." I nodded at Cassidy. "What I really am is a life survival specialist. When I was in college..." She paused, looking at the floor, then inhaled. "I was raped at a party. Same old story: too much to drink, a guy I liked but didn't know very well. No need for the gory details. You know how it ends."

"What?" I hadn't meant to interrupt, but I couldn't keep it in.

"I'm proud I can be matter-of-fact about it now. Back then shame kept me from going to the campus medical center until a week later, but only after a friend bounded into my dorm room and found me cutting my thighs with razor blades. That helped numb the pain from the rape. But then I felt ashamed about the cutting, a vicious cycle. I was captain of the women's soccer team, honors seminar, student government. On the surface, totally together. This friend saw I was sad and saved my life. She held my hand as I talked to a doctor."

"I-I-I don't know what to say. I'm...so sorry you had to go through that. I mean..."

Cassidy had actually relaxed and looked softer than I'd ever seen her. "It's OK, Marina. Well, not really, but I've worked hard to make it as OK as possible."

"How do you make something like that OK?" I asked.

"I started spending weekends camping by myself. I liked being alone. I didn't feel vulnerable, though maybe I should have. It was me, the stars, the animals. Wild things seem so much less dangerous than humans. Slowly, I started bringing less and less equipment until it was just me, a backpack with some supplies, and a tarp. After classes ended on Friday afternoon, I'd leave and be gone until Sunday evening. I even missed my graduation. I celebrated finishing college by hiking through Denali."

"So that's how you got to be an outdoors specialist?"

"Not quite. Those forays into the woods alone made me feel strong. I wasn't sure what to do with my communications degree. At one point, I thought I wanted to be a journalist or news anchor. But I knew I couldn't be stuck inside all day, so I picked the job I thought would give me the action I craved. I joined the Army."

"Wow. That explains it."

She scrunched up her face. "What do you mean?"

"Um, well, it's a compliment. You're so…disciplined. And direct. And organized." I had to stop sticking my foot in my mouth.

"Gee, you noticed." Cassidy chuckled and leaned into the sofa, stretching arms above her head, triceps and biceps forming a strong line. She sure looked good for mid-thirties. "It was what I needed at the time. I re-enlisted twice, then left to start my own outfitting company back out West. That's when a TV producer found me. The rest is history."

Now I saw why Cassidy and Arman got along so well. They both had that military precision thing going on. They both had vendettas. I'd never thought it was an attraction in the make-out kind of way and I was right. It was an attraction of minds, of philosophies, of missions.

"And my story," Kcenya said, her amber eyes boring into me so deeply that I shifted in my seat, "is that my father was a wealthy businessman in the 1990's, after the Iron Curtain fell. He paid off whoever he needed to pay to survive, but wasn't going to let the mafiya determine his future. One day he was gunned down in front of our apartment building. From that day forward, I vowed to continue his legacy. I have had to make some decisions and pay off some people I would prefer to avoid, but that is the cost of doing business. Now I have the money and power to make impact. My hands aren't perfectly clean, but I can help people in Moscow who need it. I am committed to helping the most vulnerable in my country since our government disregards their needs. Cassidy's organization will make a difference. We need your help to get Olya on board as a spokesperson."

A bell rang and the elevators doors slid open. A woman as thin and wispy as parchment paper strode in wearing all black, except for the red soles of her Louboutins. Black leggings, and black slouchy sweater revealing a bony shoulder and clavicle. Light brown hair cascaded to her waist in beach waves. Black sunglasses perched on the top of her head. She looked amazing.

The balcony doors slid open, momentarily admitting the hum of the city to Olya's gilded palace. Olya tucked her phone in her bra and sighed. "I'm sorry. Business. And stupid ex-boyfriend." I tried to look casual by picking a hair off my sweater. Olya skittered to the woman in black. They kissed on both cheeks. "This is my stylist, Lyuba!"

I nodded and wondered what craziness was waiting for me inside her bag of makeup tricks.

Three blondes bobbed in behind Lyuba, carrying garment bags and toting a suitcase. If Lyuba had that "Casually Wealthy" look, these three were rocking the "100% Artificial" look. They were a heap of hair extensions and heels, jewelry and tight skirts.

Lyuba said, "Thees are Ashas. Masha, Sasha and Dasha. They are assistants. They are to help me with makeover today."

I gave Cassidy and Arman The Eye.

Arman put a hand on my shoulder. "Marina. Trust us."

"Yes, Marina. Trust us," Cassidy said.

I had a feeling *It seemed like a good idea at the* time was going to be on my tombstone. I stood and trudged to whatever was waiting in those impossibly large cosmetics bags.

19

Two friggin' hours later, Olya took out her phone and Tweeted a selfie. I couldn't read the Russian, but she said she wrote, "@lyubalove   Thank you for your amazing work. Kisses!"

It had already been retweeted 500 times before Lyuba finished adjusting a few stray strands.

Then we stood next to each other in a mirror again. I had long, cascading curls, the chestnut of my own natural color, but now to my elbows. Our green eyes popped like Christmas lights. It felt so disorienting to have hair this long. Even weirder to have my sister from another mister standing next to me.

"Let's take a selfie! Smile!" Before I could respond, she leaned her head against mine and snapped. "I will not tweet photo yet. Not until our game is over. Now, let us go to my closet so you can find something very *me* to wear. I make escape from loading dock so I can leave town to visit my babushka. You go out front. *Spacibo*, Lyubichka! And Dasha, Masha and Sasha!"

Lyuba nodded and continued to peck at her phone. The Ashas, on the other hand, were less subtle. They took selfie after selfie and even grabbed me for a few. They were modeling lipsticks, eye shadows, snapping photos of how the makeup was laid out before they packed it up.

"So, uh, what are all the photos for?"

One of them, I couldn't keep it straight, said, "We are starting makeup business and use Instagram all of time. See?"

She shoved the phone in my face and I flicked through their account: Asha Effects. And wow – it was a beautiful account. Holy Merry Christmas! They had over five thousand followers. They were savvy with hashtags and their photos were well done. Lord, I hated my horrible habit of being too judgy. The Ashas might have looked like a clip-cloppy horde of perfumed and waxed bubble-brains, but they were smart businesswomen.

"Wow. That's pretty nice," I said.

"Thank you," one of the blond Ashas said. "Before you leave, we must to go out together. Will take you to club and dance and have fun, OK?"

"Um, sure." I tried to keep my balance as the weight of the extensions made me feel I was going to topple. My nose itched under the layers of foundation slathered on my face.

Then kiss kiss kiss. And as fast as Lyuba and the Ashas had arrived, they were gone.

"So why isn't your normal hair good enough?" I asked as Olya led me to a walk-in closet the size of my entire kitchen.

"This is my first movie role and it's important I live the character's life. Long, flowing princess hair. Is method acting."

Oh. "Uh-huh."

She pressed a button and the rack spun like at a dry cleaner's. Designer outfit after designer outfit flitted by, flapping in the motion of the conveyor.

"This. No. This. No. This. Oh, let's try all! " With a sweeping motion, she grabbed an armload of clothes and flung them onto the table in the middle of the closet. "This is going to be fun! I never had a sister to play dress up with. Let's go, Mashinka! I need to take mind off stupid ex who keeps contacting me. Is...how do you say? Creeper?"

Oh boy.

But I loved the clothes. My closet was full of things I'd maxed out my credit cards for. Still, my fetish was nothing compared to Olya's. A full hour later, we emerged, me dizzy with hunger and her giddy with excitement.

"A twin sister! I have twin sister! Arman! Cassidy! Kcenya! Come here!"

Arman grinned as Cassidy leaned against the doorjamb and guffawed.

Through gritted teeth I said, "What is so Goddammn funny?"

Olya's smile dropped into a frown. "Yes, what?"

"Nothing, nothing, ladies." Arman said. "You look absolutely stunning. And Kcenya had to leave."

So she got off easy. I, on the other hand, had to stagger around in black high-heeled boots to my knees, black tights, white mini skirt, black trench coat with gold buttons, black skin-tight ribbed turtleneck. Gold, gold, gold everywhere. My ears, my fingers, my wrists. Smoky eyes, pale lipstick.

"Do people truly expect you to go out looking like this all the time?" I felt exhausted just looking at myself. And my feet already throbbed.

"Russian women always go out looking their best."

"Then why do you get to wear skinny jeans and a pair of flats?" I eyed her outfit with jealousy, right to the tan cashmere coat draped over her arm.

"I am going to see grandmother. You are going shopping."

"What?"

"Here is credit card. Get whatever you want. Walk down street." Olya pointed to the busy thoroughfare below. "You will find many nice shops."

I slipped the black Amex into a pouch in my purse with shaking hands and a growl in my stomach. Somehow what I'd always wanted didn't feel like what I ultimately wanted.

In the living room Arman, and Cassidy tossed compliments into the air like glitter confetti. Olya beamed. I fidgeted. I hated fidgeting, so I pulled out my replacement phone. I logged into Facebook while the others were talking. No messages. Not even from Sutton.

"OK, Mashinka. Off you go to shop!" Olya put an arm around me and squeezed.

I managed a smile and shoved my phone back into her Prada bag. " Yup. Off to the trenches."

***

At first, no one seemed to notice me. I pulled my – her – coat collar up and proceeded down the street, taking a left when it t-boned. I was mixing in. Big city, lots of people. More cops with huge, scary guns. Business people glued to phones. Shoppers with bags. I was feeling kind of normal. Until I stopped to cross a street, and a group of teenage girls started screeching.

"Olya! Olya!" They skittered over holding up phones. Since my job was to be her, I'd smile all they wanted and pose as much as they needed me to. I mugged and grinned and hugged. They asked all kinds of questions, but I had not a freakin' clue as to what they were saying. So I just pointed to my throat and shook my head. Let them think I had to save my voice.

"Laringeet!" one gasped. She typed furiously into her phone.

Now I was attracting a crowd. If Olya wanted a decoy, boy, she had one. I stillettoed across the street and now even the old ladies were staring. A gaggle followed me, yelling "Olya! Olya!"

I moved on, waving. Oh Lord. How long could I keep this up? Finally, the white columns of Armani. Something I could understand. The employees must have heard my fan club before they saw me. A huge dude in a suit waited for me at the door. "Olya," he said and waved for me to enter. He then closed the door and posted himself in front of it, like a bouncer.

"Whew," I said and pushed Olya's sunglasses to the top of my head. House music thumped through speakers, giving the story a club-like feel. The floor was shiny marble and the clothes impeccably displayed. Oh my God, I felt so uncomfortable. Finally in the league I'd wanted to be in, but I would have preferred lying on the sofa catching up on reality TV. My stomach was doing flips. I tried to appear calm. Don't touch anything, I warned myself. You might leave a fingerprint or molecule.

A woman with a tight bun and tighter black dress came over and said something in Russian. I smiled and pointed to my throat, shaking my head again. Then I just meandered the store, hoping my act came across as more aloof than clueless. What to buy? I wasn't walking out of there empty handed. Something for Sutton. Yes. I glanced back at the frosted windows. People were lining up outside the store. I had to hurry and get out. I found a heavy navy sweater with leather patches on the elbows. No idea how much it cost, but — whatever. If Olya didn't care, I didn't. Plus, he'd look amazing in it. I was going to live in hope I'd see him again.

The noise from the onlookers got louder when the door opened, but I didn't turn. Nope. No conversations for me. Laryngitis. Cough cough. The man who entered said something to the clerk and she responded. Looking at the sweaters, looking at the sweaters, looking at the sweaters. At least until the crowd got tired. I sure loved sweaters.

"I must talk to you," a deep voice said from behind me.

"Eek!" I squealed and jumped. One hand slammed the hanger on the bar, sending some zillion-dollar blouse sliding to the floor. The employee skittered over and picked it up. I turned to see my admirer: the rich dude from the club who'd insisted on slow-dancing with me because I resembled Olya, his ex-girlfriend. Now he was stalking me. Creepy. Why did I always attract the winners?

On the sidewalk the amateur cell-phone paparazzi were being replaced by real paparazzi with real cameras. The store security guard, who could have passed for a refrigerator in the dark, was doing a good job keeping them out of the store. But they were getting louder, more aggressive.

Dmitry rattled something in Russian and the worker nodded and ushered us into the back. She averted her gaze, smiling as she opened a door to a dressing room. Jesus, Mary and the Carpenter. She thought we'd met up here for an afternoon delight. Oh God. Dmitry tipped the woman a wad of bills. She nodded and pivoted out.

The dressing room was all white, with a round white leather bench in the middle. White carpet. White walls. A flat screen on one side and a built in closet and shelves on the other. A silver tray with champagne on ice and four glasses. Two changing areas. What the hell? Did people have cocktail parties in here while they went shopping? Man. What a life. And here I'd thought the cushioned benches at The Loft were swaggy.

A few seconds later, I heard the clerk's heels click from the marble floor in the showroom and onto the carpet. I heard her open a cabinet, slide something out, then go out another exit. It clicked shut. Silence.

"The most expensive smoke break in the history of the world," Dmitry said. "Please, sit down."

"I'm fine. Thanks, though." I leaned against the cabinet, hoping this wouldn't take long. These pointy stiletto torture chamber boots were killing me. My toes were permanently smooshed into a V.

"This won't take long. I need your help. I was standing outside her apartment building and saw you leave. I bought her that purse as International Women's Day gift. Please help me get in touch with Olya. I need to tell her how much I miss her. She won't return my calls, emails, texts." He sat on the round bench, hands pressed as if in prayer between his knees, gaze on the carpet. A sad man, for sure. I totally believed him. We had a lot in common.

"Question: how is your English so good? I mean, most Russians here have great English but yours has hardly any accent."

His head snapped up and his nostrils flared. "First, I am not Russian. I am Kazakh."

Ekk. I always seemed to know how to hit a nerve. "Sorry."

"It's OK. Well, I am half-Russian. My father was Kazakh. But because I look more Asian than Slavic, I will never be considered a real Russian. I will always be asked for my documents, I will always be stopped for invisible traffic violations. So I am Kazakh."

"Sorry."

"No, no, it's me who is sorry." He shook his head and looked even sadder. "That wasn't nice of me. How would you know the politics of this country? I apologize. To answer your question, I have a cousin who lives in California, so I was fortunate to go to high school in America. I stayed for college then got my MBA at Stanford. Is my accent that noticeable now?"

"Ummm…no. It's kinda neutral, to be honest. Like a newscaster."

"Oh, good."

I couldn't believe this sad-ass billionaire was worried about the quality of his accent. "Listen, Dmitry. I know something about being sad. And I also don't know Olya. I don't want to get into her business." I was already in her clothes, but diving into her personal life was too much.

"Please, please. I will do anything you like in return."

My mind flashed back to Venomous Vika at the club, who'd been annoyed I hadn't wanted the affections of the billionaire she'd wanted to interview. Maybe I could help a sister out, so I figured I'd try to play relationship counselor.

And then all of a sudden, he was crying again, this male model stand-in with cheekbones I could dive off and black hair so shiny I could see my reflection in it. He'd projected all of the confidence in the world when I'd met him, with the Booty Brigade surrounding him in that plush leather booth.

"You didn't look so sad the night I met you with your entourage of porn stars."

"I was just trying to make her jealous."

"That's how you make Olya jealous? I don't think so, dude. That's how you make a woman think you're pathetic and shallow."

He pulled a tissue from his pocket and blew his nose. "Russian women are impossible. You don't understand."

"This is going to require a drink." I lifted the champagne bottle.

"Let me." He unwrapped the foil from the top and with a pop, we were drinking some mighty fine alcohol in the dressing room of an Armani store in freaking Moscow. And this was my life now...how?

"*Na zdrovya*," I said. We clinked glasses. "How long will the clerk be gone?"

"I told her thirty minutes."

"OK, lover boy, listen up." I explained how walking around with porn stars wasn't going to help. Also stalking with phone calls, text messages, etc. was out, too. Between glasses, I asked him what had happened to break them up.

Dmitry loosened his skinny black tie, then took off his coat and suit jacket. We were approaching slumber party mode. Fabulous. Break out the Ouija board.

"Well, her career is in the stratosphere. I have a lot of responsibilities as the owner of an oil and gas company. I didn't make the effort needed. It's very hard being many time zones away and only able to see each other for maybe twenty-four hours at a time. I became resentful and distanced myself. Olya needed more. I was too stuck in my old fashioned ways of how a relationship should be. I wanted her to be home for me every night, with dinner in the oven."

Needing more. Limited time together. Sounded familiar. I held out my glass for more sweet champagne. Russians sure liked the bubbly. "If it makes you feel any better, we all make mistakes like that. I think the key is to not make it a power play. You've got to give to get. From what I know about Olya, you need give her some space. She's, ummmmmm, intense. Yeah, that's the word. She wasn't happy about your texting today. Just give her some space."

"Space? Then she'll forget about me." Now the tie was undone, hanging like a garden snake around his collar.

"Not likely, Mr. Male Model."

"Please." He actually blushed.

"Dude. Seriously. Don't you get it? You're hot." My teeth were getting a little numb from the champagne. This meant I was going to start to babble.

"Well, thank you, I guess. If making myself look like the Hunchback of Notre Dame would get Olya back into my arms, I would dress up like a short, fat church bell ringer."

"Whoa — don't go that far. Step one is space. When is the last time you tried to contact her?"

"When I was walking down the street. I texted her and then checked my Twitter. I saw your hashtag."

Goddamn hashtag.

„"No more of that. For at least a week. Let absence make her heart grow fonder. It'll require amazing discipline on your part, but trust me. I need a week to think of a plan. I leave in a week. Before then, I promise I will have something."

"Can I at least look at her Facebook page?"

"Yes. But no posting. Got it?"

He nodded. "I'm trusting you."

What made him put confidence in me, I will never understand, but now I had a mission. Get him time with Olya without her being annoyed. I felt so bad for him. What a love-struck, lost puppy.

Dmitry stood and wrapped his arms around me. "Thank you so much. If this works out, I owe you." My face smooshed against his chest in an awkward hug that lingered a few seconds too long.

I heard the front door open and close. A knock on the dressing room door. He opened it, spoke to the clerk, and ushered me back to the showroom.

"Hold on." I grabbed another extra-large sweater cardigan with elbow patches. The clerk rang it up. I had no idea how much it cost, but I wasn't paying. My wildly rich twin was. If Dmitry was living in hope, so could I. Sutton would look great in this at Thanksgiving dinner with my mom.

Dmitry opened the back door that opened into an alley. Surprise! It was raining again. Stupid Moscow fall. Couldn't a girl get even a little bit of snow while she was in Russia? Jeez.

We entered the street and of course there were two real photographers waiting for us. Dmitry scowled, put his head down and wrapped an arm around me. I raised a hand to shield my face, stared at the sidewalk and let him guide me away.

I didn't respond to any of the paparazzi's comments, but then one said something that sent Dmitry flying. He flung his arm off me, told me to keep walking and charged one of the photographers. I just stood there, mouth hanging open. The Dmitry I knew – so far – had been kind and sentimental; this dude's fists were ready to knock skulls.

Both guys with the cameras kept on snapping away as Dmitry's black coat billowed behind him. *Click click click click click.* Dmitry squared up to the taller of the two, the one who must've said whatever pushed him over the edge. The other took picture after picture. Dmitry grabbed off his knit hat and threw it to the pavement. He slammed into the dude's shoulders and the guy stumbled back. Dmitry grabbed his camera and threw it against the wall of the building with such force it shattered into chunks. The guy stood frozen, staring at the remains of his equipment. The other photographer was already across the street, but attaching a large lens to the front of his camera. Dmitry took out his wallet and threw a pile of American hundred dollar bills at the photographer picking up pieces of his camera, spat near the dude's shoes, and walked away. His black hair hung limp over his eyes, shoulders hunched as he strode toward me.

He put his arm around me again. I shrugged it off. "No way, dude. You are some kinda bad news. Uh-uh."

"Don't give that other guy the photo he wants, the one of Olya shutting me down again. *Please.* You don't know what he said to me. " He pulled me back next to him.

"I don't care. What you did — that was overboard. Now get off me." I elbowed him in the ribs. He backed off, eyes still blazing.

I turned my – Olya's – collar up to shield my face, pushed my sunglasses up the bridge of my nose and pretended not to feel the pain of my toes being smooshed into the pointy heels of my - Olya's – expensive boots. The ones definitely not made for walkin'.

20

I was alone in the penthouse. Alone. Finally. In the bathroom I stripped off Olya's clothes. The tights left a ring around my waist. The push-up bra left red indentations on my ribs. The eyeliner made me look like a crazed cat. While the oversized tub filled with steaming water, I scrubbed my face with some kind of creamy wash and wished it could also scrub away the drama with Dmitry. I found a bottle of bubble bath and settled in to unwind.

I heard a door open. A thump as someone put bags down. Fine. I would immerse myself in the jasmine-scented heaven for just a little bit longer, then find out where Arman and Cassidy had been. The bubbles tickled my chin as I propped a towel behind my neck.

I was about to drift off when Olya barged in. She flicked the lights on. My head flew up and perfumed bubbles dripped into my eyes, stinging like a mofo.

"What the —? " I gasped.

Olya had fire in her voice. "One simple favor so I could see my grandmother. She is so ill. One simple favor. And you do this?"

"What did I do?"

She shoved her phone in my face. I couldn't read the article's headline but I understood the photos, taken by the second photographer. Dmitry taking the hat off. Dmitry pushing the photographer. Dmitry smashing the camera. Dmitry spitting. All quite ugly.

"I had nothing to do with that! Dmitry found me while he was looking for you. That hashtag you think is so wonderful? It backfired.

He found me, talked to me, and that got even more people waiting for us outside. That one photographer guy said something nasty that pushed Dmitry over the edge."

"You see? This is my problem with Dmitry! He is interesting man, very handsome, debonair, very loving. But he gets overprotective. He would never lay hand on me, but he flies out of control when angry. I don't have time for that. And now, *this* is all over the internet. This is public relations nightmare!"

"If it makes you feel any better, it was actually me."

She dipped her hand in the tub, which made me feel really weird. With a palm full of bubbles, she continued. "People *think* it's me. And we have, how you say? Reunited. You let him manipulate you. Why did you leave store with him?"

"Wait a second. I was doing *you* a favor!" Oh shit. Oh shit. I was naked in a tub, arguing with a major celebrity who was super-duper pissed at me. Her bodyguards in the hall could come in at any second and toss me out into the Moscow streets with nothing but a towel.

Her face relaxed and she stood. "Oh, I am sorry, Marina. Mashinka. I did not mean to scare you. You are so pale. Here, here." She reached for a towel. "Dry off and come talk. I will be in kitchen."

I didn't rush drying off and changing, hoping Cassidy and Arman would arrive and get me the hell out of here. Olya had left me a pair of black yoga pants – at least some things were internationally respected as comfortable – and a white fleece. I slathered on lotions because Lord knows I wasn't going to ever have access to all of these high-end crèmes again. I gasped when I rubbed the condensation off the mirror because, again, I'd forgotten about my new long hair.

I gathered some strength and went to the kitchen. White tile floor, white counters, white appliances, with some orange accents here and there, like beautiful arrangements of orange lilies.

Olya set out a teapot, two mugs and a tray of round cookies. "Here, sit. Please. I have not properly welcomed you to my home."

"Um, thanks." So now it was nice cop.

She set a black lacquer tray painted with red, orange and gold flowers on the table. She poured very dark tea into a mug, then added hot water from a large kettle. "Do you like your coffee sweet?"

"Yes, please."

She poured something thick and white from a can. "Sweetened condensed milk."

"Oh. OK."

"And take some cookies. Made by the bakery near grandmother's flat. Not like expensive, tasteless pastries in these expensive shops."

"OK. Thanks. So, uh, when are Arman and Cassidy coming back?"

"In about hour. Marina, let me to thank you now for helping today. You gave me chance to see my grandmother."

"Glad I could help." I nibbled the edges of a round cookie that was like gingerbread soaked in honey.

"Masha, you must understand. Visiting my grandmother isn't easy."

"I know, I know. Being *you* isn't easy. Believe me, I learned that today."

"No. When I visit her, I have to visit in prison."

"You have to— what? Prison? What did she do?" So much for the vision of the happy babushka making borscht all day.

Olya sat on a stool and stirred her tea. She stared at the ceiling, and sighed. "My grandfather died young. Too much smoking, too much work. Hard life in factory. We, my family, were trying to convince my grandmother to start dating again. She was too young to be alone. Only fifty-two.

"So she met a man who worked as a mechanic for a — how you say it? Car dealer? Yes, car dealer. I won't even say this bully's name. He started off romantic. Bringing chocolate and flowers and champagne. Seemed like nice man. His was...how you say... widower. They went for walks in park, went to ballet and symphony. Then grandmother started hiding bruises on her arms. When she avoided a family party at our dacha, summer house, we knew something was wrong. I was only thirteen, but old enough to know he was bad man. We drove to her flat. She was sitting on couch with her right eye swollen shut and cradling her left arm, crying. The bastard broke her arm. But she went back to him, like many Russian women do.

"Then one night, he was choking her. Over wanting to see us instead of being home with him. She reached for what she could find in kitchen to defend herself. It was knife. She stabbed him and ran away. My grandmother's boyfriend was the brother of the owner of big market in town. Big money, big voice. He got police to go after her. And she has been in prison ever since."

"I don't know what to say except I'm so, so sorry." Her gilded cage looking over one of the biggest cities in the world didn't seem so shiny and flawless anymore.

"Thank you. *This* is why I work with Kcenya. She is one of the only people with means who help battered people in Moscow, in Russia. We are going to launch national program about domestic abuse and human trafficking. In my culture, it is accepted to hit your wife. Boys are special in my culture. So many men were killed in the Great War, what you call World War Two, that men are given special treatment. Many people raise boys to be big spoiled babies and then get angry when they become babyish men with babyish needs and reactions. Girls marry strangers just to get out of country. Kcenya proudly calls herself feminist and people hate her for it."

If there was anything I understood, it was being angry with people taking advantage of others. I had pushed my anger down, but it was like a helium balloon, pushing its way up again. That stupid silver tooth glinting in The General's mouth, Amparo's poor, bloated body.

Olya put her hand on my arm. "Is OK. I see you are upset. Drink tea."

This trip was opening my eyes to all of the privilege in my life. Sure, I was just a girl from Nowhereville, PA, but I had so much more than so many here. My worldview was shifting. I felt like a shaken bottle of Diet Coke, with the top loose enough so that some can leak out. But you know when you go to twist, it's going to spray all over you in a million directions.

She poured me more tea and. "Here, Mashinka. Let's talk of something else. Tell me all about Dmitry."

I rolled my eyes, but felt myself relax. "Boy, Olya, you have your hands full with that one."

"Yes, I know." She tucked her legs underneath her.

"Listen, this is the second time he's told me he wants to get back with you. We were at the same club once and slow-danced with me. He started to cry when he talked about you."

"Mmmm. Always sentimental. He is, how do you say it? A crier?"

"Yes, a crier."

"Oh, my Dima. Dima, Dima, Dima." She looked into her cup of tea and stirred, smiling and shaking her head.

I let her have a few moments, then said, "So what're you going to do about him? I don't want to get in the business of a mega pop star and her oil tycoon ex-boyfriend, but — he's pretty sad and needs to talk to you."

She sighed and picked at a fingernail. "Well, that isn't so clear right now." She showed me the images on Twitter of us leaving the Armani store. "Oh, such a gentleman, isn't he? So protective of women. I remember once when…but, never mind. He will never change. I will not see him again. "

21

If I had one priority when I got back to Pennsylvania, it was to get my liver checked because I was sure it was soon going to be pickled enough to serve on top of a cheeseburger. *Cheeseburger.* Mmmmm. Sitting in the hotel bar I was officially missing home, missing all the places and friends I knew so well. I finished the dregs of my Baltika and asked Arman to order me another.

"You do it. Practice your Russian."

Cassidy grinned and drank from her pint of Guinness. "Yes – do."

"Fine." I caught the bartender's eye, smiled and held my bottle in the air. He smiled back, took it and returned with a nice, cold bottle of Number 4. I was working my way up the alcohol numbers, but since Number 1 was near-beer, this was really only number three.

Then my guts started doing the talking. "What's the plan? I'd like to have a chance to fix what I couldn't last summer. What's the deal with all this surveillance, team?"

"Team?" Cassidy raised an eyebrow and looked at Arman.

"Team. Hmmmm." Arman popped an olive martini into his mouth.

"Yes, team. With everything we have been through, we're certainly one. So, what's the deal? You didn't bring me here to sit on benches all day."

Cassidy started. "So. Russia has just been ranked a tier three country when it comes to human trafficking. The lowest ranking you can get as a government. The president, of course insists, this is politically motivated. That his country is making great strides against it. The US government, western governments and non-governmental organizations disagree. Anecdotally, the doctors from the medical team you met at the Kasha Kitchen have noticed an uptick in new tattoos on many of the girls. Not five dots like The General's had, but other tattoos. You know what that means."

I pulled my sleeve over my wrist and nodded. The girls had been marked by their pimps as property.

Arman broke in. "The western governments will tread lightly. This tier three designation would permit sanctions, but the US and other governments are not going to push Russia too hard over human trafficking. Oil? Natural gas? Sure. People? Sadly, not so much."

"OK. But I can get all this info from the internet. What does it have to do with us?"

"Our organization, Shine a Light, is going to conduct stings in various countries to break up trafficking rings. Sex trafficking, organ trafficking, labor trafficking. We must start small. Moscow will be our first. After months of planning and getting financial backing, we are ready to roll."

For the first time in months, I felt lighter, like a jolt of energy had zipped through my body. "Let's do this, superheroes!"

Arman smirked.

Cassidy outright laughed. "Arman and I were hoping brining you here would pique your interest. We may have a link to a small trafficking ring run out of an apartment building on the outskirts of Moscow. All we need is verification. We think Dmitry could find out."

"How?" Flashback to the busty gals in his booth at the club. Could they have been trafficked?

Arman jumped in. "He knows a lot of people. But we have not been able to get close to him. Who knew *you* would be the magic link. Will you see him again? Even though what happened must have been scary."

"He's literally nuts. You didn't see his mental switch flip to Crazytown with those photographers."

Arman leaned in. "From everything we can understand, he is honest, for a billionaire in Russia. There is no doubt he made his money off the backs of the poorest and most uneducated. But he did it as ethically as possible, at least compared to other business owners. He paid a wage higher than his competitors — that brought him a lot of employee loyalty."

"What exactly do we need him for? Seriously. He's literally crazy. Isn't there another way? What about Kcenya?"

Cassidy put her Guinness on a coaster. "Kcenya is one of our backers, but being a woman, she's not part of the good ol' boys club here. We need an additional financier, someone with connections. Someone who is simultaneously an insider and an outsider. Daurenov is part Russian, part Kazakh. One of the wealthiest men in Asia, also a benefactor of many causes."

"You make him sound too good to be true. The guy is sweet one minute, the next seriously violent. His brain went bye-bye when those photographers bothered us."

"Astute observation, my Marina. He could be unstable. But he is the best of the worst. And in a situation like this, we often must take the best of the worst." Armin finished the martini.

"So what is this plan?" I said.

Cassidy said, "We're are going to stage a buy. To coordinate with law enforcement, well, as much law enforcement as we can in this country. This group operates in Germany, too. We have a government connection who would fight for extradition there, ensuring their indictment."

"It's not going to be easy," Arman said. "There are a lot of wheels turning here. But Dmitry has the means to pay off whoever we need to pay off. We also have the tacit cooperation of a few western embassies, including Germany, and Interpol. The Russian federal government is not quite so cooperative, but we think our other partners can force some hands."

The past few months of my life flashed through my brain, a slideshow of the body of Amparo Rivas, muddy and bloated. The sparkle of The General's silver tooth. The thunder of the collapsing mine. The terror in my niece's eyes. I was so full of bile for these men and for what the General had done to my life that I was ready and willing to do whatever it took to take one down. "I'm in. What do I need to convince Dmitry to do for us?"

"He is our pipeline to the necessary resources, including some finances and connections. We think that if you ask him and tell him you will put him in a room with Olya, that might sway him."

Cassidy took her phone out of her coat pocket. "You are the missing link. You have Dmitry in the palm of your hand." She shoved her phone next to my bottle. In the display was a paparazzi photo of us outside Armani with his arm around me, smiling, a few seconds before he'd lost his mind. That look in his eyes — anyone who saw it could see he was in love.

Cassidy tapped out a cigarette from a cream-colored, squarish box that read DUNHILL in bold, gold letters.

"Fancy. And holy cancer, Cassidy."

"Don't judge."

I thought she was joking around, but then, wasn't so sure. I'd never figure this woman out. Never. A mystery wrapped in an enigma wrapped in a Gore-Tex raincoat.

Arman rapped his knuckles on the bar. "I am going to pose as a businessman looking for domestic help. These operations make a lot of money setting up wealthy individuals with women desperate to live in other countries. The women see this as a ticket out, but they are sold into indentured servitude or worse."

A plume of smoke snaked out of the corner of Cassidy's mouth. "The ruble is in a free-fall. Desperate times call for desperate measures. This particular syndicate is rebuilding after the murders of some of their leaders. They're the low-hanging fruit right now and they're ripe for the picking." She crushed her cigarette in an ashtray brimming with butts. "These girls will then be given support to get back home or move somewhere else, start over, have counseling. That's the crucial part. It's one thing to prosecute the criminals; it's another to heal the survivors."

The bar was now filling up with the after-work drinkers, so Arman lowered his voice. "And Sabine, my daughter. Remember her? She is studying film and is interested in making documentaries. Given her mother's role as a human rights lawyer in Germany and mine in the Kurdish struggle, she is specifically interested in human rights violations. She will be in on the sting, using sophisticated surveillance equipment to film the entire event."

Of course Sabine was a hero in stilettos. Lord, I felt like such a misfit. "Aren't you worried about something happening to her?"

"Of course. You understand my iron will? As a woman, hers is tenfold. The bargain is that she would stay outside in an SUV and monitor from her laptop, with a security team. They will be several blocks away. She will set up the equipment beforehand. We are going to wear wires. I have a communications expert who will lead. You will be in the van with Sabine, should you choose to come to the sting."

Oh. OK. I could only imagine the awkward conversation: *Hey, Sabine! I'm Marina Your dad's smokin' hot and great in the sack. You ready to take down this syndicate or what?* "Are you sure about this, Arman?"

"Not completely, to speak with veracity. Yet I know my daughter. Sabine is very strong-willed. I would rather her get experience with me, with people who are professionals, than seek out an amateur who will get her hurt or worse. The lesser of two evils, I suppose." He drummed his fingers on the bar and sighed. "Daughters."

***

Through a direct message in Twitter, I got Dmitry to meet us at a park in central Moscow. Arman and I stood under an empty band shell to shelter us from the rain and waited. Of course it was raining. Why not? I could have just gone to Scotland if I wanted rain. And people were eating *ice cream* in this craptacular weather. Ice cream. What a place.

Dmitry strode toward us, coat collar up. He shook Arman's hand and kissed me on the cheek, lingering a little longer than he should have. They started talking in Russian, while I pushed wet leaves around with the toe of one boot. Their conversation was fast and serious. They were a total match as far as intensity and intelligence. Dmitry had several inches in height on Arman, but Arman made up for it in confidence.

Meanwhile Dmitry's psycho eyes bored down at me. I still saw the crazy behind the composure.

Arman cleared his throat, "Dmitry, Marina has an offer for you."

Okey dokey. Business time. I stood taller, pushing my shoulders down and lifting my chin. "Dmitry. Listen. If I can get Olya to see you, can you help us?"

"Don't you leave at the end of the week?"

"Dude, I've put wedding receptions together in less time."

"Your American confidence is refreshing, yet not completely credible."

Arman grinned.

Now I was in client mode. This is why Prestige loved me. I could get people on board lickety-split. "Olya and I understand each other. We both know what it's like to be in relationships that, despite our best efforts, didn't work. What it's like to come from a small town and want better. Dmitry, if I am anything, I'm a romantic who gets things done." I stepped closer. My voice echoed in the band shell. People scurried past on a nearby path, buffering themselves from the wind with umbrellas.

"I know this is a huge risk, to get involved. But this type of crime will never be stopped unless heroes like you step up. You are the key. You have the connections, the credibility. Arman has the specifics, but you can grease palms, talk to people." Dmitry nodded, but didn't look convinced yet. "Plus, Olya is one of the private funders of the Kasha Kitchen. She does not like seeing the helpless beaten down. If she knows you are part of this, and are responsible for putting these men behind bars, well, you should have a shot with her. Another chance to make your love work."

His brown eyes turned dark. I wasn't sure if he was going to rage or cry. He wiped his face with a leather glove and mumbled something in Russian to Arman. He turned, smiled and waved before he walked down the steps at the side of the stage.

"So, is he in?"

"Yes." Arman zipped his maroon wool coat. The gold zipper was set slightly diagonally, fresh off the runway. He adjusted the black and cream cashmere scarf that was, of course, perfectly wrapped around his neck. "He understands the scourge these organizations are. He is reluctant to get involved because it is a very delicate balance to play in the big leagues here. But he wants Olya back."

"Well, good. Let's go, gladiator." I slid my arm in his and we walked toward the stairs.

"So what's your plan to get Olya to meet with Dmitry?"

"I have no freakin' clue." My phone buzzed. "Hold on."

It was a message from Gilly: *Hi Een – Rents are being parental. Miss u. Xoxo*

I wrote back: *Hey Bestie – Sorry. Old people suck. Love you more.*

I hoped it was just one of those things about being in your mid-twenties and your parents breathing down your neck. I just didn't get what Gilly's parents had to worry about. He was a lawyer with a secure job. Sure, he hadn't come out to them, but his parents were good people. They would ultimately be fine with it, despite their church.

Leaves crunched on the pathway as we walked to a pedestrian tunnel. "Why so sad, Marina?" Arman patted my hand.

That tiny message had me missing my little cocoon in Northeastern PA. I had a feeling that when I returned, home wouldn't be the same. And I wouldn't be the same, either.

***

After our rendezvous with Dmitry, I spent the rest of the day helping out at the Kasha Kitchen, serving meals and organizing the clothing van. It wasn't super challenging, but interacting with so many needy people just about broke my heart. It was the first time I'd felt like what I was doing was actually making a difference. A few more clients arrived with bandages over their eyes. Something about these specific injuries was bothering me.

After the meal, I went to the medical bus and rapped on the door. It whooshed open. A woman with dark skin and hair pulled back into an Afro puff said, "*Oui?* How can I help?"

"I'm looking for Jean. Is he here?"

"Jean!" She stepped back and Jean appeared a white lab coat.

"Oh, hello." He blinked at me, pushing up wire-rimmed glasses.

"Hi, Jean. Have a minute?"

"I am busy, but can manage a *menoot*." He stepped off the bus and pulled a pack of cigarettes from his lab coat pocket.

"Aren't you a doctor? Because you know cigarettes kill, right?"

He exhaled a stream of smoke from the corner of his mouth. "*Oui.* I am a cruel irony."

"Anyway, so more people are coming to the Kasha Kitchen with gauze over their eyes." I dug my hands into my coat pocket, shivering. The wind had picked up. An empty chip bag skittered over my boot. Leaves spun in a vortex in front of the bus.

Jean exhaled again and fidgeted with the gold band on his left ring finger. "It is my feeling someone pays them for corneas."

"*What?* But — but that's horrible!"

He stepped off the bus and pulled his lab coat closer, shivering in tandem with me. "We examined a few of the injured a few months ago. They'd had surgery to remove one cornea. Then, they never came back for a follow up. Now, anyone with an eye *bandazh* refuses to talk to us at all."

"How bad did their life have to be to sell part of your own eye?" I shivered again, not from the cold, but from the sheer ickiness of the idea.

Jean tapped the cigarette. The ashes were whisked away by the wind. "This is the part of my job I wish I didn't have to know anything about. You have heard of the black market, *oui?*"

I nodded. "You can buy guns, drugs, anything. Anyone."

"Well, the *red* market is for human body parts. And you, my American friend, are filling the bellies that provide them."

I remembered Arman telling me about the red market at the fight club. "These people are selling off parts of their bodies for money? But it doesn't make sense. They still have to come here for meals. So they're obviously not getting enough money to have any meaningful effect on their lives."

Jean crushed the cigarette under one brown boot. "Exactly. They are paid enough to make them happy at that moment. Then they buy food for their children — or more vodka. They receive no follow-up. And now it even seems they are being told not to see us for medical care. Or else."

"Or else what?"

"Do not be so naïve, *ma fille*." Jean's gaze held mine for a few beats. He pivoted back to the medical bus, knocked on the door and it hissed open. He looked defeated, head down, shoulders slumped, as he stepped back inside.

I knew that feeling.

26

That night, back at the hotel, I sank into a hot bath, letting the water cover my face as I slid down into the tub. My hair extensions floated around me like a mermaid's tresses. My phone vibrated on the sink counter, and I jumped out to check it, bubbles cascading to the floor. *Sutton, Sutton, Sutton,* I hoped.

No. A number I didn't recognize with a short message: *We will to pick you up at 10pm. The Ashas*

The Ashas. They were a perfume cloud of happiness and joy. I could use a dose of that. After all, I'd promised them I'd go out. Two hours of fun, then back to the hotel. That would be it.

After a long soak, I called Cassidy. I flopped back on the mountain of pillows and said, "Listen. The Ashas want to take me out tonight. We're going to be at that new club up the street."

Silence at the other end. "Whatever, Marina. Just be safe."

"Two hours. Tops. Pinky swear," I promised. "If I'm not home by midnight, send out a search party."

***

"Listen, girls. I have to be back by midnight. Understand?" The music pulsed through the front doors to Kino, the newest club in Moscow as we waited for the guards to check us.

"But the party will be just starting," said Dasha in a whine. This time, it was easier to know who was who: Masha still had the long blond extensions. Sasha's hair was pulled up in a slick bun, like the guitar-playing dancers in some old 80's video I remembered my mom watching on You Tube. Dasha's hair was now black and short, angled in a bob. She also had a little birthmark above her lip. I was sure I'd keep it straight now.

Sasha added lip gloss. "OK, Masha Two. We will have you home by *one*."

"Or *two*!" Sasha nudged me and winked.

"Masha Two, are you OK?" Dasha handed her purse to a security dude and looked at me.

"Yeah. Just a little homesick." The longing for Tommy's pizza and A-Treat soda crept up on me at the strangest times.

A few vodka and pineapple juices later, I was feeling better. I was on stage at Kino, dancing to whatever kind of song was blasting over the club's sound system. I kept telling myself that I'd get back to the hotel in twenty more minutes.

The fact of the matter was I was grateful the Ashas wanted to take me out. I missed girl time. My new best girlfriends shook and shimmied in front, behind and next to me. Masha's hair extensions whipped my face, getting in the way of me smoking my cigarette. Wait — I was smoking? How had that happened? I raised a hand over my head and waved a wrist to the music, hoping to angle the cigarette in such a way it wouldn't ash all over my new besties. The crowd pulsed, lights flashed red and blue and white. The group energy was throbbing through my veins. I shook my head in time with the music. The extensions were so much fun. I felt like a goddess.

My phone vibrated against my left boob. I yanked it out of my bra.

CASSIDY: U ok? It's 12:15.

ME: Yeahhhh! At Kino. Come on over!

CASSIDY: Off to bed.

ME: You're old!

And then I turned the phone off. I was done with Ms. Party Pooper. The cell went back in my Victoria's Secret bra and I went back to dancing.

The DJ said something and the crowd went wild. I hooted and hollered along with everyone else.

"*Davai*, Masha Two! *Davai*!" Dasha screamed. I let her pull me to the middle of the stage. The spotlight was suddenly on me and Dasha. Other brunette women were hoisted on stage by burly security dudes. I smiled at them and smoothed my shorts. I adjusted my bra and aligned the straps on my spangled tank top. The silver sequins were scraping the underside of my arms from all of the dancing. A few more vodkas and pineapple juice, and I would forget about it.

"Dasha, what is the DJ saying?" I yelled into her ear.

"Masha Two, it's Olya look-alike lip synch contest! You are going to win for sure!"

"No, no, no, I'm good. I'm good. I don't need to be in a contest."

"Come on! You ween, we sit in VIP whole night."

I looked at the girls lining the front of the stage. The other two were giving me the thumbs-up. The bass pounded. That familiar synthesized Middle-Eastern twang played again, the song I'd heard a zillion times in the past week and a half from very radio station, every cab, every kiosk. Aw, hell.

Dasha left me on the stage with the other girls. An announcer in black skinny jeans, a red t-shirt with a faded picture of some Soviet guy with a beard, and a trucker hat said something. The crowd fell quiet. The lights made it hard to see the audience but I could hear and feel them. The girls on stage with me shuffled and shimmied as the intro to the song looped over and over. Then the crowd cheered and the music grew louder.

How had Olya danced in the videos? Kind of bouncing up and down, right arm in the air, index finger pointing up. I tried that. The Ashas, in front, shrieked and waved their hands above their heads. I shook my butt and turned in a little circle. The crowd got louder. Then the lyrics started. Oh shit. I didn't understand a word she was saying. Shitshitshitshitshit. Ah! Gilly used to be in chorus and he said he just said "watermelon" over when he didn't know the words. Sweet. Watermelon it was, then.

I watermeloned it for the next two minutes through all the accordions and techno beats. Finally, a break during the mid-song rap done by some guy. I watched the other girls on stage and did what they did. Right arm in the air, index finger pointing to the sky, shaking my butt. Man, these girls were young. I was the oldest by a few years, so I sucked my gut in and shook what my momma gave me. The lights bore down like hot suns and the air was a haze through the red, blue, and white light.

Right at the end of the song, I felt another girl slide her arm around my shoulder. Then, on the other side, another hot, sweaty bare arm on my skin. I watermeloned as I sang along with the lyrics. There was no way I was winning this. The girl on my left started kicking her legs. We formed a little Rockette's kick line. Up! Whoo! Down! Whoo! Kick! Kick! Watermelon! Watermelon! The crowd went crazy, their hoots and hollers thundered down to my toes. And I was sure grateful I'd decided to not go commando like the real Olya. The song stopped and we ended with a group bow.

The crowd roared. My Ashas were blowing me kisses, all giving me a thumbs-up.

The emcee reentered the stage, clapping, too. He said something into the microphone that made the other girls on the stage giggle. I had no clue what, so I laughed. Last. Oh well.

He went on in Russian. Some of the girls held hands, others pushed their booties and boobies further out. I just stood there, trying to take it all in.

I heard "*Amerikanka,*" which meant "American female." Except his time, it wasn't a catcall. The crowd roared. The Ashas screamed. Some of the girls on stage clapped, a few hugged me, a bunch of others simply rolled their eyes and stomped off stage.

I teetered over on my sparkly platforms and accepted a pink tiara and pink sash that said something I of course couldn't read. The emcee hugged me and slapped my butt. I was an *Amerikanka* who didn't take anyone's shit, so I slapped his in return. The corners of his blue eyes crinkled and he guffawed. He said something, shrugged, the crowd laughed again. I didn't effing care. All I cared about is that the Ashas and I were going to spend the rest of the night as VIPs.

A burly dude with a brown beard and slicked-back black hair waved for me to come over. He said something and I gave him my best deer in headlights look. The Ashas swooped in to translate. Burly Dude escorted us through the crowd, pushing people away. I gave out high-fives and smiled so much it felt like my face was going to crack in two. Or maybe that was the vodkas and pineapple juice.

Our corner booth had a high back and cushiony seats, shaped like half a donut. Fish swam in the tank that served as the base of the table. Their little blue tails and orange fins flitted back and forth. The poor little creatures, spending their entire lives in an acrylic box in a night club. I stared into the water, watching bubbles from the filter zip to the tabletop and explode.

Masha snapped her fingers at me. But I was hypnotized as I watched one fish hover at the bottom of the tank, like it wanted to disappear, but couldn't. How many people's shoe had whacked their home, how many had pounded their fists, danced on its roof, or puked on these teeny fishies' transparent home?

"Marina! Wake up!" said Sasha.

"Huh?" I blinked at her. "Oh, sure. Sorry."

The Ashas chattered about the competition and how great I was. I was still thinking about the fish, feeling bummed out. The alcohol was wearing off.

"You need vodka and Doom," Dasha said. She was finishing off some bright green drink in a martini glass with a flashing ice cube floating inside.

"I need...Doom? Cuz my last summer was pretty much full of it."

"What? No. *Zoom*. Russian energy drink."

"Like Red Bull?"

"*Da*. Exactly."

"*Davai*, then." I was running out of gas and needed a little something to get me moving again. I was a VIP and wanted to enjoy it.

Three vodka and Doomy-Zoomys later, we were all on top of the table in the VIP section, dancing together. I was Masha Dva, Masha Two. I was an Asha! Whoo! I was assuming the fishes were used to the noise, so I danced on without guilt.

And on.

And on.

Burly strolled over with a tray of champagne glasses. We reached for them, but he pulled away. He nodded to a group of men in expensive suits and a table full of Cristal bottles. Sweet. More free drinks from some hotties. Burly handed everyone a glass but saved the one with a strawberry in it for me.

"This," he said, "eez especially for you, from heem." A guy with blond hair gelled into an ocean wave winked at me. Not bad. I winked back and slugged some down. Tasted a little bitter but — whatever. I closed my eyes and let my brain trickle into a trance that swayed with the music and then I just let my eyes close and I rested my head on the table and it soon was very quiet and very dark.

***

This was the hangover to end all hangovers. The dark room was spinning, though my eyes were closed. I was hoping I'd made it back to my hotel or to one of the Asha's apartments, although I had a feeling their parents wouldn't be too keen on having a wasted *Amerikanka* hugging their toilet bowl all morning. At least they were nice enough to put me in a comfy bed. Cassidy was going to effing kill me.

My tongue was a dry sponge, my stomach was a Tilt-A-Whirl. I had to get to a bathroom. I tried to roll over, but couldn't. My arms were tied down with something. So were my legs. I wiggled and strained and finally screamed. Stars formed in front of my eyes, and I ran out of breath. I struggled against the restraints. As my eyes adjusted to the darkness, I made out something tall next to me. Metal glinting. A metal pole, a bag of liquid attached to it. I tried to slide my arms down the restraints, but a gigantic pull on my skin that made me scream. What *was* that?

A metal pole. A bag of liquid. A *needle* in my arm? Oh my God. Oh my God. My breath caught in my throat and everything went even darker.

27

Light behind my eyelids. *Make it stop. Make it stop. Make it stop.* My stomach heaved and I turned my head to puke. My arms and legs were still restrained, but luckily it was only a dry heave. I opened my eyes to small slits. I was in a white room, and an IV drip was attached to my right arm. I was in a hospital gown, white with blue stripes. My clothes lay folded on a chair. Horizontal windows lined the top of one wall, so high all I could see through them was sunlight. I had no idea where I was.

Well, in a hospital. That I much was clear. A hospital in Russia — but still, a hospital. What had happened last night? Where were the Ashas?

"Help! Help!" I screamed and screamed until someone turned the doorknob.

A woman in white lab coat, gold-rimmed glasses perched on her nose, entered. She spoke to me, but I had no idea what she was saying. A gray streak ran through the front of her black hair, which was pulled into a clip. Her lips were pressed in a straight line, wrinkles radiating from her lips. She looked like a pack-a-day grandmother. She shook her head and said something else.

"I don't understand. Where am I? Please?"

She sighed and adjusted the needle in my arm. I yelped and she sighed again, as if annoyed.

"What's going on? Where am I? Where are my friends?"

She glanced at numbers on the monitor next to the bed, jotted something on a clipboard, and pivoted to walk out.

"Help! Help! I need someone who speaks English! Heeeelp!"

Muttering in the hallway. Footsteps tapping closer. The knob clicked and a tall man with blond wavy hair and black thick-rimmed glasses entered.

Maybe he'd tell me what was going on. I collapsed onto the pillow. "Come on, dude. Someone's gotta tell me something. What happened? Why am I in the hospital?"

His Russian accent was light, with some type of British accent overlaying it. "Well, young lady, you need a procedure."

My heart stopped, I swear. *Time* stopped. I'd never had surgery in my life. "I am not getting any kind of procedure. Let me out of here."

He removed his glasses and rubbed the bridge of his nose. "I assure you, you are in the best medical facility in the city. Nothing to worry about. Now, our anesthetist is going to arrive and put you to sleep. It will all be over quickly."

"What will? What surgery do I need?"

"Your appendix is about to rupture. We must to remove it."

"Nope. Hell no. Get me out of here. I don't need surgery. Why am I restrained?"

He crossed his arms over his chest. "Because you were brought in thrashing all about in a fit. The restraints are for your safety. If you do not have this surgery, your appendix will rupture. That feeling is far from pleasant. Dying from internal bleeding or septicemia is even less so."

"I haven't had any pain. How did I even get here?"

"Your friends brought you. You are very ill." He picked up the phone on the wall, said something into it, and frowned. "The anesthetist has had a small delay. To my mind, that is not a good thing. We need to take care of you as soon as possible."

"I want to call my family."

"Afterward. Ah, here is the anesthetist." A middle-aged man with a comb-over strolled in. He didn't even bother to greet me.

"She is ready, Ivan Borisovich."

"Don't you want to know my medications? I take Adderall. How will that react with the anesthesia?"

The anesthetist didn't look at me, just fiddled with some equipment. He put a clip on my finger and looked at a screen. His gray goatee matched his eyes. The blood pressure cuff squeezed my upper arm and the *shh shh shh* of the pump bounced off the walls. I didn't want this to happen. But what if my appendix *was* going to burst?

On the flip side, what it if wasn't? Something wasn't right. "Excuse me, sir? Doctor? I haven't given my consent. I need to think about this, OK?"

He ignored me and checked the monitor. I heard the beeping rise with my racing heartbeat. The anesthetist shook his head. The doctor with the glasses nodded. At least I hoped he was a doctor. He opened a cabinet and took out a vial and a syringe.

"No, no, no, no, no!"

The anesthetist broke his silence. "You will be fine. Just relax." His bedside manner left a lot to be desired.

I whimpered and closed my eyes. They snapped open when someone lifted my head. Oxygen mask. The elastic band tugged at my hair. Then another needle in my other arm. Another IV.

The men stood near the monitor, talking very quietly. As if I could understand them anyway. At least the fluid from the IV was making me feel a little better. This had to be the worst hangover of my life. All I wanted was a glass of 7-Up with ice, some toast, and my comforter.

Their facial expressions were typical Russian serious. They could have been talking about my guts or their dinners. Who knew in this crazy-ass country? The one with the glasses pulled the curtain back on the wall opposite, revealing a window looking out into a hallway. In a room across from me, with its curtain open, a man in another bed was hooked up to the same machines as me. He was staring at the ceiling.

Where hell was I? This was not like any hospital I'd ever visited.

A woman in a brown fur coat passed my window, peered in at me, picked up a clipboard that was evidently hanging near my window and read the papers on it. As she flipped through the documents, she looked me over and frowned. The man in the lab coat who was escorting her put a hand on her back and ushered her over to look at the man across from me. She picked up his clipboard and, after a minute or two, nodded. The doctor gave a quick nod back. She walked away, smiling. Then some people in scrubs entered the room, unhooked the guy and wheeled him out.

"Where is he going?"

"Oh, him?" The anesthetist said, hooking his thumb toward the guy's room. "He just has to get a procedure. Do not worry about him."

But I was. *Very* worried. Especially when a few more people walked by my window, picked up the clip board and stared in at me. I felt like was up for auction.

After the fourth gawker, I started screaming, "Help! Help!" I flailed my arms and legs. It hurt as if someone was pulling knitting needles through my veins, but I didn't care. I needed to get out of there. The anesthetist pressed a button on the phone. The woman with the gray stripe in her hair returned and jabbed me again with something. The last thing I saw was the pink lipstick smeared on her yellowed front teeth.

28

It was quiet. So quiet. And so, so cold. How long had I been out? No idea. Did anyone know where I was? What about the Ashas? This time I was the fish trapped in the table, watching people walk by. Who were they? What did they want? A woman in a black fur coat stood in front of my window, checking her phone. Wait. I knew that face. It was MY face. Olya. Olya was here? I tried to yell for her, but my voice wouldn't work. I was swimming in a sea of molasses. Olya looked in at me and her eyes widened. She said something to the lab-coated escort next to her and he nodded. She picked up my clipboard, flipped through the pages and pointed to me. The escort walked away. Olya stared at me and gave a tiny, teeny nod. What the hell did that mean? I was too tired to make a fuss, so I could only keep my eyes trained on my Russian twin.

Gray Stripe Doctor appeared next to her and extended a hand. She even blushed, probably because she was meeting *The* Olya. Olya offered her a graceful smile and walked off in the direction Gray Stripe pointed. Gray Stripe keypadded her way into my room and started unhooking me.

"Well, well, aren't you lucky!" Gray Stripe said as she pulled the needles from my arms. "I know you can't talk right now, but that is famous music star, Olya. Her grandmother needs a new kidney and *you* are giving it to her. How wonderful is gift of life? And you look so much like her! After a few days of recuperation, you will leave here with several thousand dollars and the joy of knowing you saved a life for someone famous."

I tried to respond but the drugs me made me still feel like I was screaming from the bottom of a dark sea. Anger fizzed in the few corners of my brain that seemed to be working. Olya. Olya. *She* had all of this planned, planned to get me in her good graces, to get me to trust her. Then WHAM – kidnapped at the club to donate a nice healthy kidney for her grandmother. The only problem is, I was supposed to have been too drugged up to notice.

But I couldn't fight back. I couldn't punch Gray Stripe and run. I couldn't even make a fist.

Someone knocked and peeked in. Another guy in a white coat. Where did I know that slicked-back hair from? Gray Stripe popped the door open and said something. He shrugged. She shook her head and pointed to me. This dude didn't look like he belonged on a hospital staff. He looked more like the member of a motorcycle gang. The edge of a blue tattoo peeked out from under his collar. He said something else and Gray Stripe froze. She gulped and dropped the blood pressure cuff. He backed away and grunted. She slid like a ragdoll down the wall as he tossed a syringe into a trashcan.

Slick Hair grabbed my right wrist, flipped it, looked at the tattoo of the five dots and grunted. He then rattled something off in Russian. I had no idea what he was saying, nor could I respond. But the drug seemed to be wearing off. Just a little. My view of the world was less stained-glassy now and more fishbowly. What choice did I have? Stay here and get cut open? Let Slick Hair get me out of here for some new fate? Go it alone, barefoot and bare-assed? Let frickin' Olya's grandmother have my kidney?

He put an oxygen mask over my face and wheeled me out of my room. This was no regular hospital hallway, more like a neonatal nursery, where you could look at the cute babies through a window. Except we were all adults, each in his or her own single. Every window showed someone in a hospital bed. Some appeared to be unconscious, others were reading magazines or watching TV. A clipboard hung outside each room. Like tour guides, workers were escorting well-dressed people past the windows. I counted sixteen rooms and four visitors as Slick Hair wheeled me down the corridor. Olya was nowhere to be seen.

The visitors stopped at each window. No...not visitors...shoppers. Olya was *shopping* for a kidney for her grandma. As we passed another patient's room, I saw a young man with gauze over one eye, sleeping. Like the bandaged eyes of the people at the Kasha Kitchen.

But was this by choice or by force?

I tried to yell at Slick Hair to stop, but the words wouldn't come out. My heart was pounding, all the blood in my body whooshing to my brain, making my head throb. With a whack, he slammed the gurney through stainless-steel double-doors and booked it down the hallway. The rattling gurney all of a sudden slammed into a wall. My arms and legs flailed. I wanted to scream obscenities but my tongue was still a Kettlebell in my mouth. Then Slick Hair heaved me out of the bed and slung me over his shoulder. I felt a cold draft on my bare ass. Nice. My arms hung down his back and my legs bobbed as he sprinted down the corridor.

Sirens whined and lights flashed. He busted through an exit and we entered an airplane hangar, with two white private jets parked inside. Like the kind you saw in action movies waiting to take the bad guy away. Coolers with biohazard signs were stacked next to the gangways. Shouts echoed off the concrete floor and men in dress pants and leather jacket swarmed toward us.

A black Escalade was idling in front of one of the jets. Two men in black tactical gear tore out of the rear and aimed machine guns at the guards pursuing us. Slick Hair popped the cargo door and tossed me in the back. What fresh hell had I gotten myself into? The guys jumped into the SUV and slammed the doors. I still couldn't speak or move much, so I hoped whatever was going to happen next would be over quickly.

***

I woke up in a torrent of rain pounding on the roof, the car creeping up a dark road. I was officially over my panic. The situation was what it was. It was out of my control.

I lifted my head over the seat, hoping for a clue as to where we were. Fog limited my view, but I could make out fields punctuated by patches of trees. Lightning bolts scraped across my head and I groaned as I collapsed back into the cargo area.

Gravel crunched under the tires as the vehicle stopped. A large man in black Kevlar opened the door and motioned for me to exit. I tried to move, but it was like swimming through Jell-O. Luckily, I could at least mumble now. "Do you speak English?"

"*Nyet, dyevushka*," he said in that gravely, mumbly Russian some of the men spoke here. *No, young lady.* He cradled me in his arms and I was too tired to argue. My hospital gown was revealing whatever it was revealing. He sloshed through puddles to a brick building, my now-wet bare butt still exposed to the world.

The dude knocked four times. Another muscular dude opened the door. They muttered to each other and he carried me inside. A hallway with multiple doorways. I saw a chalkboard through one. Another revealed am empty gymnasium. An old school?

The dude walked into a room with empty desks, the kind where the wooden desks and seats were fastened together by a metal bar. He plopped me onto a cot and covered me with a heavy blanket. His footsteps trailed away as I fell asleep.

29

I woke to the patter of rain on barred windows. I was in the back corner of a classroom. Besides the desks bolted to the floor, there was also a wooden teacher's desk and globe. A new guard was sitting on the other side of the room, smoking a cigarette and tapping around on a tablet. He turned to me and I waved. He got up, stretched and opened a closet. Came out with a pair of black sweatpants, gray sweatshirt, plaid slippers. He shrugged and left.

They smelled clean; the slippers still had tags on them. Better to change than sit around in a hospital gown. Hmmm....no underwear. No bra. The sweatpants were two sizes too big, the sweatshirt a size too small. At least the slippers were comfortable. I got dressed, then remembered every hostage movie I'd ever seen and sat with my back against a wall, facing the door. And waited.

Footsteps in the hall. Men talking. Then someone else strolled in, and walked to the teacher's desk, where he ran a gloved finger over the top. He turned and smiled at me.

There was no mistaking him.

His hair and beard were now all white, but the face was the same. And those soulless eyes.

The General said, "Marina. Marina. Well, well, well."

Instead of sinking into the fetal position, I found myself automatically standing, chest out, hands on my hips. "What am I doing here? What are *you* doing here?"

"Am asking myself the same things, my darling."

"How did you get out of the mine?"

"Fate. And air duct. I found my way out and crept out of coal mine. And here I am."

"I'm confused," I said. "Why did you save me from that crazy medical place?"

"I did not mean to." He leaned on the teacher's desk. "I received a call from one of my men. He said there was a girl dancing at the club who had one of my marks."

"Oh. Yeah. That." I rubbed the tattoo on my wrist.

"Yes, that. It is interesting you gave yourself my brand, yes? You must have fond memories of me." He smiled and his silver tooth glinted. "That club is not part of my territory, so I sent men to get this mystery woman. The owner and I have had financial disagreements in past. I couldn't take the risk of the owner doing something to one of my assets. But it was too late."

"How did you know I was in the hospital?"

"My men followed them. And make no mistake: I do not enjoy your company or find you as engaging as your friend, Arman, finds you. And I do not need that man's money."

"How about letting bygones be bygones and let me go, huh?"

The General shook his head.

"Just let me go and I won't say anything. Pinky swear."

He snorted. "Pinky swear? The pinky is the smallest finger. That says a lot about your promises."

"No one will know about this. Just get me home. Your secret is safe with me."

"Fine. I can do that."

"Great. Great." Relief came in a wave. I just needed to get back to the hotel. This wasn't going to stop me from participating in the sting with Arman and Cassidy. If anything, this abduction was giving me even more strength. Something was shifting in me. I shouldn't have felt so centered in this abandoned school with a psychopath a few feet in front of me. But I did.

He cleared his throat and snapped me back to the situation. "Marina. You know my nephew, the one you called The Husky, did not make it out of the mine collapse. You owe me for his death."

A train horn blared nearby and I could hear the rumble on the tracks. His nephew's different-colored eyes, one blue, one green, flashed in my mind and I shuddered. I wasn't going to apologize for that maniac's death. The asshole had it coming.

"He was very loyal to me. He was like son." The General turned toward the windows as he spoke. "But what matters is the here and now. You have provided me with an important opportunity. *Misha!*"

Footsteps echoed down the hallway. In walked another dude in a black leather coat, this one carrying a black duffel bag. He plopped it on the desk The General was leaning on. The General unzipped it and curled a finger to invite me over. Inside the bag were what looked like hundreds of flat sugar packets, each stamped with the word "Peace" in red block letters.

"You will deliver these to a location in Moscow. Misha will tell you where."

"Um, OK. Looks easy enough. What are they? Some new age mumbo jumbo herbal remedy pyramid scheme you're invested in?"

"No, my dear. This is not a health scheme. These are packets of heroin. You are to deliver to the owner of the club you were dancing at. This will be my *peace* offering to him. Understand?" He grinned and pointed to the stamp on the packets.

Sutton loved to watch *Locked Up Abroad*, this show about tourists who did stupid things in foreign countries and spent years in dirt-floored cells, starving, bug-infested, desperate. I'd always told him those people were morons and deserved what they got. Now I started to mentally plan my own episode. From what I'd seen so far, I had a pretty good idea what a Russian prison would be like, especially for a twenty-five year-old female drug mule.

"There must be another way. Come on, General. I am a horrible liar. I'm going to look all sweaty-palmed and shifty. I'm gonna have the police in my face so fast that—"

He stood from the desk so fast it shook. He was now inches from my face. I squirmed and wrinkled my nose as his spittle dotted my face. "Let me be clear, *Amerikanka*. The man you called in the media 'The Husky.' He was no dog. And now you pay for my nephew's passing."

"Then I'm done? Forever?"

"*Da*. Forever."

A few weeks ago, I would have collapsed on the floor, a ball of tears. Now I was looking my nightmare in the face and I was going to be rid of him once and for all. "What exactly do I have to do?"

"Ah ha, *dyevushka*. I am glad we see eye to eye. Now, let's get you changed into something more acceptable. And then you will go on train. To *Leningradski Vokzal*. Someone will meet you."

"Leninwhatskizalwho?" Oh, Lord. If I couldn't pronounce it, how would I find it?

The General sighed. "*Lenin-grad-ski Vok-zal*. Leningrad train station."

I remembered faint music, a few lines from some Billy Joel album my sister used to listen to. "Fine. What's the plan after that?" It was like a weight had been taken off my shoulders. The time spent cowering under The Big Cow and curled up in the fetal position in the office were floating away. I was facing the focus of all those endless nightmares, his face disappearing suddenly in a flurry of coal, his hands reaching out to me. He would be gone after tonight. After I went to wherever it was I was supposed to be going.

"Marina! Marina!" The General snapped his fingers. "Pay attention!"

"Sorry. So where am I going again?"

He sighed. Maybe regretting getting tangled up with me again. My, how the tables had turned. To the same extent he probably didn't know the difference between a salad fork and a dinner fork, I didn't know anything about geography. It was amazing I'd gotten to Moscow, period.

"It is simple. The train station is a few miles away. Misha will drop you off. You will get on train, private, first class car. You will be by yourself. Door will lock. You will talk to no one. You will get off in Moscow. The conductor will let you know it is your stop. You will get off the train and be perfect *Amerikanka* tourist. You will use this map to get to Puskhinskaya Square. You will meet my contact there. The password is "*Kroshka mya*." Then hand over the bag. And leave."

"*Kropka hiya?*"

"I will write it on the map. *Kroshka mya*."

"*Kroshka mya*," I repeated, extending each syllable.

"*Maladetz.*"

"*Spacibo.*"

"You speak some Russian now." He pushed his bottom lip over his upper lip and tilted his head in surprise.

"*Choot choot.*" Just a little.

He exploded into an uncharacteristic belly laugh. I have no idea what was so funny, but hey — points for the *Amerikanka* drug mule.

30

Twenty minutes later, I was in "American tourist" clothing: skinny jeans, bright pink running sneakers, a hot pink fleece, and black baseball hat. I had no idea where he'd gotten the idea this is how I should dress because all I did was stand out. A fluorescent pink beacon. But I guessed the goal was to make me appear as innocuous as possible. All the pickpockets in the entire city would descend on me. But maybe looking clueless and spacy would keep the police away.

A few more hours and I'd be back in my hotel, and then, the sting with Arman and Cassidy. If anything, this escapade had solidified my need to see these psychopaths behind bars. The next task would be packing to go back to my little house in little old Edwardsville, Pennsylvania. Bumblefuck had never looked so enticing. Fall festivals, apple cider, taking a road trip with my mom to see the leaves turn.

The General said, "Misha will walk you to the train. This will be impossible to mess up, *Amerikanka*. Once more: you get on train, lock your compartment. Wait until conductor gets you when train stops in Moscow. Take get map, walk to statue in Pushkin Square. You say password. Give the person the bag. And then — you are free. Very simple. *Ochen prosta*."

The last time told me something was going to be simple, I'd ended up in a mine collapse, running for my life with my best friends and my niece. Nothing in my life had ever been *ochen prosta*. Nothing.

***

The drive to the station took us through a depressing village. Patches of grass surrounded by mud. Mud. And more mud. A few factories huffed smog in the distance. Squat apartment buildings, rusty playground equipment, and derelict-looking shops completed the place.

While we waited on the platform, I tried to make small talk with Misha, but he either didn't speak English or was ignoring me. When the hell would this train come? I was tired of standing, so I took a few steps backward and plopped onto a large boulder with remnants of yellow paint under a map of the train tracks. It was all gibberish to me.

Someone tsk-tsked, a universal sign of disapproval. Shuffling to my left. A babushka wearing a bright, floral scarf tied under her chin waddled over and hit my shoulder with a newspaper.

I turned my head and narrowed my eyes.

She hit me again! Then again, this time on the butt. Then she started to shove the folded newspaper between my butt and the boulder.

Misha snickered. Out of the side of his mouth he said in slightly accented English, "You will not be able to have babies if you sit on bare stone. It will freeze female parts. Do not fight old lady. *Babushki* always win."

"Geez, *now* you speak English." I stood and looked at the old girl. Her round face had a gray cast but her blue eyes sparkled. Tufts of gray hair poked out of her headscarf . Her sun-roughed face had deep wrinkles. I said, "*Spacibo.*" She shuffled back to her friend, shaking her head the whole way. Everyone on the platform was now looking at me.

At least my ovaries were safe.

A train whooo-whoooooed in the distance. Thank God. I couldn't stand the thought of people contemplating my fallopian tubes one more minute. Everyone stood, checked purses, hugged loved ones, and hoisted bags onto their shoulders.

Misha picked up the Duffel Bag of Doom. I could feel people watching. I mean, I was a walking freaking Easter egg in these stupid pastel sneakers and pink fleece. Everyone else was in black coats, dark pants, black boots. Not a single baseball hat among them.

Misha slipped the bag over my shoulder and then, in a move straight out of a romance novel, grabbed my face and laid one on me. A kiss that took me so unexpectedly I kind of went with it. He was quite the kisser. Now everyone *was* looking at us. The mobster and his American girlfriend. Or rather, *Amerikanka* whore.

He slid his mouth to my ear and whispered, "You must get this to Moscow. Understand?"

From afar, it probably appeared like we were lovers saying goodbye. That I was sad because I was leaving.

***

I heaved myself and the bag of heroin packets onto the train. When I showed the conductor my ticket he frowned. He said something in rapid-fire Russian. I shrugged and pulled the bag closer to me. He repeated himself, this time louder. Since I wasn't deaf, that didn't help, either. I turned to get help from Misha, but he was already gone.

The conductor waved for me to come along, a circle of sweat in the armpit of his shirt. He pointed to the door of a compartment. #6. At least numbers were the same in English and Russian. Finally. I just wanted to lock myself away and be alone. The conductor inhaled and held his breath as he opened the door. As soon as the smell of vomit and pee hit me, I tottered back and gasped. He closed the door and exhaled. I had no idea what had happened in compartment number six, but I was not going to investigate.

My forehead was dotted with sweat. I shifted my lovely bag of contraband to the other shoulder. Where was I going to go?

He said, "*Daviatye*." At last, a word I knew. *Let's go*. So I followed him through the first-class compartments into the second-class area. Four bunks per compartment. Then into third-class. Instead of doors, each area was an open arrangement of two lower bunks and two uppers with a window in the middle. Below the window was a table. It was so loud. So many people, so little deodorant.

I sighed and nodded. The conductor pointed to a set of bunks where only one was occupied — by a tiny, wrinkly babushka wearing a red and orange floral scarf. The same one who'd shoved the newspaper under my butt. I nodded hello and threw my bag of drugs

on the bed across from her. The old lady spouted a bunch of words I
didn't understand, except for *nyet*. Her eyes narrowed. She shook her
head. A gnarled index finger pointed up. I sighed and hoisted the bag
to the bunk perched five feet above the floor. After hoisting myself
onto the bed, I pushed the bag between me and the wall and pretended
to fall asleep so no one would talk to me. With my butt facing the
world it should have been clear didn't want to chat.

And then someone poked me. "*Amerikanka! Amerikanka!*" he
slurred.

A woman said something I didn't understand, shooed him off in
the universal language of Disapproving Wife and they left. Jeez, how
did they know I was American without hearing me talk? Oh yeah, my
Easter egg outfit.

The cheap seats filled up and I heard a voice in the bunk below.
The babushka and her friend were chattering away. I hoped the
rocking of the car would put me to sleep. But then I remembered what
was in the bag. There would be no sleeping, only faking it so no one
would bother me.

Fat chance. Heavy steps approached. A deep, male voice spoke. I
rolled over and was eye-to-eye with a spokesmodel for Hitler Youth.
All blond crew cut and ice-water eyes. He rattled off something in
Russian.

I just said, "English?"

Aryan Nation replied, "Passport."

Fuck. I hadn't taken my passport to Kino, so I didn't have it.
Heck, I didn't even have the bra I'd worn to the club. I decided to buy
time by searching slowly through my pockets. I also smiled and batted
my eyelashes. What if he wanted me to open the bag? My episode of
Locked Up Abroad was already writing itself.

Aryan Nation shifted closer to me and put his hand on my knee. I
froze. His fingers crept to my thigh.

And thank God, thank Krishna, thank whoever was watching over
me that day, but the two babushka in the bottom bunks went off at
him like school marms. Fingers pointed, tongues clicked, heads shook
back and forth. Aryan Nation turned red, put his hands in the air, and
stepped back. The old ladies crossed their arms over their chests, chins
sticking out. He backed up and strode away.

The train car lurched and up came bile. I swung off the bunk with my bag in tow. I nodded at the ladies and ran to the bathroom, hand over my mouth. The restroom floor was already spackled with pee, the sink was plugged with toilet paper and stagnant water. I puked in the reeking toilet and cried. Someone pounded on the door. I pushed one cheek against the cold metal of the wall and took deep breaths, trying to gain some self-control.

I steadied myself against the chug and rumble of the train and opened the door. A punked-out girl with half a shaved head snapped something in Russian and pushed past me. With the Duffel Bag of Doom secured across my chest, I wobbled back to my bunk.

31

The old lady with the floral headscarf patted a spot beside her on her bunk. I shrugged and sat. I set the heavy duffel on the floor and wrapped the strap around my calf. The ladies watched me prepare this security system, screwed up corners of their mouths, and looked at each other.

The one with the floral scarf poured tea out of a beat-up, seafoam green thermos. She pushed the metal mug toward me.

"*Spacibo*," I said in my shaky Russian.

"*Pazhalsta*," she replied in a soft voice. She dug in a plastic bag illustrated with a heavily lip-glossed woman and pulled out a plastic container. She opened it and offered a cookie. I smiled, took a small, brown disk, and dunked it in the tea. The first food I'd had in almost twelve hours.

I took a bite, sighed. They smiled.

"Olga Mikhailovna," the red scarf woman said, pointing to her chest.

The lady with the floral scarf pointed to herself. "Lidya Ivanovna."

A muddled *zdrastvuyte* came out of my mouth. Priviet was so much easier, but I'd learned *priviet* is only for friends. "Marina."

"*Maladetz*, Marina." Olga offered me another cookie.

I smiled for the first time that day.

I looked out the window as the two ladies prattled on about who knows what. The gray landscape rushed by. All gray skies, leafless trees, clapboard, paint-chipped shacks leaning to one side like an old man with a bad leg. Every train station was the same. Chipped gray concrete platform filled with dour women, grey-skinned men in leather jackets, and teens wearing ear buds, all traveling to the big city. The train chugged on and I dipped cookie after cookie into my tea. A new one always appeared, and my cup was never empty.

"Marina, Marina," Olga said, shaking my shoulder.

My heart jumped and I lunged for the bag. It was still there.

Olga's gnarled index finger pointed out the window. We'd pulled into a station. How I hadn't been woken by the clamor, I had no idea. Voices were shouting, bags being heaved and tossed around. On the platform passengers were embraced by loved ones with warm, generous hugs and kisses on the cheek. Warmth despite the endless fall rain. I was insanely jealous of that love fest. What was my family doing right now? It was fall in Pennsylvania. They might've been on an apple-picking excursion or enjoying a hayride at a pumpkin patch. What was Piper going to be for Halloween? I'd always supplied her with the princess dresses and crowns her mom refused to buy due to her stance on pigeonholing girls into gender stereotypes. I mean, come on, when you're a little girl, pink and glitter are fun. You can't deny a kid that.

Well, maybe you could. I was, after all, the poster child for too much fun.

Lidya wrapped a few cookies in a napkin and put the tiny bundle in my hand. I thanked her and stepped off the train. The station was a riot of people and deep puddles. I pulled the bag close to my chest and wove through the humanity. Techno blared through speakers jerry-rigged on rickety posts by kiosks selling vodka, dill-flavored potato chips, cheap electronics and bootlegged Blu-Rays.

I desperately needed a bathroom break so I found the sign with that spidery X that announced zh — for *zhenshini*, or women — and pushed open the door. Thwack, right into a woman's back. I offered what I hoped was the international weak smile for "sorry" and she glared in the way Russians liked to glare at me. As if they'd all received a letter ordering: give Marina Konyeshna a hard time, *konyeshna*.

I scooted out of her way, gripped the strap of the duffel and did the Peepee Dance until it was finally my turn. Muddy footprints dotted the tile, but I managed not to slip.

Sweet relief flooded through my body as I opened the stall. Finally! But where was the toilet? I saw only a hole in the ground with two metal plates on either side. This was a joke, right? I was on some type of Russian reality show. I looked around for hidden cameras, but saw none. I poked my head out to a line of impatient women who needed to empty their bladders as much as I did. So I closed the door and searched for a hanger for my bag. Hahahahahahahahahahah. Like a hook would be there, when the main appliance wasn't even there, either.

The floor was covered in liquid. Water, mud, pee…well, it was a bag of heroin, not priceless art. This seemed in fact like its natural environment, so I decided I'd pull some toilet paper and set the bag on top of it. Hahahahahahahahahahahahahaha. Of course. No toilet paper. So I pulled my pants down, crouched to my finest squat from Zumba class, pulled my jeans and underwear away and peed into the hole, hoping for the best. Everything was an ordeal in this goddamn country.

I pulled up my jeans, and opened the stall door. I trudged to the sink and stared at my pale face in the smudged mirror. No fucking toilet paper, not even a toilet SEAT. I'd had enough of this stupid, rainy, awful, mean country. I couldn't wait to hand off my bag of goddamn horse and fly the hell back to Nowhereville, Pennsylvania. Sure, there wasn't much to do there, it housed more mullets and backwoods hicks than an international truck pull competition.

And having a father dying early on you didn't make things easy. My mom had compensated by giving me whatever I'd wanted. She'd stunted me, in the end. And when she'd finally gotten a clue after I left for college, she moved on to a craft room and book clubs while I was still stuck in Mommy's Little Girl mode. That'd all come crashing down last year, which had led me to Arman and that geocaching competition and Amparo's body lying dead by the river.

In the mirror I saw a woman who should have been at work planning a party while waiting for a text from her amazing boyfriend about what they were going to do that weekend. Instead I was hunched in a stinky train station bathroom, drying my hands on my jeans, a bag of heroin packets at my feet. I'd never quite understood the term rock bottom until that very moment.

The bathroom exit popped open into the marble lobby of the train station. The same scene as every other station in this godforsaken country – people wobbling around with overloaded plaid bags, black jackets, and music blaring from the kiosks. Except now, I also noticed the militsia with the huge guns strapped across their chests. Kalashnikovs. I pulled out the map Misha had given me and played the tourist card. Well, I *was* lost. Also prime pickpocketing bait – large bag, clearly a dopey foreigner in her hot pink jacket. The bag full of drugs just made it total lose-lose. I just needed to get to the designated square and be done. The map was a crinkly mess from riding in my back pocket and it was hard to read. What an effing day.

Someone cleared his throat. I turned.

A militsia officer with his huge weapon. A high peep leaked from my mouth.

He took a step back and swiveled the strap so the weapon hung behind his back. "EEExcuse me. I see you are tourist. Can I khelp?" He smiled. Even bobbed up on his toes, like a boy asking his crush to a dance.

Oh boy. Time to lay it on thick. Take advantage of his flirting. I blinked and smiled. "Oh, thank you! Thank you! I am just SO horrible at reading maps. I need to get this square."

"Oh. OK, very simple." I handed it over, and he flipped it around to the right spot. "Here. Go out of train station, turn left, and follow street here. Not far. Is Pushkinskaya Square. Pushkin, important and interesting Russian poet." And then he started reciting what I was guessing a Pushkin poem.

I stood and smiled. I nodded, wanting to be polite. After what seemed like six stanzas later, I said, "Why, thank you so much! Russian is such a beautiful language."

I let my smile linger, felt his gaze on my ass as I walked away. Fine. Whatever worked.

I plowed down the street, squinting in the unexpected sunlight. Amazing to have a day of sun. Color me hopeful.

So...a whole square named for a writer. That was cool. My mom said my dad used to love to read Cold War spy novels. Dad would have been proud to see his little girl traveling the world. My mom always said he'd always wanted to make sure we got out of The Valley for a real purpose, not how he did it – as an eighteen-year old drafted for the Vietnam War. But surely, this is not the way Stan Konyeshna would have wanted his baby girl to see the world. I took in a deep, shaky breath.

The buildings here were so old. The pastel green and yellow buildings always surprised me. Still standing from an era when everything was done by hand. No backhoes, no machinery. Just good ol' elbow grease, as my Aunt Yelena used to say when I'd clean her claw-foot tub with Comet and a sponge. I missed her, too.

Traffic whizzed around me, people crowding the sidewalks. And I looked at the stones that made up the wall of a church and realized it was probably the oldest thing I'd ever seen, outside of an artifact or painting in a museum. Older than the Constitution or the Liberty Bell. I propped my elbows on the top of the wall around the church and gazed at its gold dome. The rough concrete prickling into my skin gave way to a churning in my stomach. All of a sudden I felt dizzy. The last time I'd felt concrete under my elbows like this, I was leaning on the railing of the Market Street Bridge, back home, watching the swirling currents drag tree branches downriver, while police searched for the bloated, bruised body of a murdered girl.

Even though this trip was the very definition of a nightmare, maybe it was what I needed to do to finally grow up. I'd buried myself in charity events at work, as if selecting fancy napkins and table centerpieces would somehow fill the hole in my heart. It wasn't just my heart, though. It was like a hole in my soul, a place I couldn't even see, but felt the tug from every now and then. A chamber in my chest weighed down by a box dangling on a string. *Amparo.* I'd never done anything real to honor her memory. Sure, hearing the story of her family's flight from El Salvador put a face on immigration for me. But I never *did* anything about it. Instead it had all been about me me me me me me me me, I I I I I I I I.

My poor mom, poor Gilly, poor Kendra, poor Sutton. I'd let myself wallow mired in a vat of me —and they'd let me do it, too. Did I feel angry about that? No. They were just doing what people who love you must: take care of you. Help you. Let you do what you need to, even stupid stuff. In my case, get buried in work. In Gilly and Kendra's case, push me a little, nudge me in the right direction. And how had I thanked them all? By freaking out and leaving the country. How had I honored Amparo's memory? By working myself into a stupor, hoping raising some money for charities would cross out the bad on my scorecard.

A rounded leaf, green with red speckles, fluttered off a tree. Sick and tired of being whooshed into the wind. Sick of life taking me to such hard places. I wanted to go where *I* wanted to go. Where that would be, I had no idea. But it did not entail delivering heroin or having another desperate roll in the sack with Arman. I mean, it sure was satisfying but I belonged in Sutton's arms. Or maybe no one's arms for the time being. More importantly, I had to rebuild my relationship with Janna. I'd given my sister space, but now I needed to work to get her back. Along with that part of my soul back that had been sucked away in one awful weekend.

So —deal with the darkness, face to face.

The rat-tat-tat-tat of drums and a chorus of shouting broke my pep talk. I turned to see a parade walking down the sidewalk. Led by an old man carrying a crimson flag crossed with a gold hammer and another symbol. Sickle. That was it. The flag of the Soviet Union. But the Soviet Union had dissolved years ago. A whole bunch old folks were marching, wearing brown and black coats. Hmm. According to the map, they were going in the direction I was headed, too.

No one seemed to care about this band of seniors. People either looked, then went on with their business or didn't seem to notice them at all. But I couldn't stop staring. I had no idea what the posters said, but many bore pictures of some guy with beady eyes and a pointy beard. The placards bobbed up and down and their chanting got louder as we approached the square. Lenin. That was the guy on the signs.

When I stopped at a corner, I bumped into an old lady who was hunched over, carrying a sign and wearing a red vest with gold and red pins all over it. At the tail end, and she seemed to be losing steam fast. She sighed and spoke to me, but I didn't understand. She said something else, this time louder, as if it would make a difference. I shrugged. She sighed and jabbed the sign in my direction. Oh, right. She wanted *me* to carry it.

"OK." Seemed like we were all going to the same place anyway. Oh my God, focus, Marina. The duffel. I had to get this awful shit to its rightful dealer. Right now, *this* was my life. But I still couldn't say no to the babushka. The old ladies here had been like guardian angels to me. Time to pay it forward.

She laid a wrinkly hand on my forearm and said, "*Spacibo, dyevushka.*"

Finally something I understood. "Thank you, young lady."

I smiled at her. As we crossed the street as she stood a little taller and shook her gnarled hands out. The sign was heavy. I wondered how she'd carried it. The stake it was attached to was super thick, almost a 2 x 4. I rested the bag of heroin so conveniently strapped across my chest and marched on.

As we approached the square, more people had cellphones out and were taking pictures. Mostly younger guys and gals, though. Hmmm. This must be amusing to them or something. A lot were pointing their phone cameras at the old lady holding my arm. Awww. Maybe they thought I was an upright citizen or something. Maybe she's some famous local activist. I had no flipping idea, but wanted to get rid of the evil bag and move on with my hot mess of a life somehow. I couldn't possibly resemble Olya in this getup.

Drum beats echoed as we passed through an archway between buildings. The amplified noise made my head throb. The old lady's voice got louder. She pushed my arm higher. I took this as my signal to raise the sign. She grinned and yelled even more loudly. So I raised it even higher and bobbed it up and down. Right on.

We entered the square. The skies were still sunny and blue. I saw the statue in the distance, tall marble dude, curly hair, wearing a cape, arm tucked in his shirt. That was it. My destination.

With my rendezvous point within eyeshot, I tried to hand the old lady's sign back, but she was now playing an accordion. Where the hell had that come from? Her arms pumped in and out as the people around us started singing a song, circling us. Oh. My. God. I needed to get out of this geriatric ring-around-the-rosy and get to that damn poet statue. But louder and louder they sang, warbly old voices and all. More and more people gathered around this knot of singing old folks and took photo after photo after photo. Why was this so interesting to everyone? Who *were* these people anyway?

Just then, they all started chanting, "Olya? Olya! OLYA!"

Oy. Oh no.

They still thought I was the pop star.

How was this still a thing?

Should I wave and smile? Or run for it?

No, that would just call attention and the last thing I needed was attention. Time time to dip. Since the group of grannies and grandpas were clearly at their stopping point, I put the sign down and excused me-ed out of the throng. Their singing turned into yelling and clapping. An old man wearing an army olive jacket studded with medals moved to the center of the circle and started shouting through a megaphone. The breeze made his white comb-over wave like a hair-sprayed wheel flap, but he was too into his groove to notice.

I kept my eye on the statue of the poet. A bunch of people were hanging out in front of it, taking pictures. I started to jostle my way out. I readjusted the strap across my shoulder and broke free from the crowd of senior citizens fighting for the right to party or whatever they were rattling on about. The cool air felt great and I took in a deep breath as I sped toward the statue. The dude had one hand shoved in his waistcoat, like Napoleon. Weird. Poets rule, I guessed. At least that's why my eleventh grade English teacher had told us. I guess she'd been right.

Running footsteps behind me. A crowd of younger people with cell phones, snapping away and yelling, "Olya!" over and over and over, as if saying the name a set amount of times would make me spin around and smile.

Instead I pulled the baseball hat brim down closer to my nose and started trotting. But they trotted, too. Until I could actually feel them behind me. I waved my arm to signal them to back off. Nothing. I was now close enough to see how many people were around the statue. Which one was supposed to pick up the bag? Most of the men mulling around it looked alike. It was like a frickin' uniform: black leather jackets, dress pants, black dress shoes, cigarettes plugged between lips or fingers. There were some women, too. A lady with a baby carriage pushed it back and forth, as if she were waiting for someone. Oh, how I longed to switch places with her. A simple walk with a baby. Simple was good.

The adoring fans behind me continued to yell, "Olya! OLYA!" and a bunch more stuff. I couldn't outrun them, but I had to be here to hand off the bag. So I stopped in front of the statue and let them take photos and tweet and Facebook and Snapchat whatever the hell else they wanted. Soon, they had to realize I wasn't The Real Olya, anyway.

The Real Olya. If they only knew she shopped for human organs like they shopped for produce.

The horde of people with cell phones extended like permanent appendages to their hands pressed in. I backed up closer to the chain. Pretty soon, my butt was using it as a seat and I was searching for a way out. The wheezing accordion from the parade started up again. The protest crowd's calls swelled and swelled, along with the calls from others for Russia's beloved pop star.

A man started shouting from behind the crowd around me. He pushed people away. He spoke into a walkie-talkie. Like Moses parting the Red Sea in that old movie my family would watch during Holy Week, my adoring, misinformed fans backed off. He had a blond buzz cut and wore a charcoal gray coat with some insignia on the chest. His gray pants ballooned out where they were tucked into his black combat boots. And an automatic rifle over his chest. He marched toward me. I put my arms over the bag and pushed back against the chain, with nowhere to go but over.

I was totally and utterly screwed.

He rattled off something gruff. I shrugged, hoping the clueless tourist bit would buy me time. To do what, I wasn't sure. But I knew I couldn't go to the police station.

"Excuse me, young lady," he said in English. "I am sorry these people are bothering you. To my mind, you are making important delivery."

OhmyGodohmyGodohmyGodohmyGodohmyGodohmyGodoh myGodohmyGod.

This was it.

I would indeed be on *Locked Up Abroad*, if it was still on cable when I got out of the hole with my name on it. But I'd try for an Academy Award nomination, first. "Um —delivery?"

Silence.

People were still lingering, taking photos of the beloved pop idol in her Easter egg outfit with the studly police guy.

"Yes, delivery, *kroshka mya*," a woman approaching from my right said. *Kroshka mya*. That was the password. "Means 'my little crumb.'

Term term of love in Russian. Now, *kroshka mya*, put bag in here, where it belongs."

What the hell? It was the lady with the baby carriage. Her hair poked out of a black fur hat, and she wore a short leather jacket. Her jeans were tight and her heels high. She was the most non-mom looking mom I'd ever seen. She popped back the carriage's visor and handed me a bundle of blankets. Inside lay....a doll. She shoved the plastic-headed baby at me and I had no choice but to take it.

"Take care of my little girl." She handed me the doll. Then she tugged at the duffel bag and I bent so she could pull it off me. She set it in the carriage, covered it with the pink blanket, even tucking it in and patting it. "Good baby. Good baby."

"*Spacibo*," she said as she sauntered off, singing what was probably a lullaby as she stroked the lump under the baby blanket and smiled. Her swaying butt got smaller and smaller until she blended in with the rest of the mob in the square.

I turned back to the guy in the uniform, but he was gone. So were the amateur photographers. It was just me, the square, and this doll. No trash cans in sight, so I held it to my chest and took the chance to think. A whole lot of not thinking had gotten me into a whole lot of trouble lately, so a few minutes or possibly hours of thought would be fine. The soft baby doll was oddly comforting. It even smelled like talcum powder. A moment of sheer horror: *was* it a real child? I had to unwrap it again, hands shaking, to reassure myself it wasn't. Jeez, I was really wrecked. Still, I stood there cradling it across my chest, then over my shoulder, like I'd held my niece when she was tiny.

I saw an empty bench and wobbled over. As I sat, the adrenaline ran out of my body and I closed my eyes.

32

After a few minutes of just being still, I pulled my baseball hat down, stood up straight and strode to the street, like I knew what I was doing. Life had already been too much before I'd gotten here and now my cup of adventure was overflowing. I was pissed off. I wasn't sure where to direct this anger, but it was slowly, finally seeping out of every pore. I crossed the street using my "city walk," trying to exude a don't-mess-with-me attitude as looked for a taxi.

Someone grabbed my arm. I shook the hand off and continued walking. Enough already.

"Marina! There you are." Cassidy held onto my biceps, tapping her foot. "I *told* you not go to that club."

"Well, it's nice to see you, too." I walked faster. "How did you know I was here?"

Cassidy held up her phone to display a Twitter feed with a hashtag I of course couldn't read. But there were pictures of me at the club, on the train, getting off the train, grimacing in the bathroom, walking in that parade, even of the bag/baby handoff, me sitting on the bench looking like a dazed Easter egg. The most recent, taken two seconds ago, was of Cassidy holding onto my arm.

I looked behind me, wondering who snapped the picture. "What the hell is this?"

"You, my friend, are a hashtag gone wild."

"What do you mean?"

"You're still being mistaken for Olya, so someone created a new hashtag: #Olya? I'm so relieved to see you. Arman was going to have his security consultant find you if you didn't show up. My bet was that you hooked up with some guy and—"

I suddenly felt very warm and mushy. "Arman hired a security consultant to find me?"

"He did. And, despite my best intentions, you've grown on me, too." Cassidy rolled her eyes. "I'm glad you're OK. There. I said it. Come on. Let's get you out of those awful clothes. Then you can fill me in."

I suddenly noticed people taking photos of me and hammering away on phones, posting into the universe. I pulled off the baseball hat and shook my hair loose. "First, here. For you."

I tossed the doll and Cassidy's reflexes kicked into gear with a quick catch. "A baby doll? Why the hell do you have this?"

"Long story."

"Dasha, Masha, and Sasha said you were blitzed. You'd been hanging all over some guy who bought you a drink. You told them you were going to dance with him. And then you disappeared."

I shuddered. "I don't recall any of that. But I sure as hell remember a lot of other stuff. I need to tell you it all. But first I have to talk to Olya. You have to take me to Olya. And gimme your phone."

Cassidy frowned. "You lost the replacement?"

"I'll tell you all about it later." I put my palm out and Cassidy placed her phone in it. "Thanks."

***

As we entered Olya's building, I pointed to the bar. "Stay here until I come down. Got it?" Cassidy shrugged and took a stool. She plopped the doll on the bar top and waved over the bartender.

The elevator dinged and the doors whooshed open, leading me back to Olya's golden palace of a penthouse. I leaned on the doorbell. Olya barked something. I just kept my finger on the buzzer. I could do this all day.

A door opened behind me and a big guard with an earpiece cruised over. "Mees, you must leave." His voice was a fist made of gravel.

Good thing I was a steamroller. "*Nyet.* I'm not going anywhere until I talk to Olya." I made sure to say this next part very loudly, near the intercom. "I know where she was yesterday. When she was out of town. When she was *shopping.*"

The door flew open. Olya's face was bright red. She snapped something at the security dude, then gestured with a large, sweeping arc to come in.

We stood in the foyer, floor and ceiling covered in mirrors with gold filigree scattered throughout, like veins in marble. My voice echoed on the tile floor and off the silvered glass. "So, that was the Olya you don't want anyone to know about? The one who shops for illegal organs for her sick grandmother like she shops for new fur coats?"

She stepped back, face drained of all color now. She leaned against a mirrored closet door and slid to the floor. Kicked off her heels and picked at her big toenail. Ew, gross. I had to look away. Who picks at their feet in front of other people?

"*Da*, it's a nasty habit. My pedicurist takes care of it, but after the other day, I just can't stop."

"I'll bet."

"You must to believe me. My friend. He told me there was hospital where people volunteered to help those who need medical aid. Volunteers. I would just pay fee to cover medical costs and a stipend for the donor. He swore it was legitimate. My grandmother needs new kidney." She was starting a nice pile of toe skin on the gleaming floor. "Or she will die."

"I was no volunteer, Olya."

"I felt shock to see you. Like looking in mirror. You must to believe me when I was going to call for help."

"Right. I bet. But you didn't, did you?"

She looked up, green eyes bloodshot and red-rimmed. "I am not bad kind of person. I promise you. Money can buy anything in Russia. I would not do anything illegal. But when the doctor said there was hope for my babushka, to fix her kidney failure, I was ready to hear anything. I believed those were volunteers."

"Here's the deal, Olya, my twin. First, you will call Dmitry and invite him over for dinner. He wants to talk to you. He misses you. God knows why. But I promised him a face to face meeting with you."

"I will never see him again. He broke my heart."

"Hearts are made to be broken, honey. That's how we are able to fit more stuff inside them, eventually."

Her voice gathered strength. "I will never—"

"Never mind the fact he doesn't deserve you. *Just do it.* Second, you are going to work with Arman and Cassidy to shut that evil excuse of a hospital down. Then, if you do, you can stay here in your pretty penthouse and go on your concert tours."

"You cannot make me—" Olya rose.

We stood nose to nose. I rubbed my finger on the white fur collar of her sweater. "The Ashas make you look so beautiful on the outside. Too bad you're ugly as hell on the inside."

Our similar reflections repeated dozens of times in the mirrored walls and ceiling. "And how are you going to make me, Marina? You, some girl from nowhere who thinks she can order me around?"

"I'll tell everyone you were there, at the hospital. It's just a tweet away."

"So, go ahead. Who is going to believe you? I have many people at my disposal to discredit you."

"Discredit me? Seriously. I'm just a girl from Nowhere, Pennsylvania. I know a pissed-off Russian reporter who would love to get her teeth in a story that reveals Russia's beloved pop star icon is visiting her murderous babushka in prison on the weekends." Venomous Vika from the salsa club would dive on this.

Olya's face turned as red as a brick. "Murderous? He wanted to kill her!"

"No doubt. But no one will believe that. It's much more juicy to call her a criminal. And after what I know of you now, baby, I'm not so certain that story is one hundred percent accurate, either."

She stepped away and pushed her hair out of her face. "Listen. We can make this work. How much do you want? I can pay you anything to keep quiet."

"I don't want your stupid rubles. There are plenty of others who need your help."

"But—"

"But nothing. You meet with Dmitry. You shut the hospital down with Cassidy and Arman. Got it?"

Olya looked around her gilded apartment, twisting the emerald ring on her left index finger. Her lower lip quivered. "Who do you think you are?"

I fished Cassidy's phone out of my jacket pocket. "Excellent question. I'm just starting to figure that out. One thing I do know: I'm smarter than you. I've recorded all of this."

Olya's heels clacked as she jumped for the phone. I pushed her away, sending her clattering to the marble floor. "Here, take it, Olya, but I have it backed up to the cloud. So, good luck with that."

"Fine. *Fine.* I will meet Dmitry. I will help Cassidy and Arman."

"I'm thrilled you understand. Cassidy will be here in a few minutes to get the address of the hospital. All you have to do is give her the information she needs, supply the cash and then you can sit here in your pretty gold palace and pick your toes all day long."

People here had thought it was cool I had a Russian "twin sister." At first, I'd thought so, too. But now I realized the one sister I had was more than enough. As soon as I got back, I had to make amends with her. I needed her. My real big sister.

Olya slammed the door behind me. The security guard pushed the *down* button.

"*Das vidonya,*" I muttered as the elevator doors closed. I hoped never to see her again.

Back at the bar, I sidled up to Cassidy. "Your next mission is all paid for."

Her turn, finally, to gape. "What?"

"Trust me." I told her about the club, The General, the hospital. "Olya generously offered to be part of Shine a Light and also to fund your next mission: to shut down an organ-harvesting operation for good."

Cassidy sprang up and hugged me. There was a first time for everything. "How did you get her to agree? She's so generous!"

"Generous. Yeah, that's one word for it." I said. "Don't worry about how I got her to agree. Let's just say she owes me." I fished inside my hoodie pocket and handed Cassidy her phone.

"What did you need it for?"

"Just in case. But I forgot to ask you for the security code."

33

After much prodding, I filled Cassidy in on the night's events. I wasn't sure if I was ready to relive them, but she needed to know. Then I told her I needed time to myself and went to my hotel room alone. After scalding and scrubbing several layers of skin away, I slipped into yoga pants and a tank top, ready to gorge on room service. I lifted the silver dome over my plate, smiling, anticipating a fluffy pile of steaming pancakes, with a dollop of whipped butter sliding across the golden discs of glory. Instead, there sat a floppy pile of deflated whitish-pancakeoids.

I grabbed the menu and double-checked my order: "Pancakes topped with fresh fruit." If you could call five strategically placed blueberries a fresh fruit topping, and, yes, these had clearly been made in a pan, then they were indeed fruit-topped pancakes. I stabbed at the pile with my fork and shoved a chunk in my mouth. Ugh. I was devastated. All I'd wanted was something comforting, something to remind me of home. I popped the blueberries in my mouth, one by one, and collapsed back into the soft comforter.

I'd felt trapped at home. I felt trapped here. Maybe there was a connection to the trappedness. Yes. That connection was clearly *me*. Only I was in both of those equations. Something had to give. I had to stop letting things happen to me. To get out from under the shadow of last summer. Breaking up with John had been the easiest part. The competition, Amparo, that we couldn't save the girls, the mine collapse, Aunt Yelena passing away. Piper being abducted. That was the one part I wasn't allowing myself to fully reckon with. I had been putting it all on Janna, believing she was being ridiculous. But *I* was the ridiculous one. The one who was being horrible, the one who never apologized.

Wow. I'd traveled all this way to realize I needed distance from me.

The shame welling up felt like a hundred snakes shoving their way up my windpipe. I choked on my tears as I slid under the covers. Why had I let this all pass over me instead of diving into it, figuring it out, why it had all happened? My mind became movie screen: Arman talking to me at my cubicle, playing bingo with him, Amparo's dead, bloated hands, the Hello, Kitty bracelet, fleeing The Husky in the pouring rain, The General pushing me down in the bed during the geocaching competition, the mine cave-in, Aunt Yelena in her coffin. Sure, I found Cassidy's crankypants attitude annoying. I was even beginning to find Arman's fancypants attitude not as sexy as I thought before, but they were the only two I could trust to end this. They would shut the hospital down, at least. I could leave this country knowing I'd done something to ease someone's suffering.

And then the sting. It was set for tomorrow. I was ready.

I flipped the pillow to the cool side and closed my eyes, hoping for sleep. I finally dozed off, but tossed and turned, dreaming of martini glasses with eyeballs instead of olives, of climbing a snowcapped mountain, and of open wounds, oozing with blood.

23

The next morning, I met Cassidy at room 727. I had nothing to do with the set up. My role had been the behind-the-scenes gal with Dmitry. They mainly had me along for the ride so I could try to clear up my own business, my own trauma. *Fight it straight on*, my counselor said. I didn't think *this* was exactly what he'd had in mind. But my way of dealing with things was kind of like 80's hair: bigger meant better, so here I was.

Rush-hour traffic hummed outside the hotel window. Arman was getting wired up with teeny, tiny receivers that fit anywhere. He had some in the buttons on his shirt.

I picked one up. It was half the size of my fingertip. "How can these be so small and still work?"

The tech dude with the waxed mustache, Don, said, "Pretty cool, huh?"

Arman buttoned his shirt and nodded at me. "I am relieved you are OK. Cassidy informed me immediately when she found you."

Sheesh. I was expecting at least a smile or something. He was Mr. Serious now. "Are you mad at me, Arman? I mean, I'm here. I'm alive."

His lips were a straight line. "You were reckless. I do not have time for reckless." He looked in the mirror and adjusted his collar. Yikes, Captain Cold Shoulder.

"Marina, so you know what to do, right?" Cassidy said. She had her feet propped up on the end table near the bed, checking things off a list on a clipboard.

"Stay in the van and don't leave."

"Good girl."

A knock. In walked Sabine, long, black hair cascading down her back in loose waves, her designer black trench coat cinched tight at her tiny waist. Skinny jeans and black ankle books. Arman's face lit up at the sight of his daughter. My stomach tightened because I wished I could look at my father that way. Dying of cancer when your daughter was five put a damper on that.

"Sabine, let me introduce my American friend Marina. Marina, Sabine."

I extended a hand and she gave it a firm shake, then leaned in for a kiss on each cheek.

"A friend of my father's is a friend of mine. It's nice to meet you," she said in perfect English, with a hint of some accent that was probably a blend of German, British, Turkish, and perfection.

"Nice to meet you, too," I said.

The door clicked open. Hasan entered, nodded at us, leaned against the wall, all Addams Family Lurch in his black, leather motorcycle jacket that seemed to fill the entire entryway.

Arman slipped a wad of American hundred dollar bills the size of a brick paver into Hasan's messenger bag.

St. Anthony and the Virgin. This was real.

"You both will be safe and sound several blocks away," he told us. "In the van. And that's where you stay." He stared at Sabine.

"Yes, Father, I will," she said, gaze downcast.

Uh-oh. I knew that look. The some one I'd given my mom when I'd wanted to stay out past my curfew.

Arman looked at me next.

"Yes, I get it. I am with Sabine. A few blocks away, safe and sound."

24

Arman left first, in a Maserati that made my mouth drop open. It was so slick, so streamlined. Hasan took his usual post at the wheel and Arman got in the back. He slid on his aviators, waved goodbye, and powered up the window. "See you in a few hours," he said as it closed.

Cassidy would oversee the back up at the location. She and Waxy Mustache Don were responsible for coordinating with local law enforcement. They were doing some type of strategic-positiony stuff. And all I had to do was stay in the van and observe. Easy-peesy.

Sabine and I would share the communications truck with Anu, who, after she'd escaped trafficking in Estonia, had joined the military to become a communications specialist. We were also joined by a dude named Max from Ukraine, and a guy named Arik from Israel. They were ex-special forces, security to the comm team. I didn't know their credentials, but bulging muscles and serious faces were all I needed for proof. Arman and Cassidy assured me they'd spent a lot of time and money vetting them, so I was clearly in good hands. I also suspected that being next to Sabine was probably the safest place in the world. Arman was not going to let anything happen to her. That was the only sure bet of the day. After what had happened at Kino, I was totally fine with the sidelines.

The communications vehicle was a boxy black delivery truck. Nothing that would stand out. The dark tinted windows revealed no hint of the technological fortress inside. The screens in the backs of the seats were all monitors for the operation. There was a super-fancy tablet at the front of the vehicle, like the kind cops use in their cars. In the back, other monitors and screens.

My adrenaline was pumping. I was more than ready to put someone behind bars. To give two women their lives back.

Max was the driver, Sabine riding shotgun with a tablet, talking to her dad on the headset. We all had those on, but talking to Cassidy, Don, Arman and their team had to be limited. So I just sat in silence and waited. That was new to me, sitting and waiting. My mom would have been proud of me for practicing such self-control, not even occupying myself on my phone. I missed her so much.

We parked in front of a nondescript Soviet-era apartment building, a façade of rectangular balconies. I sat in the back with Arik, who flicked on screens divided into four sections. One for each member of the sting who had cameras and mini microphones in their clothes. My heartbeat speeded up to the cadence of the bass drum in a polka. I realized I was holding my breath when I ran out of air.

Thanks to some fast work by Dmitry, Arman had made the final connections with the traffickers. Dmitry said he knew someone who needed household help in England and vouched for his intentions. The traffickers didn't care about intentions; they just wanted Arman's money.

"OK," Cassidy said. "Everyone is in position. Get ready. Arman's walking in."

Through the camera planted in Arman's shirt button, we saw him open the apartment building front door and enter the tiled lobby. Like Kcenya's mom's, it was dumpy and grimy. Seeing it in stark black and white made it even less inviting. His finger pressed the UP arrow. The door opened, the elevator hummed. It stopped at the seventh floor and Arman got out. He rang the bell for apartment number 33. I switched to Hasan's camera, which was pointed in the same direction.

Slow and steady. Slow and steady. Traffic whizzed by our van and made it shake, but I hardly noticed due to the drama unfolding on the screens in front of us.

A buzzer sounded, and Arman and Hasan entered a hallway. Arman rang another doorbell. A lock tumbled. A tall man with dark hair and five o'clock shadow opened the door. We entered. The transaction was entirely in Russian, so who knew what was being said, but the cameras showed a small living room where two gorgeous girls were sitting on a sofa. Arman and Hasan were checking them out. They wore tight skinny jeans, strappy sandals and spaghetti strap tank tops. They looked away from Arman and Hassan. The guy with the five o'clock shadow said something and the girls turned to Arman and Hasan with weak smiles. Arman spoke. Five o'clock Shadow repeated it. The girls slowly got up and turned in a circle.

I was shaking. How could human beings put other human beings through this? I would never be able to understand this cruelty.

The girls sat down again and looked at their hands. Arman and Five O'clock Shadow talked.

In Cassidy's corner of the monitors, she and her team crept up a pitch-black staircase, except for some blinking lights at landings. They pushed open the door labeled SEVEN and sneaked into the hallway. A teenage boy carrying a trash bag stopped, stared, and whipped back toward where he came from. Someone stepped in front of Cassidy and picked the lock to the hallway. One by one, the six people in her team passed her to line the left side of the hall. She trotted past and held up a palm to signal them to wait.

Arman said the code words, "*Nu ladna, davai*," which meant "Well, OK, let's do it." Cassidy's camera showed two men with a battering ram slamming into the door. After four smashes, it flew open and the team rushed in. All of the body cameras showed different things: an empty kitchen, one of our guys dragging a guy from a bedroom, an empty bathroom, opening the closets. Five O'clock Shadow, his buddy, and the girls were forced to the floor and tied with zip ties. Cassidy bent to the girls and whispered. They nodded, looked at each other, and relaxed.

Once everyone got the signal, Cassidy escorted the girls to the kitchen. The rest of the team hauled the traffickers off the floor.

They'd done it!

And then the driver's side window of our van exploded and someone threw in an egg-shaped thing that spewed smoke. I started to choke. I couldn't see anything. More smashing glass, bright light. Yelling, the thump of punches landing on bodies. Everything sounded like I was underwater. I heard a scream, also muffled. The smoke swirled around me, burning my eyes.

The back doors slammed open, sunlight flooded in. I was blinded by glare but I felt the shocks on the van dip as someone bounded into the back with Max and me. Through my squinting, I could make out the figure of a guy in a black ski mask. He reached for Max. I barged into his chest, sending him flying off balance. Then Max pinned me down and yelled in another language to the guy in the ski mask. Max pulled a ski mask over his own face, his eyes a cold, piercing blue beneath the two holes in the black fabric. Then he leaped out the back with our attackers.

And just that quickly, it was over. Cars rushed by, honking, and the smoke dissipated. It was just me and Arik and Anu.

Sabine was gone.

25

I leaped from the back of the van. Cars whizzed past, close enough to feel the rush of air, the rumble through my body. Someone pulled me back. Anu. Her silver hoop nose ring gleamed in the sun.

My voice boomed. "Where is Sabine? Where is she?"

"Shhh, Marina. We don't know. Get back in the van. Come on."

We climbed in back and sat on the bench. I leaned over, trying to catch my breath.

Arik shook his head as fiddled with buttons and wires. "They were coordinated. They attacked the van, took Sabine, and jammed our communications at the same time."

We all stared at each other, in shock.

"Sabine!" Arman yelled from the sidewalk. He brushed broken glass off the driver's side window and peered in.

Anu opened the rear doors. Arik and I followed her out. My ears were still ringing from the blast. My eyes were burning from the smoke.

"Where is she? Where is she?" Arman screamed at Arik, grabbing his shoulders.

Cassidy stepped between them. "Arman. Screaming isn't going to help. What happened out here?"

Arik said, "Just as you finished the sting, our windows were smashed. Someone threw in a smoke bomb. They knew where Sabine was sitting and they dragged her out. She fought like a devil. I swear she did. It all happened so fast."

Anu moved next to Arik. "Max was in on it. He was a mole. They jammed our communications simultaneously. That's why you couldn't reach us."

"Who has her? Who has her?" Arman's face was red. Veins bulged from his neck like angry fault lines. "Who was that bastard Max with? *You* brought him into our team." His face was in Arik's now, eyes narrow.

Arik took a step back, hands at his side.

Cars rushed by. I was praying a police car wasn't among them.

"Arman. Wait." Cassidy stepped between the pair. She pulled out her phone and texted someone.

A few seconds later Pavel stepped out from behind a bus shelter. I'd had no idea he was in on the operation. "Arman," he said. "I recorded the license plate. I am not sure it will get you anywhere but it is a start, my friend."

I pulled Arman to the side. "Are you *sure* Pavel didn't have anything to do with it? I mean, how he just kind of appears out of nowhere. How much do we honestly know about him?"

"Trust us," Cassidy said. "Pavel is on the up and up."

"But are you sure? I mean, he's homeless. He might be persuaded by some money."

Arman's eyes narrowed. "Pavel, please come here....Pavel, Ms. Konyeshna seems to think you have something to do with this." Arman's breath heaved.

Pavel's gaze dropped to the pavement. He hung his head like a child being scolded.

Arman cleared his throat, hands on his hips. "Pavel, I know you had nothing to do with this. You have been a crucial part of our team. Ever since that day I saw you pull the Skinhead off the African student at the metro station, I knew you were one of us. You have never let me down. Please know that, despite what Marina thinks, I know you are a trustworthy man."

Pavel looked at Arman and smiled. "Thank you, my friend."

Arman's angry expression softened. "Thank you, Pavel. You have always been very helpful to us. Thank you. Now, what did you see, my friend?"

Pavel said in a gentle voice, "I would have been useless against those hooligans. Maybe it was cowardly, but I decided to just sit and watch. To remember their license plates."

Cassidy put her hand on his shoulder. "Pavel, it's OK. You couldn't have physically stopped them. Max was working us from the inside. They were always a step ahead."

Pavel turned and walked back to the bus shelter and sat on the bench, hunched over, rocking.

"Jesus, Marina." Cassidy glared at me.

"I didn't know all that. I'm sorry. I feel terrible. I'm a little freaked out, you know."

"If you're going to work with us, you need to hold on to yourself in crisis situations. Blaming someone without proof is devastating. And wrong. Learn from this mistake."

Arman was on his phone, speaking a rapid-fire German. Probably to Sabine's mom. Then in Turkish, I guessed. Cassidy leaned against the van, looking left and right at frequent intervals. Anu and Arik stood at the front and back of the van.

"Where are the girls?" I asked Cassidy.

"Being taken to the Bulgarian embassy, so they can go home. They will receive support when they get there. If they left for safety reasons, like abuse, our partner in Sofia will help."

"Thank God."

"Yeah."

Arman turned to us. "I called Sabine's mother. We are using a private response company. We have always had a plan in place for this. It's the cost of doing the business I do. Let us go now, Hasan."

"Wait." I grabbed his arm. "Who would do this? Why *now*?"

"There is a long list of people who dislike me, Marina. How could I have been so stupid and naïve?" He spoke through a stiff jaw. "Let us go, Hasan."

And that was it. They strode away down the sidewalk.

"What happens now?" I said, turning in a circle to look around us. Not a siren to be heard. I wasn't sure if that was good or bad.

Cassidy sighed. "Well, first, in these situations, the security, or response, as it's sometimes called, consultant will ask for proof of life. In the movies, you see hostages holding that day's newspaper. They can also pose questions that only the kidnapped person can answer.

Who was their fourth grade teacher, or the name of a beloved pet. Then, there's negotiation. Knowing Arman, his security firm will drop off the money and then get her at a different location.

"So I'm not sure if Arman and Sabine's mother will even alert the authorities. They have the means to take care of it themselves. If Sabine's lucky, the kidnapper just wants the money and will treat her well. But if this is payback against Arman or me for trying to take down a trafficker, or retribution for anything he's done to piss off some of his international rogues...well, her safety might not matter so much."

"Which do you think it is?"

"Let's believe it's for the money."

Arik and Anu started the van. Cassidy waved them off and Anu steered into traffic. Piles of smashed glass marked where the van had been parked.

"First, sit down. You look pale," Cassidy guided me down to a bench. I leaned my head back and looked at the bright blue sky. The breeze was cold and my face stung. "Honestly, the girls truly are safe with the embassy. Kcenya has a team that liaises with governments of high-trafficking countries. Bulgaria especially, has been a vital partner. Once the girls return there, we have partners in the U.S. embassy in Sofia who will follow through, too. So, we should probably pack up and get out of here quickly, until we know who's responsible for Sabine's abduction."

"Do you think The General is behind it?"

"Not likely, honestly. Like I said before, he has his tail between his legs now. He was a big fish in Pennsylvania, but here, he's a bottom feeder in the Organizatsiya. He bungled so much back there that when he returned here, he'd lost respect of most key players. That bullshit he pulled with you, I have no idea what he was thinking. And anyway, he doesn't have the clout anymore to make something like this happen. Let's get back to the hotel, get some sleep and pack up. We should get on the next flight home, as soon as possible."

"Agreed." I hoisted myself up. "I'm ready."

Cassidy glanced over one shoulder. "Uh, oh. I hear sirens."

We took off down a side street, slipping away just before two cruisers pulled up, lights flashing.

26

Kcenya's assistant took care of the plane tickets, but it still was a few hours before Cassidy and I had to be at the airport. Fydor had shown up at my hotel with a hot coffee, a croissant, and an invitation to go souvenir shopping.

This last-minute run to a street filled with tourist-trap shops had been awesome. Fydor was not just a great guy, he was a hell of a last-minute guide. Plus, he knew how to haggle. If I came home without souvenirs, I would have felt terrible. And even though there was so much I didn't want to remember about this trip, I was certain it was a turning point in my life. So yes, I wanted a few reminders for myself. So then I suddenly had one of those plaid bags full of matrioshka dolls, scarves, blue and white Gzhel figurines, and more. I decided on only one bottle of vodka. Times, they were a-changing for me.

I was leaving a different person.

Now we were taking some final photos. The wind whipped and I pulled my coat collar closer.

"A little to the right, Marina …OK…smile!" Fydor snapped away in front of St. Basil's Cathedral.

All of a sudden, snowflakes whirled and danced around us. They stuck to our hair and were transforming the city into a picture-perfect greeting card. I smiled and posed with the fairy tale blue, white, mustard, green, and red spires rising behind me. The clouds above were now finally heavy with snow. Flakes dropped to the bricks below our feet and dissolved. My cheeks hurt from smiling.

Cassidy, ever the buzz-kill, said, "Come on. Make this quick. We have to get to the airport."

"Oh boy. Don't wreck this with your signature doom and gloom. You know you want a picture with me!"

Cassidy rolled her eyes but still sidled up. Even cracked a faint smile

"You look like beautiful Russian snow princesses!" Fydor said as he snapped more photos.

I even got Cassidy to make a kissy face and a peace sign. She actually loosened up.

Miracles happened.

"Our turn," I said to Fydor. "Thank you so much for being so nice. I felt so out of place here and you went out of your way to welcome me to your country. I had fun with you. When you come to America, please let me know. My house is your house."

He raised his hand in a high five and I slapped it. "Cassidy has invited me to be part of Shine a Light, so I will be in America for training this summer. Can you believe it?" he said. "I look very forward to seeing you again."

"Awesome!" I gave him a hug and a kiss on both cheeks. We wrapped our arms around each other and Cassidy snapped a few more pictures.

I turned to look at the cathedral and its winding spires, the swirling onion-top domes, like fires, spiraling to the sky. The snowfall was picking up and I took one last look at the brick expanse of Red Square, the towering walls, the rectangular mausoleum of Lenin, and the Kremlin roofs peeking out from behind its walls. I had no idea if I even still had relatives left in Russia. I had no idea of how to go about finding them. But I did feel a connection to this confusing, beautiful country. Maybe one day I'd return to discover more about my past.

But now, I was more concerned about my future. I was ready to go home.

But first I had to make a stop.

34

Marina, we don't have time** for this."

"Sure we do, Cass. The plane leaves in three hours."

"Don't call me Cass. And it leaves in two hours and fifty minutes." Cassidy-not-Cass crossed her arms over her chest and leaned into the back of the seat as the Mercedes zipped through downtown Moscow traffic.

"Hey, Cass."

"*Jesus.* It's Cassidy."

I giggled. "I know. Just playing. Anyway, thanks for making this stop."

We rolled up to the orphanage for the start of lunch. Galina smiled and waved us over. She was actually quite beautiful when she wasn't scowling. Cassidy told the drive to wait there and we trotted to the van to help her and Pavel unload.

"Um, Pavel," I said, a little shaky.

"Hello." He pushed up his glasses with an index finger that poked through a black glove, and continued loading the cart with plates, napkins, utensils.

"Listen, I'm going back home and I wanted to offer an apology. I have no idea why I said those awful things when Sabine was taken. I was in shock. But it was wrong. And I'm really sorry."

He put his hand on my shoulder and said in his soft voice, "It is OK, Marina. We all make mistakes. This country can take a person and flip him upside down."

His kindness to me was a miracle. I felt so humbled and lighter. I sank to a step. It was nice to hear someone tell me it was OK.

"Come with me," Pavel left the cart at the bottom of the steps and turned toward a line of trees. I wasn't sure what to do. Past experience had taught me not to go into the woods with a stranger. Just then, Galina and Cassidy popped their heads, looking for us.

"Pavel wants to show me something. In the, um, woods." I bit my bottom lip.

Cassidy looked at Galina, who nodded. Cassidy trotted down the steps. "Sure. Let's go. Pavel's cool."

"Yeah, I wish I'd figured that out earlier."

We jogged through the parking lot. Pavel was waiting at the edge of the trees, pulling his navy knit cap lower against the snow, which was falling harder by the hour. I hoped our flight could still take off. We followed him into the woods and after a few hundred feet we were in a clearing. He followed its edge to a small stone structure the size of a shed. Graffiti covered the outside walls. Used syringes littered the ground.

"Hooligans. I apologize." Pavel pushed the trash to the side with his boot and opened the door. There was a planked floor. Small windows lined the top near the ceiling. Their panes were smashed, the remaining glass jagged teeth. A red and blue flannel shirt in the corner and some empty beer cans added to the very creepy décor.

Pavel crouched and pulled on one floorboard. It lifted, along with several others, to reveal a hatch.

"Be careful," he said. "And watch your head."

The last time I'd been underground, a mine had been collapsing around me. I wiped my sweaty palms on my jeans. "I'll stay here, Cassidy. You can report back."

She shrugged and backed down the ladder. I heard her tell Pavel I was claustrophobic. A moment later, she called up. "Marina, get your behind down here. You'll be fine. You have to see this."

Her voice was closer than I'd thought it would be. I took a deep breath and descended. The rickety ladder gave me palpitations. The last time I'd been on one, I'd ended up covered in a mafioso's blood and with a gun pointed at my head. Luckily, this one only went down about a dozen rungs.

The room was probably ten by ten and furnished like a mini museum and library. Three walls were lined with cases that came to my hips. They were filled with books. Their spines had titles in English, Russian, and other languages. The walls were covered in artwork from magazines. Abstracts, portraits, and more. A cot hung on the wall next to the ladder, along with a propane heater, the kind I recognized from camping trips.

"Welcome to my little home. The entrance closes quite solidly and seamlessly, so no one knows I'm here. I've been living here a year."

Cassidy smiled. "You are a better survivalist than me!"

"How do you mean?" Pavel frowned.

"Well, I used to have a TV show in the US called *Wild Woman* where I'd be helicoptered into desolate places and survive for a week."

"Please, sit." Pavel pointed to two wooden chairs. "You did this... for fun?"

Cassidy blushed. "Um, yes."

We sat. Pavel searched through pages of books. He said, "Hmmm. And they paid you?"

Cassidy swallowed hard. "Yes."

"Smart lady! Good for you! And to think — just a week!" He laughed and ruffled the pages of a large book with a red cover. "Ah-ha! Here they are!"

He pivoted back to us and held out two coins, then nodded, so we put out our hands. He dropped them into our palms. They were almost the size of a half-dollar, heavier than they looked. On one side was an eagle with two heads, one facing left and the other facing right. On the other side, the number one hundred framed by two sheaves of wheat. The date on the bottom read 1993. Someone had punched a hole in the top of each coin.

"I have been saving these and thought you'd like them. The Soviet Union dissolved in 1992, which led to very unstable times. They still are for many of us, as you have seen. So the year 1993 is a reminder for us that life can be difficult but you will persevere."

I had so many questions to ask of him but I didn't have that right.

Pavel continued. "The side with the eagle has many interpretations. To my mind, I prefer the one where one head looks to the East and the other to the West. To the past and to the future. You can't have one without the other. But the future is where you should be looking, my friends."

From behind another book, he pulled a bottle of vodka and three shot glasses. "I know you must get to the airport, but permit an old man a proper goodbye." He raised his glass and we followed. "To Russia, to America, to friendship, to mistakes, to the future!"

We clinked and drank.

I was still dumfounded. "Pavel, why are you being so kind to me?"

"Because when I needed someone to be kind to me most, people were kind. I enjoy paying that debt back. That's why I help at the orphanage and other assorted business. Be kind to yourself, Marina. We all make mistakes. Look always to the future."

I got up from my chair and hugged him. He stiffened, then hugged me back. I kissed him on his scruffy cheek.

"*Dos vidonya*, Pavel," I said.

"No, it is not goodbye, Marina. It's *uvidemcya skora*."

"Oh. What does that mean?"

"We will see each other soon." He smiled and walked back to the ladder.

Cassidy hugged him. "Pavel, I know you don't want any handouts. But why won't you let us get you a real apartment?"

"Ah, Cassidy. This is my home for now," he murmured. "You concentrate on the people who truly need help."

She hugged him. "So we can count on you to continue surveillance for Shine A Light?"

Pavel put his hand on his heart and bowed his head. "Anything for you."

I sniffled. "*Uvidemcya skora*, Pavel. *Spacibo*." I was indeed grateful for his grace. I looped the coin through the gold necklace I was wearing and tucked it into my sweater so I could feel its weight against my chest.

∗∗∗

As the ten-seater bounced through the clouds on our descent to the Avoca airport, I tried to forget every bit of air-crash footage I'd ever seen on the news. I turned up my earbuds and leaned against the window. I was still aghast someone hated Arman so much that they would kidnap his daughter. Who was he, really? What else didn't I know about him?

I saw her today at the reception, Mick Jagger sang.

I felt sudden comfort looking down on the ground below me: house, backyard, house, backyard. Maybe the backyards were wide and hilly, maybe there was a pool or a shed. Cars in the driveways. Sidewalks. Black roads that curved and turned. The gray-white roof of a shopping center and a parking lot full of yellow school buses. This was what I knew, what I loved.

At her feet was a footloose man, Mick continued.

It had taken several thousand miles to get to that truth. I wasn't sure what else was waiting for me when I got off the plane, but in that moment I had a bag full of souvenirs and gifts to give away. I wanted to go to Dunkin Donuts and get a real coffee. I wanted a shower in my own bathroom, and I wanted to get—

You can't always get what you want, but you'll find sometime, you just might find, Mick explained.

"You get what you need," I whispered into the window. I drew a heart with my finger in the cloud of haze on the pane.

***

Stuck in traffic on 81!!!!! Overturned ketchup truck!!!!!!!! Gilbert and Kendra should be there!!!! Xoxoxoxoxoxoxoxoxoxoxoxoxoxoxoxox

A few weeks ago I would have rolled my eyes at Mom's overuse of exclamation points in her texts, but today it was definitely on my top ten list of things I loved. I couldn't wait to hug her, smell her hair spray. And Gilly and Kendra. I had so much here to be grateful for. I stepped onto the escalator, heel wobbling on the metal conveyor as I balanced my carry-on and the big red, white and blue plaid bag I couldn't leave without. Everyone in Russia traveled with these. I was the only one at this airport with one. In fact, I was one of the few people here, on this sunny fall afternoon. Not at all like the crowded terminal in Moscow, or the connection in Paris or the loud hustle of Dulles. A few weeks ago, I would have scoffed at the lack of travelers at our local airport, but today I got it. *Finally.*

And there was Gilly with a bright yellow poster board that read WELCOME HOME MARINA!! And there was Kendra on her tippytoes, waving, her baby bump all of a sudden so much bigger than it had been two weeks ago. I hauled the straps of my bags over my shoulders and skittered down the escalator. If I broke my face, I broke my face. Too bad. I couldn't wait for their hugs.

Clop clop clop down the metal stairs and into their arms. We were a rocking, screeching cluster of happiness. Gilly parked a big fat kiss on my cheek. Kendra took a photo of me giving the obligatory peace sign. Then she took a selfie of all of us together, and typed furiously on her phone. "There. I told everyone I'd post a pic when you landed. Everyone wants to go out!"

The air was clean here. No one was smoking. It was so bright. Everything was written in English. I understood what was being said around me.

"Uh, Marina?" Gilly snapped his fingers.

I smiled. "Yes! Yes! Sorry! Let's do it. I want to see everyone. But not tonight. I need to just chill. I'm going to go for a run. Tomorrow night. For sure."

Kendra shook her head and whistled. "Look at you, Marina. Taking time to relax. What happened in the Old Country that's making you slow down?"

"That's a story for over a long dinner."

Kendra smiled. "Deal! Now look at those boots!"

I stuck one pointy-tipped, high-heeled black leather foot out. "One of my souvenirs."

Gilly nodded at Kendra, who smiled. What were they up to? It felt like I was going to be proposed to. Gilly rolled up his sleeve and exposed the golden koi tattoo on his forearm. He tapped it. "Look."

Five of the scales were shaded into the five side of a pair of dice.

Just like on my wrist.

I was confused.

"I can't get another tattoo right now because of my delicate condition," Kendra said as she chomped on a Swedish Fish, "but I did get this." A silver bangle with a wide, flat top that had the five dots stamped into it.

"Wait...I'm getting this thing," I said, as I pushed up my coat sleeve, "Covered up as soon as possible. I'm going to ask my cousin, Joann, to take me to her tattoo artist next week. I need to get rid of it. You have no idea."

"Listen," Gilly said. "It wasn't right of us to give you such a hard time before you left. We are all dealing with things from the fallout of the geocaching competition. *You* were the one working through it and *we* were the ones denying it. *You* were the one processing it. *We* tried to move forward too fast."

Kendra looked at the floor. "Yeah, I'm sorry. It wasn't right of us."

"Guys. I don't know what to say. I mean, I got us into an awful mess. And then over there in Russia, well, it all came together in ways that are even more complicated and, well, it's just a lot to tell right now."

They grabbed my hands. Gilly said, "This is always going to be a part of us. Denying it isn't going the help. So, listen. Go home, relax, call Sutton."

My heart fluttered hearing someone say his name.

"And," he added. "We'll talk about how we can all work *together* to move forward."

"Well, I'm moving forward," I said. "Cassidy and Arman started an organization to fight human trafficking. I'm going work for them, eventually."

That was met with a chorus of wows and awesomes. I'd tell them more it in the car. Because at that moment, I needed a bathroom and a milkshake a.s.a.p.

And then I heard her. "Marina!"

I dropped my bags and ran over to my mom — well, running in those boots wasn't much of an option, so I kind of skittered and tottered over, with my arms wide-open. As hers wrapped around me in a force field of safety, my eyes welled up.

She kissed my cheeks, my forehead, my temple, even my nose. That familiar smell of perfume and fabric softener took me over the edge, and that was it. Tears flowed like fall rain in Moscow.

She patted my back and said, "It's OK."

35

A few hours later, after a humongo chocolate milkshake, three pieces of pizza, and a long shower, the time difference kicked in. I was antsy and couldn't rest. It was only seven P.M. so, off I went for a run. I needed to get my brain together. I'd stop by Gilly's parents' house. They were my family away from family. Their perfect white house on Reynolds Street with its formal dining room and columns and sweeping staircase was my second home.

Kingston was in full Halloween mode, with scarecrows, pumpkins, hay bales, cobwebs, and fake gravestones staked into front yards. I'd forgotten how much I loved this holiday.

When I trotted around the corner, there were four cars in the driveway and three parked in front. Uh-oh — was I disturbing a dinner party? Thump thump thump thump up the side stairs.

Mrs. Tomlinson opened the side door a sliver and peered through. Her reading glasses caught the porch light. "Oh, Marina! Welcome back!" She leaned in and looked past my shoulder. "No Gilbert?"

"Uh, no. Just me." What was that all about?

Her face relaxed. "Welcome home, sweetie! Come in, come in! I can't wait to hear all about your trip!" She poked her head into the dining room. "I'll be right back. Gilbert's friend, *Marina*, is here."

"Oh, Marina?"

"Hmmmm…"

"Hi, Marina! Welcome home!" Mr. Tomlinson entered the foyer and enfolded me in a huge, rocking embrace. For a compact, skinny guy, he'd always had one heck of a bear hug.

"Hi, Mr. T." I always got a kick out of calling him that. With his bony frame and comb-over, he'd definitely be voted Least Likely To Say I Pity Da Fool. The A Team. My mom once said in passing that my Dad used to love that old show, so I used to watch episodes on YouTube.

We entered the kitchen. "You look really nice. That's a great suit." Gilly's mom had a tiny size four frame and such style it made me jealous. I swear she could wear winter white dress pants through a dust storm and come out looking perfect. "Sorry I interrupted your party."

Mrs. Tomlinson opened the stainless steel refrigerator and took out a bottle of water. "No problem, dear. Here you go. Actually, we were just talking about you!" Her smile quivered, then decided to reset itself. "Come on in and meet our friends from church."

Oh boy. Stand up straight. Watch your language. Smile like a good girl.

China coffee cups clinked against saucers. It was a sweater vest and blazer convention. "Everyone, this is Marina, Gilbert's best friend. She just got back from a business trip to Russia."

The AARP cardholders cooed and ahhed over me. What was going on? Even being a drug mule had felt a little more comfortable than this bizarre, stiff gathering.

A lady with poufy black hair spoke first. "Well, Susan, she's just as beautiful as you said. Even in that tomboyish outfit!" She winked at me.

Tomboy? Who said that anymore? And what was wrong with running tights, a fleece, and a baseball hat? I was exercising, and Poufy Hair looked like she hadn't seen her own feet since the Eighties. Insert pageant smile here.

"Help yourself to some dessert, dear. On the sideboard in front of the window." Mrs. Tomlinson pointed to cheesecake, brownies, and star-shaped sugar cookies with a maraschino cherry stuck in the middle.

I stuffed one into my mouth and sighed, spraying crumbs all over the lace. Oops. I dusted it off. Great. Work on new superpower: Not being a mess twenty-four hours a day. And of course Poufy Hair had been watching, as evidenced by how startled she looked when I turned around. Lovely.

Mrs. Tomlinson was sliding orange pamphlets into a tote bag.

"Sorry I interrupted your, um, meeting," I muttered.

"Dear, not a problem at all. As I said...just some friends from church." But her hands were shaking. "Please, sit."

I took the only empty seat, which was between an unshaven man in a Hawaiian shirt and Mr. T.

Mr. T put his hand on my shoulder. "Meet Pastor Fleck. Pastor, Marina Konyeshna."

"Nice to meet you." I'd heard stories from Gilly about this new minister. Eternal damnation and fiery brimstone bubbled underneath his relaxed surfer dude exterior.

"Great to meet you, Marina. *Great* to meet you." The pastor nodded and smiled — not at me, but at something over my shoulder. Way in the distance. Definitely not Reverend Social Skills.

"So, uh, who made the cookies? They're delicious." I fiddled with the napkin in my lap.

"Mrs. Fitzgerald," said Mrs. Tomlinson. A lady raised a cane to identify herself and winked.

What was with all the winking? Man, it was time to go. "Well, uh, I feel tons better now. Hard run. Thanks for the water and dessert. Carbs will keep me going. Runners need carbs. Again, sorry to interrupt."

The guests twittered goodbyes and said they hoped to see me again – more winks and nudges. Must be some weird Protestant thing, I decided. But I had to make a pit stop before I fled. "May I use the bathroom, please?"

"Of course, dear. But you'll have to go upstairs. We're painting the one down here."

The stairs were literally grand with a thick oak railing and a landing with enough room for a table with a vase of silk flowers. I'd loved walking down it when Gilly and I used to play prince and princess. We'd always fought over the tiara. Mr. T had always made sure I got to wear it. He'd been my staunchest ally.

The steps creaked as I stopped midway to look at family pictures. Gilly with his moppy brown hair, holding a baseball bat. His parents' wedding photo, his mother with bologna curls and his father in a white tux and bushy mustache. His older brother in a high school graduation picture, taken a few months before he'd died in a car crash. He and Gilly had the same wide smile. The Tomlinsons had joined Grace

Fellowship a few months later. They'd been kind of consumed by Jesus and the Bible after that.

I skipped over the last three steps, just like Gilly and I used to when we were younger. Of course, I overshot and stumbled. I knocked into the table at the top. One of Mrs. Tomlinson's orange pamphlets fluttered to the carpet. I picked it up.

God's Pathway To Manhood:
Helping A Loved One Overcome Unwanted Attractions

Say what?
I flipped the pamphlet open.

In a recent study of men who want to overcome their homosexual tendencies, a significant number said their relationship with their father and mother significantly contributed to their sinful inclinations. Path Of Manhood Ministries dedicates itself to liberate these men from their temptations.

What the hell was this? My face grew hot. I folded the flyer into a tiny sliver and shoved it into my running belt.

A tap on my shoulder. "Marina, we're here tonight to formulate a plan to help your best friend emerge from his sin and find his better, truer self," said Pastor Fleck, without looking me in the eye. Now he seemed to be gazing at the bathroom door. "The Tomlinsons and their Faith Circle think you might be an integral step in rescuing Gilbert. They've always thought you'd make the perfect wife for him." He placed a hand on my shoulder and squeezed. My skin crawled underneath and I flinched.

Was that why Mrs. Tomlinson had seemed relieved Gilly wasn't with me? And the winks. The chorus of cooing over me. OMG. I muttered, "Gilly's amazing just the way he is."

"Don't be angry, Marina. God hates the sin, but not the sinner."

I shrugged out of his grip and pounded down the stairs, but the pastor leaned over the railing. "Marina! Wait! I know this is hard!"

I was almost out, but Mr. Tomlinson stood in front of it with his arms crossed. "Marina, please. Listen. Pray with us. For our sake, if for nothing else. We know Gilly's struggling in his soul. You can help us help him."

"Please, Mr. T, please just let me go."

Gilly's dad stepped back. He'd always been like the dad I no longer had. And suddenly the man who'd always had everything under control, from making sure we got to our swimming lessons on time to telling us stories to distract us through thunderstorms, seemed old and scared. "Yes, it's too much. For all of us. I understand, I understand." He moved out of my way.

"Marina, please help us." Mrs. Tomlinson wiped tears with one of the monogrammed napkins.

The screen door slammed behind me.

I shoved in my ear buds, cranked up the volume, and sprinted to Gilly's. Oh, no. Poor Gilly. What had he been dealing with? Why hadn't he *told* me?

His apartment was only a mile or so from his parents' and, based on the thumping of my heart, I reached a personal record for my running that night. My breath came out in puffs of haze as I rang the doorbell, put a hand against the brick façade to prop myself up. Just as I was wiping sweat from under my bra, the door rattled open. Light from his living room filled the small side porch. I noticed boxes on the hardwood floor.

"Gilly. We need to talk." I panted. "Your parents. They've gone off the deep end." I had no idea how I was going to continue this conversation, literally the most difficult one of my life. I mean, how do you tell your bff that his parents are secretly plotting to convert him from being gay – and they want him to marry me, hot-mess me?

Gilly shook his head and let me in. Not only were there empty boxes on the floor, a pile of newspapers sat on an end table. All of his picture frames and art were off the cranberry-colored living room walls.

"Hey, what's going on here?"

He motioned to the sofa. All the nights we'd spent here talking, drinking, playing games, watching movies. Doing nothing. Or the morning I'd found Amparo Rivas' body, the morning that had changed everything. I was being overcome with this profound feeling of loss. I wasn't sure what to make of the hole that was now making an appearance in my chest.

Gilly leaned back into the arm of the sofa and slid his glasses to the top of his head. "You ran into my parents and their prayer group."

"Yes. Why didn't you mention this?"

"Well, I kind of tried. That text where I said my parents were getting on my last nerve? And I didn't want to take away from your trip or your homecoming. I was planning on telling you tomorrow."

I kicked an empty box. "Where are you moving to?"

"DC."

I sprung up from the sofa. "*Washington, DC?*"

A black and white picture strip taken at a photo booth in Ocean City, Maryland a few years ago was propped on a bookshelf. In square number one, the two of us were smiling, my sunburned nose, his already-tan face grinning. Square two was of us dead serious, mouths set. Square three we were sticking out our tongues. In square four our heads leaned together, arms around each other's shoulders, complete with easy smiles.

I caught my breath and wiped away a tear. I was sick of crying. I didn't come home to cry. I wasn't ready for this.

"Marina. When you left, I took it as a sign that I needed to do some prioritizing, too. I mean, that was the first time I ever saw you actually do something for yourself that didn't involve a credit card or a manicure. You did something different. Took a risk, took your life in a new direction. Do you remember that message I sent about my parents being parental?"

If only I'd known then what I knew now. I took a deep breath. "Um, yeah, of course."

"In the process of dealing with what happened last summer, well, I came out to my folks."

I put the photo strip back in its place. "I thought you were going to wait for me to tell them."

"I was, Een. I was. But I then couldn't wait. Things with Pete are getting serious."

Finally, a reason to smile. "They are? He's wonderful!"

"Yeah, he's great." Gilly grinned for a second. "Great enough that I had to tell my parents. It wasn't some dramatic scene I'd envisioned, with me showing them photos of me and Pete or anything like that. Just a plain, old Tuesday night. We were clearing the table after dinner. And I just kind of blurted it out. 'So, Mom and Dad, um, I'm gay.'"

"And?"

"And she continued to load the dishwasher. My dad continued to put the leftover chicken parm into plastic containers. Finally he said, 'Yes, we know.' My mom went to the basement to put the laundry in the dryer. My dad turned on the TV. And I left."

"What? I mean, really! Who does that to their child?" I felt my face get red. I threw my arms around him and squeezed. His muscular arms were tight around me and I kissed him on the cheek. "You know I love you. It will be fine. And screw this fricking conversion committee."

"Well, how they ever thought me marrying you was a sane idea is beyond me. I mean, really. I've been taking care of your house while you were gone and let me tell you, Ms. Konyeshna, you need to invest in some Clorox wipes and a better vacuum cleaner. We'd never work."

I stuck out my tongue at him. "Not to mention the whole you're-not-into-vaginas thing, either."

"Yes, there's that. So, I avoided my parents and a few days later, they called and asked me to come over after work. At that point, I was so, so hopeful. I mean, they'd had time to think about it, deal with it. But no. I walked in and there was that pastor. Did you see the scruffy surfer guy?"

I nodded. "He has terrible social skills! He didn't make eye contact with me when we spoke."

"Yeah, so that's the leader of my mother and father's church."

"He's an asshat. And he doesn't matter."

"He does and he doesn't. He does because it took *him* to make me see I have to get out of here. At least for a while."

I tried not to slip into Selfish Mode, because this wasn't about me. But it *was* about me. But it wasn't. But it was. Argh.

"Pete and I decided to move in together," Gilly said.

"Sorry I'm not squealing with delight, but — this is very sudden, don't you think?"

"Maybe. But I love him, Een." His face relaxed. "And I need to start something new for myself. All these years I felt like I had to stay here, because my brother died. I had to watch over our parents. Now, for all I care, they can move to fucking Alaska."

"Oh, Gilly, you don't mean that. Come on."

"Yes, I do, Marina. I do."

I was trying to take the Less Is More Approach, not babbling on and on like I usually would.

He filled the silence quickly enough. "Pete is settled in DC. He owns a huge townhouse in a nice neighborhood. I'll be living in a huge city. I can be me."

OK, so now I knew he was serious. But I had one more angle. "It sounds nice and all. But now that there's marriage equality, things will loosen up here, too, right? And what about running for office? Last summer you said that was still a priority, that you could make changes around here."

He leaned back into sofa cushion. "That could still be in the plan. I'm only twenty-six, you know. If I want to change things, I need to see what change is possible. To know how it is to live freely, to be myself – at work, at home, walking down the street. I can't do that in the Valley, not like I want to. It feels so wonderful to hold Pete's hand and just walk into a restaurant. Can you imagine us doing that here?"

"Well...um."

"Exactly."

Again, I left room for silence. I'd been doing this quiet business a lot lately. Maybe I was finally growing up a little, learning that every tiny pause didn't have to be filled with words. Or club music. Or the sound of my purse unzipping so I could get to my credit card. Or the clink of empty cotton candy vodka bottles landing in the recycling container. Silence wouldn't kill me. So I wasn't going to blurt out anything.

Gilly drummed on his thighs. "You're uncharacteristically quiet. I was expecting waterworks and gnashing of teeth and pulling of hair."

"Yeah, well, I needed some changes, too."

"What happened in Russia?" He leaned in.

I let this new friend called Silence linger until I found the right words. Gilly lowered his chin and looked at me over the top of his glasses. He seemed just about to speak when I said, "Listen, when you get settled with Pete, I will come down. And we'll have a big sleepover, and I'll tell you all my secrets. I need to process it all first."

"Over Double Stuf Oreos, right?" He grabbed my hand.

"Hell yeah!" At least our marathon friend-therapy sessions of junk food would still be a constant.

Gilly embraced me again. I couldn't hold back the waterworks anymore and neither could he, so we just hugged each other while I tried not to snot on his polo shirt. I cried about missing him already, the lives we were leaving behind, and the new lives in front of us.

36

Red and blue lights filled my narrow street. I picked up the pace. Police were in front of *my* house. What the? Jesus, I'd only been home for like eight hours. There wasn't time for me to do something stupid. My neighbors were out in full force, leaning over the fences to get a solid look at whatever was going on. My next-door neighbors, the ones with the concert-loud music, were in a clump in front of my retaining wall. The mom saw me and yanked on her daughter's hoodie, who then said something to the cop. Now all of them were looking at me.

Great. Great. Great. Great.

I trotted up. "Um, hi? What happened at my house?"

It was Eddie Jankovich. He'd graduated with my sister and now was an Edwardsville cop. His neck puffed over his too-tight blue shirt collar. His face was spidery-veiny red. Lord. He was one hot wing away from a heart attack. Still, he was a good guy. I was glad it was him. "Eddie. What the hell is going on?"

He smiled, but only with his mouth. His gaze shifted to the side and he fiddled with his flashlight. "Marina Konyeshna! How's your sister?"

I didn't have time for this. "Fine, thanks. So, uh, can you please tell me why the cops are here?"

"Due to the diligence of your neighbors," he hooked a thumb in their direction, "We caught someone trying to break into your house. The lurker Gil Tomlinson called me about."

Chills ran the length of my body. My chest sucked in. I needed one person, right now. I pressed her number. "Mom. Please come over. Now."

Eddie put a hand on my shoulder. "Now, Marina. It'll be OK. We got the guy."

"What? Where is he?"

"Over there. In that cruiser."

"Who is the son of a bitch? Lemme see!" I didn't get roofied, almost organ-harvested, and forced into being a drug mule to have myself killed in my own home. I knew it. I knew The General would be still after me. Liar.

As I pivoted to the car, Eddie grabbed me with sausage fingers. "Marina. Wait."

"No." I shrugged free. I strode over. Two cops were talking near the hood, so I had clear view of the jerk. He was wearing a dark hoodie, his head tilted down. I pounded on the window and he shot upright. He turned his face and I saw pale skin. Blue veins under his eyes. Not a speck of hair and a weak smile. He lifted a hand to wave and I saw a hospital bracelet poking out of the sleeve. I gasped and took a few steps back, bumping into someone.

"Sorry," I mumbled.

"It's more than OK," he said. It took a second to register.

"Sutton?" I turned to see him, in a black coat, towering behind me.

"Marina."

So should I hug him? Kiss him? I had no idea. None.

I didn't have to choose. He squeezed me in the biggest hug of my life and kissed my cheek.

I planted one on his lips. "We have to talk, Mister. But we have more important things to discuss right now. What the hell is going on here?"

"Well, that guy was trying to break into your house. Won't say why."

"He looks familiar. I can't place him, though. Is he sick or something?"

"Yeah. Says he has cancer."

Flashbacks to my Aunt Yelena withering away before she died last summer. "But what does he want from me?"

"Not sure. He won't talk."

Eddie walked up. "Hey, Cicero, the creeper says he wants a word with Marina."

"Tell him he can talk at the station."

"Wait, wait, no. It's OK. I have to know."

"And I know better than to get in your way." Sutton waved me toward the cruiser.

I knocked on the window and the cop in the driver's seat powered it down. "So, what the hell do you want from my house, huh?" I asked the guy in the hoodie.

"Listen. I gotta tell you something. But I don't want to get you in trouble."

"Listen, buddy. I know what trouble is. *You*, my friend, have no idea. So get to it."

Sutton leaned against the back quarter panel and grinned.

"Marina. Don't you recognize me from your Aunt Yelena's funeral?"

"Huh?" Not the answer I'd expected. "Well, uh..."

Sutton pushed off the sedan and came to stand next to me.

"I was in the group that arrived early. We gave you that note from your aunt."

I flashed back to the beginning of her viewing. I'd thought I was alone, but it'd turned out she'd had an entourage from her cancer support group keeping vigil already. But yeah, this guy had been in that group. Except now he was, well, so very sick. He didn't look the same at all. His face more pale and puffy. His eyebrows were gone.

"Listen, they're going to take me to the station soon. You have to go down to the basement. Alone. Or with your bodyguard there." He lifted his chin toward Sutton. "I've been trying to get that stuff out of the basement so you didn't get in trouble for it. Shouldn't be your problem. Yelena and I had a plan but she got so sick so fast. It's behind that coal room door. I'll tell the police it's all mine. Because it is. Yelena was just trying to do what was right. "

"What's down there? I don't have patience for this. I'm jet lagged. I'm cranky." I turned to go into the house, but Sutton grabbed my forearm hard enough so I couldn't move. Under the right conditions, that would have been majorly hot. But now, not so much.

"Yeow! That hurt, dude! Let go. I have to see what's in the basement."

"Marina." Uh-oh. He'd gone all Officer Cicero now. I knew that tone. "Listen, you don't know this guy from Adam. He's sending you into the house. What if there's something dangerous in there? Don't go there until it's clear. Stay here."

He strode over to Eddie and the atmosphere turned cop very quickly. Within a minute, a tape perimeter was set around my house. The cruiser with the Lurker in it sped off. It was a cool, October evening, and the leaves were rustling in the wind.

And everyone was on their goddamn phones, documenting this mess for the world to see. The leering jack-o-lanterns on people's porches were totally freaking me out.

"Excuse us, excuse us, please!" My mom's voice brought me back. I hugged her tight. She was all bundled up in her old tan coat that had all of these pockets and bungee cords. She took tissues out of one pocket, and a granola bar out of another. And then, to make the night even more crazy, Janna was behind her, in a fuchsia knit cap, nose red from the cold.

"Uh, hi." I said to my estranged sister.

"Hi," she said back, looking anywhere but at me.

"Listen, you two. I've had enough of your bickering." Mom shook her finger at us.

The crowd got quiet. I zipped my fleece and pulled it up to my nose, hoping to hide. Janna looked at the ground and turned up the collar of her coat.

"Ever since you were little girls, you fought over stupid things." Mom sighed. "It's time to get your acts together! It's been three months since this business went down. You can be angry, Janna, but in the end, Piper is fine. Perfectly fine. And you, Marina, you have to stop actin' like you don't care. Because you do. Runnin' off all the way to Russia! Saying you have to work all the time. Ha. You two need to sit in a locked room and hash this out because here we stand, in front of your beautiful Aunt Yelena's house with the police everywhere and—"

There was simply no completing that sentence. Mom started weeping. She fished out more tissues from another pocket in her jacket. Janna and I caught each other's gazes. We both started to smile. The Anna Konyeshna Guilt Show always got her what she wanted.

I was about to say something to Janna when Sutton sauntered over. He crooked a finger in my direction and lifted the yellow tape. My mom, Janna and I ducked under it and followed him into the house. One cop was sitting on my sofa, using his cell phone. Hmmmm. Didn't seem dangerous so far. Muffled voices rose from below the orange shag rug – I *had* to replace that. Holy embarrassing.

Sutton opened the basement door and we descended. The stairs shook, my heart raced. Was there a body hidden all of those old Christmas decorations I'd never sorted?

Holy embarrassing again. I'd never got to clean out all of my aunt's junk and then had added my own. When I'd moved in, I'd filled at least ten recycling containers with old *National Geographics,* expired coupons, and empty margarine containers from the kitchen alone. I hadn't gotten to purge the basement yet, so there were boxes full of stuff, stuff, and more stuff. Paint cans, jars of old screws and nails, a dusty toolbox, and stacks of mismatched patio furniture cushions.

And then all my boxes, too. This was the equivalent of getting hit by a car, going to the hospital and having your laundry-day undies on. But with a police force and your mom and sister looking on. And your... boyfriend? Former boyfriend?

At the far end, past the artificial Christmas tree covered by a dusty tarp, a shelving unit made of two by fours covered the wall. To its left, that padlocked room, where delivery trucks would dump coal in ages before electric heating. I'd never gone in there since I moved in, even when Sutton had mentioned it a while ago. There was a padlock on it. I kept writing *bolt cutter* on my shopping list but had always ended up with another bottle of nail polish or more cheese puffs instead.

Janna giggled. "Hey, Marina. Remember when we were little and you'd annoy the crap out of me and I'd threaten to lock you in Aunt Yelena's coal room?"

We stared at each other and a few beats passed. Laughter sputtered out of my mouth. She shook her head, still giggling. Our eyes reconnected. Sister Power was back on.

And the coal room door was now wide open. We stepped closer.

"Yo, the owner and her family are here. Can you give them some space, please?" A guy and a woman in suits exited and nodded at us. I nodded back. "Go in," Sutton said.

The tiny stone-walled room was filled with three tables, really just plywood over sawhorses. The tables were lined with huge flower pots. Except the plants were now brown crumbles of dried leaves. Rows of long tube-shaped light bulbs were suspended from the ceiling. All kinds of plugs and extension cords snaked everywhere.

"So your aunt was growing weed." Sutton entered the coal room. "Metal halide bulbs. She knew her stuff. Crazy."

My mom and Janna were uncharacteristically quiet as they scanned the tiny space. Janna, probably at all of the weed; my mom probably at all of the cobwebs on the walls and in the rafters.

I reached over one table to touch a plant and Sutton pulled my forearm away. "Uh-uh. This is a crime scene, Marina."

"Why would she grow marijuana?" I was so confused. She smoked cigarettes, guzzled coffee, and played cards, but she rarely even drank wine. She wasn't all four-twenty or anything.

Sutton said, "Well, based on the condition of this room and the condition of the dude who says this stuff is all his, I think your aunt was giving him space to grow medical marijuana."

Oh. Then it all made sense. "All these strange people were stopping by, asking for my aunt. It was getting to be odd. So this was why?"

Janna looked around the stone-walled room. "Just when you think you know someone."

And then I saw the pink flamingoes propped in a corner. I pointed at them. "Wait. The pink flamingoes. She wasn't just storing them in here. Oy vey." I rubbed my forehead.

"What?" Mom said, picking one up by its metal stake.

"They were, like, code. The flamingos were *code*."

"Huh?" Janna said, picking one up, inspecting its pink plastic body.

"It's all so clear now. People only came by when I started putting out the flamingos again. These must have been the signal the product was ready."

My mom hustled out of the coal room, cheeks flaming.

"Yeah, so." I stared at the mess in front of me.

"Um, yeah." Janna put her arm around me and I leaned my head on her shoulder. Leave it to Aunt Yelena to find a way from beyond the grave to get us to reconcile. We stood in silence for a few beats.

Sutton cleared his throat. "So, I gotta be honest. I'm not sure what's going to happen now. I know the police will want to talk to you. Plus, you're going to have DEA and FBI here. And whoever else. So if I were you, I'd go make coffee and be ready for a long night."

As he spoke I heard the words, but it was hard to concentrate. All I wanted to do was put my arms around him.

A female detective popped into the coal room.

"Hey, Lopez. What's up?" Sutton said.

"Just wanted to give you all an update. The kid is saying no one sold it. That there were no financial transactions. He swears. He says the old lady—"

I glared at her.

Lopez cleared her throat. "The former owner of the house just let him use it to grow the weed to give to people in their cancer group."

"Does that make it any better?" Janna asked.

Sutton looked around the room. "Not sure. Maybe. With medical marijuana legal now, I'm not sure how a judge will look at this."

Lopez knocked on the door frame and waved as she left.

"Marina," Janna said, a hand on my shoulder. "I'm going to tell mom to go home. I'll be here with you until the bitter end. Oh — and you should probably call Gilly, since he's a lawyer and all."

I put a hand over hers and squeezed. "Thanks, Jan."

She squeezed back and smiled. I never would've guessed we'd make up while standing in my deceased aunt's marijuana farm.

37

We were told to clear the house again, so we shuffled back outside. The crowd had gotten even bigger. Now a news crew was setting up. Hello again, small town.

Another news van pulled up and Laura Jacobs popped out of the passenger side. She waved. I beckoned her over. She skirted the crowd and approached, hand out to shake. "Nice to see you again, Marina. Well, not under these circumstances, but you know what I mean." She looked around. There was a lot to see – the spectators, the cop cars, the agents in navy and black jackets hustling around in and out of the house.

"You, too, Laura." After the evil geocaching competition, when the local sex trafficking ring was busted, Laura had done an hour-long special on it. She was OK in my book.

"So, what's going on?" she said, iPhone ready to record.

"Well." I paused. Man, I was so proud. I *paused!* I didn't just ramble on. I had actually stopped to think.

"Hello, Ms. Jacobs," Sutton suddenly said from behind me. I got all tingly just hearing him. Janna gave me a thumbs-up. "Miss Konyeshna can't talk right now. Ongoing investigation."

"Excuse me," said a voice from behind us. Someone tapped my shoulder. "Um excuse me? I'm Yesenia, your next-door neighbor. My mom said to come out of the cold and wait with us."

The crowd was expanding and more people than I could handle were taking photos of my house.

"Oh, OK. Thanks." I followed Yesenia around the crowd. I was getting nervous and appreciated the offer. Mom and Janna followed. Yesenia's brown hair was pulled into an immense, loose bun on the top of her head. Her black hoodie looked a size too small. She wore yellow Sponge Bob pajama bottoms and pristine red, white, and blue Jordans.

I crooked a finger at my mom and sister. Together we walked up the stairs to Yesenia's porch. I could hear the TV through the walls and when Yesenia unlocked it, broadcast Spanish spilled out. No loud music this time. A little granny in a pink, white and blue housedress sat with hands in her lap, staring at a TV screen where a woman with long hair rode a horse down a beach. Sweeping orchestral music played as she galloped toward another horse. This one was ridden by a broad-shouldered, shirtless man with dirty blond hair and an eye patch.

Yesenia must have seen me give a cockeyed look. "My abuela's *novelas*. Her soap operas. Yeah, that's Brutus. He got his eye poked out when he tried to kidnap his children back from his ex-wife. The one who ran away with a circus elephant trainer."

"Uh-uh," I said. "Got it."

My mom said, "Hiya!" The old lady just raised her hand as if pushing her away. She was the long lost grumpy sister of Mamichka. We scooted out of her way and Yesenia laughed.

"She doesn't miss an episode. Come on in. Hey, Mommy!"

We followed the clattering from what was probably the kitchen because the layout was just like at my house – long living room, stairs to the second floor. The walls were covered in framed photos, presumably all family members. School portraits, blurry color photos taken in the eighties and nineties, just like my mom had hanging up. A crucifix here and there, a few portraits of the Virgin.

The aroma of onions cooking in oil made my heart warm. After such a craptacular night, it was like my nervous system was on caveman setting. A little bit of warmth and food and I'd be OK. My heartbeat had finally slowed. We passed through a narrow hallway into the kitchen and there was a woman in blue skinny jeans, a hoodie with WVW Spartan Marching Band across the front and big, red fuzzy slippers. She was wiping down the stove.

"Mommy," Yesenia said. "They're here!"

Her mom wiped her hands on a towel and fired off something in Spanish. My mom, Janna and I both looked at Yesenia and she smiled. "Mom said it was about time I invited you over. She says sit down and relax."

Her mom rattled something else off. "She isn't even asking if you want to eat, she said she's getting plates ready for all of you."

Finally, Anna Konyeshna had met her match. The other mother no one could say no to.

Their kitchen was just like mine – tiny and overflowing with stuff. Don't get me wrong, it was neat. But these coal-cracker kitchens weren't designed with today's lifestyle in mind. As if back in the day, you had four plates, four glasses and — done. Yesenia showed us to chairs around the dark wooden table. Her mom said something else, waved hello, pointed to the fridge.

"What would you like to drink? We've got water, soda, milk, juice." Yesenia opened a cabinet and took out glasses.

We all said water was fine. It was unexpected to have culture shock again, so soon, in my own neighborhood. It was awkward to not be able to say something to Yesenia's mom. But then again, I'd already learned so much about silence, I just stayed quiet. My mom fumbled with her watchband while Janna petted the little white moppy dog that bounced at her feet.

Yesenia smiled. "That's Frankie. He's the one who noticed there was someone at your house."

My ears perked up. "What do you mean?"

She set the glasses down and took the chair next to me. "Well, when you left. I mean, the whole neighborhood heard you leave."

I sank in the chair, the wooden spindles pressing into my back. "Oh. Um, that's embarrassing."

"Nah. Don't worry about it. Family has a way of doing that to you. Hold on. *Wela!*" Yesenia rattled something off in Spanish and the TV volume lowered. A little.

Yesenia's mom came to the table with three bowls full of steaming rice and beans. "Please," she said, smiling, cheeks dimpled and eyes bright but a little tired.

"Thank you for being so kind to us. My name is Anna," said Mom. "This is Janna, my oldest daughter And this is Marina, my youngest."

Yesenia's mom put a hand to her chest and said, "Zoraida. No speak much English. Sorry." Then she added a few words in Spanish.

Yesenia translated as Zoraida smiled. "My mom says she hopes you like the *arroz con habichuelas* – rice and beans."

"It smells great," said Janna, and dug in.

It *was* wonderful. Total comfort food. It was hot and a little smoky. We took a few more bites in silence.

The front door rattled and a man's voice boomed through the house. Whoever he was, he sounded angry.

"My brother, Axel," Yesenia murmured. "Sorry. He's not usually like this."

My mom, sister, and I stared at each other. We gradually stood to leave. Zoraida looked to the living room, back at us, and said something to Yesenia, who told us. "My mother says to please stay. It's too cold out there."

Zoraida went to the front while Yesenia made small talk with us. They were from Puerto Rico but had lived in Philadelphia, New York, then back to PR, as she called it, and now hopefully were permanently here because Axel just got a good job at the Tobyhanna Army Depot. Her mom cleaned office buildings. Yesenia was a junior at the local high school.

We heard footsteps above us, going upstairs. Zoraida returned, face red. She rattled something off and Yesenia put an arm around her mom, pulling her close.

"Eat, please," Zoraida said. She opened the back door and stepped outside.

Yesenia sighed. "My brother just noticed someone wrote NFHS on the side of his truck in black Sharpie."

"What does that mean?" Janna said.

The shower started upstairs and we could hear Axel singing along with the radio. Time to break the tension. I held back a smile but then couldn't hide it. "Wow, your brother and I could totally be contestants on Bathroom Idol."

"Oh yeah." Yesenia plucked a bean out of her bowl and popped it in her mouth. "When the window's open, we can hear you, too"

"Uh," I said, twisting my hair. "Good to know." Gulp. What else had they heard?

"You're not that bad," she added.

We all laughed.

Janna said, "But seriously, what is NFHS?"

Yesenia's smile disappeared and she picked at one sparkly, blue acrylic fingernail. "Not From Here Scum."

"Oh, my. That's...terrible." My mom's voice quavered.

"Yesenia. Wow. That's horrible. How mean." I didn't want to add I wasn't at all surprised, given the political climate here. For God's sake, my best friend had to move four hours away to be able to live openly as a gay man. A Pennsylvanian candidate for Congress had recently supported a bill to construct a wall at the U.S./Mexico border. He'd won his primary. And not to mention I'd been a big, fat jerk, making pinheaded assumptions about them.

Awkward silence descended.

Yesenia spoke first. "Would you like more?"

We all said it was delicious, but we were full.

I jumped in. "So Frankie. Like, how did he let you know there was someone at my house?"

Yesenia leaned against the sink. "He's usually pretty mellow. But some nights he'd jump on my bed, look out the window and bark at your house. And then tonight we saw that guy trying to get in through a basement window, so we called the police."

I had been so, so rude about this family and here there were, being good, helpful neighbors. While I'd been a judgmental ass.

A knock at the front door. I heard Sutton ask if we were still here.

He walked into the kitchen and I leaped up. "Hi, Mrs. Konyeshna. And, uh, Janna."

My mom smiled at him. "Hello, Sutton."

"Hi," Janna said, grinning. She nodded at me. That was a sister high-five.

Zoraida said something and returned to the stove. Yesenia translated. "My mom said you were good about watching Marina's house. She said Wela would watch you when you stopped by to check everything. My mom wants you to eat. And you can't ever say no to my mother."

Zoraida gave him a heaping bowl of rice and beans.

"*Muchas gracias,*" Sutton said.

Zoraida smiled.

"How come I didn't know you speak Spanish?" I said, both shocked and oddly kind of turned on. I mean, given the situation, I shouldn't have been, right?

"I dunno. Never came up?" he muttered through a mouthful of rice and beans. "*Delicioso.*"

The TV was suddenly quiet. *Abuela* made her way into the kitchen to see what the fuss was about. She looked at Sutton, adjusted her housedress, and pinched his biceps. "Uh uh," she said and gave a thumbs-up.

We all howled with laughter.

Axel entered the kitchen, his hair slicked back from his shower. "Wow. Who's the party for?"

Yesenia said, "This is Marina, who lives next to us. This is her mom, her sister, and her..."

"...boyfriend?" Sutton said, glancing at me, one eyebrow raised.

The last time someone had tried to stick the girlfriend label on me, it had ended up with a screaming match and smashed family heirlooms. This time, I let the word sit there. I made myself sit there, too. Did I like the sound of that word? Yes, I did. I gave a little smile and he winked at me.

"Right. Boyfriend." I punched his arm and he pretended to wince.

"My mom told me about the guy trying to get in your house. I'm sorry," Axel said. He was so skinny his light blue t-shirt hung off his frame. He had a few tattoos on his forearm and a little goatee. Zoraida handed him a bowl of food. He kissed her cheek.

"Sutton, do you have anything in that cop car of yours that can take off graffiti?" I asked.

"Actually, I do. Why?"

Axel filled him in. Sutton's expression turned grim. He shook his head. "Some of the people around here are so ignorant. No one's done that to me yet. Not to my face. But I'm waiting. Word of advice: don't ever read the comments on the local news articles. Never. Anyway, come on, let's see if what I have will work."

"Thanks, man." Axel clunked the bowl into the sink, kissed his mom on the cheek again, and waved goodbye to us. As he and Sutton left, I realized there was a whole part of my...boyfriend's life we'd never discussed. He was *waiting* for someone to do that to him? He'd never mentioned that to me.

"Marina! Hey!" Janna poked my arm. "Let's go see what's going on."

"Um, *gracias*, Zoraida," I said, my tongue a fumbling mess.

"You're welcome." She said something else Spanish, so I looked at Yesenia.

"She said to come back soon."

My mom, Janna, and I said our goodbyes. Abuela was still watching her show. She raised a hand and gave a little wave. Maybe just to get rid of us — who knows. She made me miss my Aunt Yelena. Same housedress, same intensity when watching their shows.

Sutton and Axel stood at Axel's pick up, rubbing cloths over the area that had been vandalized. The entire driver's side door. Axel had driven over an hour home from work with that on his truck. My heart sank.

A woman in a dark coat with DEA stenciled in yellow on the chest called my name. "Miss Konyeshna. I'm Agent Sparr. We can't let you back in your house for a few days. We have to do some tests, some investigating. It's clear from the decay these plants have not been touched in months. The suspect's story is matching up. We do need to question you, though."

My stomach churned. I'd been down this road before. A few months earlier. The questioning had felt endless. *No, I didn't know anything about this sex trafficking ring before I got involved in the geocaching competition and then it was too late. Yes, I would have alerted the authorities. Yes, I lied about The Husky telling me to be quiet when the body was found. I had to protect myself.* My deposition had cleared me of any wrongdoing. But I hated being on the receiving end of the law.

"Fine. Let me call my attorney" I pressed his number. "Gilly. You need to stop packing and come over now, please."

***

Two hours later I was allowed back in the house to pack a bag to last me a few days, under three conditions: I couldn't leave the area, I had to be reachable by phone, and leave a temporary address. U.S. Attorney Pumpernickle could add some more monitoring to his list. My mom, Janna, Gilly, Sutton, and I said our goodbyes in front of an unmarked police van. The media was here and I need to skedaddle.

"Marina, Piper would love to see you. You're welcome to stay with us," Janna said. Astonishment nearly knocked me over.

Gilly jumped in. "Well, you know I'm leaving for DC tomorrow and—"

"What?" Mom said. "But what is Marina going to do without you, Gilbert? You are her life coach!"

"Ma!" I rolled my eyes.

Gilly smiled. "Mrs. K, she will be fine. She keeps me in line, too. I have some job prospects and well, I'm going try some old fashioned domestic cohabitation with my boyfriend, Peter."

Janna said, "Good for you! Get outta here and live your life."

My mom hugged him, perched on tippy-toes with arms around his neck. She planted a kiss on his cheek and said, "Good for you, Gilbert. Good for you. And forget about your parents. They're so wrong. You deserve to be happy."

His smile turned to a frown. "Wait. How do you know about my parents?"

"Gilbert, you know this is small-town. People talk. It's about time those two come around. The next time I see your mom in Price Chopper, I —"

"Ma!" I said. "Jeez. Give the poor guy a break already."

Sutton said, "Marina, you can come stay with me, too. But you know my place is a true bachelor pad. I eat tuna out of the can and have a pile of frozen dinners, but it's yours if you want. I'll be working a lot, though. That undercover job went in another direction, so I'm back in the Valley for now."

"Thanks, Sutton. Thanks, Gilly and Janna. All of you. But I think I need my mom."

She squealed. "Back to roomies! Yeah! When we get home, just give me a minute to clear out my Scentables from the basement so you have a place to sleep."

"Your...what?"

"Ooh, they're lovely scented wax discs that make the house smell real nice. Just a few boxes. I thought I'd make some side money. You can help me my first sales party tomorrow night!" Mom's eyes gleamed. She was happy to have this boomerang back in her house. And me? I was happy to be boomeranged.

38

A month later my heels clicked on the courthouse marble floor, the echo magnified by my nervousness.

"Marina, it's going to be OK," Gilly said.

I unraveled the tangle of hair wound around my index finger and nodded. "Thanks for coming back from DC to be with me for this."

My house got the all clear when the grower, Dustin, insisted it was all his. But instead of being locked up, he was at General Hospital for his chemo. I wondered if I could see him because I'd been told he probably wouldn't make it to Christmas.

I was back at home, working at Prestige, and in contact with Cassidy about Shine a Light. Sabine was still missing, but Cassidy said Arman had strong leads. I hadn't heard anything from him, didn't expect to and was completely fine with that.

I was also making sure Sutton and I had actual dates now instead of Netflix and chilling.

The heavy mahogany doors of the courtroom were open and we walked right into the cavernous room. It was just like a scene from *Law and Order*. High ceilings, paneled walls, wood seats, the judge's bench at the front on a raised dais, prosecution and defense tables in front. We took a seat behind the rails. People in suits fussed about with papers at the front.

"Miss Konyesha." A voice I recognized. I stood and offered a hand. Time to put a face on U.S. Attorney Pumpernickle.

"Nice to finally meet you. USA McNichol."

He was much younger than I'd expected, his hair combed hard to one side as if it were on a mission. His shirt looked a little too big around the neck, and his pants were a little too long. *This* was what had intimidated me for months?

"Is this your attorney?"

"And my friend, Attorney Gilly Tomlinson."

And there was Ruby. In a suit that had become two sizes too large since her stint in county jail. No makeup, her hair an un-gelled, frizzy mop. Her nails short and natural. How unnatural to see her like this.

If I'd learned anything in the past few months, it was to trust my instincts. I looked at Ruby again — her hair unkempt, her gray suit hanging off her, the suit that had once been custom-tailored, no make-up, no lacquered fingernails. Her skin blotchy and sallow. But she talked to her lawyers, she nodded with the same self-assured grin that had always made me so uncomfortable. All those days at work I used to tell myself I needed to get over it, that it was all in my head. But no, I'd been right. Maybe another thing I was learning was to slow down and trust my gut.

"Gilly, let's go. I want some lunch. Let's see what's on the menu at What The Fork today before you drive back to Pete."

"But don't you want to hear it all? Don't you need the closure?"

"You said she made a deal, right?"

He nodded. "That's my understanding."

"Well, then I've seen all I need to see. Let's go. Take care, Mr. McNichol."

Gilly put his hand in mine and we stood.

We walked out and I left Ruby behind me.

***

After we had lunch, Gilly drove back to his new life with Pete in DC. I wrapped my scarf around my neck and stuck my hands in my coat pocket as I walked on to The Dike. I sat on a bench and watched the river, tree branches bobbing in and out of the tiny crests. The clouds were thick. Maybe a Thanksgiving snow. Cars zoomed by on the Market Street and Pierce Street bridges. On the opposite bank, a woman with blond hair was watching a tan dog chase a black one up the hill. The two dogs ran in arcs, up and down, up and down. They were having fun. It was time for me to have fun back in my life. I'd punished myself enough.

The General was somewhere in Russia, having promised to leave me alone. If I didn't take him at his word, I would drive myself crazy. I had faith Shine A Light would shut down the transplant hospital. Arman's team would find Sabine. Not sure if all of the endings would be happy, but I was certain of closure.

I played with Pavel's coin on my necklace and remembered his advice: *look to the future*. The future was hope. I would keep hope alive for Sabine. I would keep hope alive for Kcenya and her work with the Kasha Kitchen. I would keep hope alive for Pavel.

I opened the photos on my phone. At the airport, leaving for Russia, a selfie with the departure/arrival board behind me. One of Cassidy, knocked out on her sleeping pills, mouth open, on the plane. Shots of Red Square. The hotel. With Kcenya's family and the massive spread they'd prepared for me after the hotel fire. A snowy pic with Cassidy and Fydor. I flicked the screen to enlarge the shots.

Ding. A text from Cassidy. *Anu found this on a website:*

Then she sent a screen shot. Sabine. Staring into a web cam, in a black push up bra, her eyes glazed. The date was yesterday. She was alive.

!!!!!!!!!!!! That's terrifying and hopeful. How's Arman?

Cassidy: *A walking ball of fury. Now we trace the IP address.*

Fingers crossed. Hope Olya is still cooperating. Saw Hong and Dolly yesterday. Hong had her first week of English lessons!

Cassidy: *Olya is paying the bills for the search. And you rock for however you made that happen.*

I learn from the best. xo

I pulled the hood over my head, fake fur soft against my face. The Old Marina would have deleted Sabine's photo. Would have just gone to her car and would have just said — not my problem anymore.

But I wasn't that same girl.

I slid the bracelets from my left wrist and looked at the five dots that tattooed my skin. Five little dots that meant nothing to most people, but so much to me.

The only thing I knew was I was still alive. And hopeful. Maybe more so than I'd ever been in my life.

THE END

Acknowledgments

The act of writing is solitary, but it takes a village to make the manuscript come to life. First, to everyone who read HOPE YOU GUESS MY NAME: it was a totally different experience to write a book having you behind me. I hope I did you proud in the sequel and I can't wait to get you Book 3. Thank you for your encouragement, Tweets, Facebook messages, hugs, and reviews.

I'd be nowhere without David Poyer and Lenore Hart for their belief in my writing and their love of Marina's adventures. Thank you for making me part of Northampton House Press.

Thank you to Dr. Bonnie Culver and Dr. J. Michael Lennon, of the Wilkes University Creative Writing Program, for nurturing an inspiring community of writers. And to all of my fellow Wilkes creative writing grads and current students who are too numerous to list here, I'm so grateful for the fellowship we have created. Keep writing!

Thank you to all of the following people who shared their expertise and creativity with me. From informational interviews to translations to brainstorming to offering input on a draft to creating my cover, I owe you all so much: Jim Gwynn, Sylvia Gordon, Michele Shuey, Susan Riggs, Lance Lauchengco, Jason Moorehead, Brett and Zina Morrison, Jennifer Howard, Vanessa Sassani, Suzie Bichovsky, Johanna Hollway, Carrie McAdams, Vickie Bartkus, Kristin Weller, Ashley Supinski, Lauren Stahl, Megan and Scott Snyder.

My time in Russia as a Peace Corps Volunteer from 1997-1999 helped shape this part of Marina's adventures. Bolshoi spacibo to the Peace Corps, the School of Self-Determination, and the Center For Humanitarian Aid for providing me beautiful opportunities to grow as a teacher and person. I am forever grateful to Nina Eremina, Susana Artyoonina, Angelina Voskovskaya, and all of the other amazing Russians who filled my two years with laughter, friendship, vodka chased by pickles, dancing, and life lessons. I hope we meet again. And to my fellow Peace Corps Volunteers, especially Russia 6, thank you for being part of this story, too.

This book is dedicated to two special people from my time in Russia. Bonnie Brush was a fellow volunteer from Michigan. She was known for her great sense of humor and dedication to teaching. She was a great friend to me and was taken too soon when she passed away at 43 in a car accident. Vladimir was a homeless man who often ate and volunteered at the Center For Humanitarian Aid, an organization that supported the homeless and poor in Moscow. Vladimir is the inspiration for Pavel. He was like a grandfather to me and I will never forget his kindness and gentle nature.

The character of Sutton Cicero is partly informed by the experiences of my cousin, Corporal Harvey C. Snook III, of the Arlington County (Virginia) Police Department. Harvey died from lymphoma in January 2016, most likely caused chemical exposure during his work as a 9/11 first responder at the Pentagon. The night Harvey and I were supposed to have a more in-depth interview for this book, his condition worsened and we were never able to have that conversation. That's why I'm so grateful for my college friend, Dr. Tom Lembo, for setting me up with an interview with his father, Sargent Thomas Lembo, Retired (Union, NJ). Sargent Lembo graciously shared details of his career with me, from the basic minutiae of police life, to humorous stories, to serious situations. I am deeply indebted to him for his honesty and I hope I do right by him in this book.

To the long list of people in my husband's family, the Dopkins and Nowaks, who always support me and cheer me on. To my family, the Harlens and Brizgints, who provided me with great memories from growing up in Northeastern Pennsylvania. To my brothers, Jason and Ryan Harlen, for coming to my readings, time after time after time. Big hugs to my mom, Rosemary Harlen, and my dad, Bill Harlen, for always believing in me.

Last and certainly not least, to my husband, Mike Dopkin. Thank you for supporting me, for letting be hot mess when I need to be, and for always understanding. You're still my favorite.

About the Author

Heather Harlen is a writer and teacher. Her two years in Russia as a Peace Corps volunteer inspired much of the Marina Konyeshna series, of which *Hope You Guess My Name* was the first volume and this novel the second. She holds an MA in Creative Writing from Wilkes University and is a National Writing Project Fellow. She lives near Allentown, PA with her husband. You can find out more at www.heatherharlen.com.

Northampton House Press

Established in 2011, Northampton House Press publishes carefully selected fiction, lifestyle nonfiction, memoir, and poetry. Check out our list at www.northampton-house.com, and Like us on Facebook – "Northampton House Press" – as we showcase innovative works from brilliant new talents.

www.ingramcontent.com/pod-product-compliance
Lightning Source LLC
Chambersburg PA
CBHW022043240626
47154CB00007B/2536